John F Plimmer's

The Secret of Annie Crockett

Another Richard Rayner thriller from the Victorian Detective's casebook series

'It's not me who can't keep a secret. It's the people I tell that can't'.

Abraham Lincoln

Chapter One

It wasn't until Frederick Morgan stepped closer to his daughter, that he realised she was sobbing. The Head of Scotland Yard's Detective Branch was puzzled after being asked by Estelle to meet her at the docks of all places. Now it became obvious, whatever the reason it had to be of the greatest importance: she turned and looked at him, with rivulets of tears cascading down each side of her young face.

Until recently, Morgan didn't even know he had a daughter, the girl having been born after he and his lover of twenty years previously had gone their separate ways. At the time, the red-headed Chief Superintendent had been a dashing young officer in the Coldstream Guards with the enticement of adventure and excitement still in his blood. Having left her mother, a Jamaican lady, Dorothy Roland, in Liverpool, where she had been born and raised, Estelle secured herself a position at one of the many 'Ragged Schools' created by Quinton Hogg for destitute children in London. She was fortunate to be now living with her father and step-mother, Sally-Anne, in the prosperous district of Richmond.

"What in Heavens name has upset you my dear?" Morgan asked, remembering his wife Sally-Anne's stern warning never to swear in front of his daughter, "I got your note back at Scotland Yard and wondered why it couldn't wait until we saw each other at home tonight?"

"It's my friend father," the girl gasped, "He's gone missing and I fear something terrible has happened to him."

"Christ, and there was me thinking it was a bleedin' matter of life and death," he blurted out, forgetting momentarily his wife's words of caution.

"But it is father, I know Ralphie wouldn't just disappear like that; he's been gone for about three days now."

"Who is he, Estelle?" Morgan asked, looking down at the industrious scene of the main London Dock, beneath where they were stood.

His daughter hurriedly described, a tall, thin youth of West Indian origin, who was an itinerant and pushed an old handcart around the streets of London, searching for any discarded object he could sell on for cash.

"His name is Raphael Dickens father, and he's the most nice and humble person you could ever wish to meet, but I just knew last time I saw him there was something worrying him."

"That's a fancy name for some street muffin darling," her father remarked, "When and where did you last see this Raphael, and what made you think he was in some kind of trouble."

"Last Tuesday father, but I see him every day when arriving at my school in The Strand. He's always around and usually greets me with a broad smile, only Tuesday, he looked terrified. When I asked him what was wrong, he told me some men were after him and he had to go. I haven't seen him since and neither have any of the kids who know him well at the school." She paused, "Father, I just know something terrible has happened to him and it's most upsetting."

She began to sob again and Morgan placed an arm around her, before asking why she had preferred to meet him at the docks.

"Because this is where he sleeps at night, somewhere inside one of the docks and I thought we could start looking for him down there."

"And what of school young lady, you must have used up your dinner break by now, surely."

"I still have a little time left, will you help me find Ralphie, father?"

"Of course, but you know, these street muffins have a habit of disappearing for a time and then reappearing once their problems have been resolved."

"This is different."

As he continued to console his daughter, trying to reassure her that her friend would be alright, Morgan noticed his Detective Chief Inspector, Richard Rayner, standing on one of the quaysides down below from where he stood. The renowned detective, who had a reputation for always being smartly and immaculately tailored, had with him his two Sergeants, Henry Bustle and Jack Robinson.

Grasping his daughter's gloved hand tightly, Morgan realised at that very moment, his pleasurable excursion and sense of nirvana he always experienced when in his daughter's presence, was at an end.

"Isn't that Richard down there, father?" Estelle asked, watching as the three Scotland Yard men approached a small group of uniformed constables standing at the far end of North Quay.

"I believe it is," her father answered, before suggesting he should return his daughter back to the school room and promising he would do all in his power to find the missing Raphael Dickens. He was well aware that whatever had brought Rayner and the others to London's dockland, would in all probability not be suitable for Estelle's eyes.

Not wanting to go against her father's wishes, the young lady agreed and the couple turned back, slowly walking towards where Morgan had earlier left his driver and carriage.

The uniformed Sergeant, who first approached the three detectives had a flushed face with the bottom half almost completely hidden beneath a bushy walrus moustache, obviously his pride and joy. He stood with a posture that confirmed a military background and spoke with a loud, gruff voice.

"What have we Sergeant?" Richard Rayner, the dandy of Scotland Yard enquired, known by that label as a result of his flamboyant attire and being forced to hold on to his top hat, as a determined breeze coming off the water tried to snatch it from his head.

"Sah!" the man snapped back, as if presenting a parade to an inspection party on a drill square at some Army barracks, "Murder, bloody murder, is what we have ... sah."

"Show me," Rayner instructed the rigid figure whose face was so crimson, the Chief Inspector thought for a moment the Sergeant had stopped breathing. The man in temporary charge of the scene was prompted to turn and lead the way into a large wooden shed with a loading bay, which was one of many lined up along that particular quay. In the darkness, towards the back of the structure was the body of a man, lying amongst a pile of hessian sacks. The corpse appeared to be dressed in working man's clothes, a woollen jacket, trousers and a collarless shirt. When Rayner looked more closely, he could see dried blood at the back of the victim's head causing the hair to be matted and presenting the detective with his initial assessment of how the man had died.

"I fink the geezer was hit on the head with this, sah," the same Sergeant said, picking up a metal bar and about to hand it to the Chief Inspector, before being abruptly stopped and admonished for having touched the item with his bare hands.

"I suspect Sergeant, you have just managed to wipe off any finger impressions the killer might have left for us to find, that's if it is the murder weapon." Richard Rayner was never shy in offering constructive criticism, if sufficient to make a point, rather than a tongue lashing that only resulted in embarrassment for the recipient.

The speed in which the officer dropped the bar on the floor, indicated it might well have just come out of a fired-up kiln and he apologised profusely, causing Rayner further diversion away from his priority, which was to make a cursory examination of the body.

"Never mind, we can all learn from our mistakes, Sergeant," he suggested, not wishing to chastise the man further.

"Sah."

The senior detective envisaged the officer speaking to his wife in a similar brusque manner at breakfast, or when dining on a bowl of stewed dumplings in between his shifts and smiled to himself at the bizarre thought. If it came to that, perhaps his wife responded to her husband in the same fashion.

"Has Doctor Critchley been sent for?" he asked, referring to the pathologist.

It was quickly confirmed that the physician was expected to arrive at any moment.

Rayner crouched down at the side of the dead man to look more closely at the face and hands.

"Looks like he's been in a fight," Henry Bustle suggested. The Detective Sergeant had been a close friend and confidante of the Chief Inspector's for a number of years and could almost read the senior detective's mind.

"Perhaps, Henry," Rayner quietly answered, before turning back to the uniformed statue who was still standing close by, motionless as though waiting for a fly to settle on his nose so he could squat it.

"Who discovered the body, Sergeant...?"

"Beeching sah, Reginald Beeching out of Cannon Row at your service, sah." The man then clammed up, as though he'd forgotten what the question had been.

"Who found the bleedin' body, Reg?" Bustle prompted, a little more forcefully than how Richard Rayner had put the question.

"Sorry sah, me mind was elsewhere." The Sergeant glanced at his notebook and read out the name, "Patrick Cronin, a dockyard labourer, sah. 'E says he found the cadaver at about ten thirty this morning when coming in 'ere to pick up some rope...sah." His words were punctuated, which was a little frustrating for Rayner, but he was a patient man.

"Is he still here, Sergeant?"

"I believe 'e is."

The tall and impressively handsome Richard Rayner nodded to Henry

Bustle, signalling for his right-hand man to get Sergeant Beeching to introduce him to the witness and elaborate more on what Mr. Cronin had to tell them.

When both men had disappeared, leaving the Chief Inspector to continue his initial examination with young Sergeant Jack Robinson remaining and standing well back from the senior man, a familiar sounding voice spoke from the open doorway.

"Might I assist, Chief Inspector?" It was Doctor Albert Critchley, the pathologist and elderly physician who had worked with Richard Rayner over a long period of time and was well acquainted with the Chief Inspector's methods. The grey-haired specialist was warmly welcomed by the senior detective, who stood back to allow his professional associate and friend, the room he required.

Within a few short minutes of investigating, the pathologist stood to face the Scotland Yard man and explained that it was difficult to confirm the actual cause of death, prior to making a more detailed examination of the body back at the mortuary at St Mary's Hospital, where Doctor Critchley worked.

"I suspect that blow to the back of the head might well have caused his fatality though, Richard," he conceded, "But I need to examine the brain and skull."

Rayner indicated the iron bar so negligently handled by Sergeant Beeching, and the physician told him he would take it with him back to his mortuary for purposes of comparison.

"What about the time of death doctor?"

"It's quite obvious the victim has been dead for a number of days, possibly two or three. I can be more accurate later."

That assumption surprised the Chief Inspector considering the body had only just been discovered.

"I'll make the appropriate arrangements to have it transferred to St. Mary's and meet you there later." Rayner then requested Jack Robinson to direct a couple of the constables to remove the corpse, before leaving the scene in search of Henry Bustle.

He found his senior Sergeant standing on the quayside, talking to another man who the Chief Inspector assumed was Patrick Cronin, the individual who had first discovered the dead man. Whereby Bustle was a short, stocky man with a face that resembled an experienced bar room brawler, rather than a Scotland Yard detective, an appearance supported by a scar running down the left side of his face, the witness was even smaller, a wiry ferret faced looking man, wearing a brown cow-gown.

"Mr. Cronin here, knows the deceased sir," the Sergeant confirmed, "His name is Joseph Kelly, and he was a Stevedore working here on the docks."

Rayner asked the man if he knew anything about the dead man's background and was told that Kelly was a mild-mannered Irishman, who lived somewhere in Whitechapel with his wife and two daughters. When pressed further about how well he actually knew Mr. Kelly, the witness confirmed he was a work colleague and nothing more, and that he was usually employed in the adjacent dock, St Katharine Dock, mostly involving loading and unloading on the quayside there.

"Did he like a drink?" Rayner asked.

"No more than the rest of us Inspector," Cronin answered.

"It's Chief Inspector," Henry Bustle corrected him.

"As far as you are aware sir, was he ever involved in altercations with any of his workmates?"

The man shook his head and confirmed, "It's like I said before, Joey was a mild-mannered sort of a bloke who kept himself to himself, if that makes sense."

"Who did he work for?"

"The Port Authority, like most of us. They keep a rota system and call us in whenever there's work to be done. They pay us an hourly rate on a day-to-day basis."

Rayner then enquired how it was possible the body of Mr. Kelly had been left inside the warehouse for a period of two to three days, without being discovered. He was told that it wasn't unusual for a building to be left secured and unattended, until required for storage purposes.

"I only opened this one up because we are expecting a shipment of grain to come in sometime today," Patrick Cronin confirmed.

The Chief Inspector thanked him and suggested they might want to speak with him again in the future.

"We need to be at the post mortem, Henry," Richard Rayner directed, as both detectives were making their way back to their carriage, having left Jack Robinson to continue searching the area around the scene. Robinson was thin, almost skeletal in build, with a thin moustache and in his mid-twenties. He was married with a young daughter and the most enthusiastic detective Rayner was aware of. The senior detective also instructed him to trace the victim's home address in Whitechapel and inform his widow, as soon as he had finished at the docks.

"Find out as much as you can Jack, about Joseph Kelly's background but without distressing his wife too much."

"Yes sir, leave it with me."

Henry Bustle looked a little pensive and expressed his view that he thought the dead man had been involved in a fight and had bitten off more than he could chew.

"But I have a sneaky feeling you are thinking there is more to this than just an altercation between some blokes?"

"We shall see."

Before going on to St. Mary's, they returned to Scotland Yard at the senior detective's instigation. Rayner needed to update Frederick Morgan, on what was beginning to look like London's most recent murder and found the Chief Superintendent sitting smoking his pipe in his Chief Inspector's office, located next to his own on the first floor.

The senior man looked pale and Rayner detected a hint of anxiety in his features, so much so, he enquired if Morgan was feeling well.

"Of course, I'm feeling well, Rayner," the Head of the Detective Branch snapped back, obviously not appreciating his Chief Inspector's concerns for his health, "Why the bleedin' hell shouldn't I be?"

"Very well sir, if you say so. Did you manage to meet your daughter over lunch?" The Chief Inspector recognised all the signs frequently displayed when his senior was suffering from the kind of discomfort that transformed him into something resembling an irritated demon.

"Yes, I met her down at the docks where we saw you lot, but I had to get her back to the school. She was going on about some missing kid she was worrying herself sick about. For the life of me, I'll never understand how a young lady's mind works."

"Really, sir, that's unlike Estelle."

"Oh, it's just some street muffin by the name of Raphael Dickens, a black lad who goes around pushing some old cart, you know the type Rayner, looking for anything he can pick up to flog. With a name like that he should have had a career in oils and canvas."

"Why is Estelle so concerned about this particular chap?" Rayner asked.

Morgan told him how the last time she had seen Dickens, the lad had looked fearful and told her some men were looking for him and she hasn't seen him since.

"He'll turn up though, they always do. So, what have you got for me?"

Rayner gave a brief rendition of what they had discovered so far regarding Joseph Kelly's death, emphasising that there should be more detailed information coming from the post mortem.

"Was he pissed at the time he was topped?" Morgan asked, bluntly, never being one to choose his words with a great deal of thought.

"I'm not aware of that, but I'm sure Doctor Critchley will be able to throw more light on that possibility a little later."

"Very well, Rayner, I'll leave it with you." It was obvious the Chief Superintendent was in some discomfort from the way in which he winced as he rose from his seat.

In recent weeks it had been noticeable how more aggressive the Chief Superintendent appeared to have become. He certainly wasn't his usual self and Richard Rayner had no idea of the reason why. Of course, the man from Porthcawl, who had the kind of powerful build that supported any notion he could readily look after himself, was never anything but abrasive most of the time, but to his colleague and friend, Richard Rayner, something outside his understanding was wrong with him; some kind of physical or mental discomfort was dominating the way his friend was behaving. It was known throughout the detective branch that Morgan suffered from toothache from time to time and then there was the occasional pain he suffered from inflamed haemorrhoids. It might just be that one of these afflictions had raised their head, but Rayner had other stuff to worry about at that moment.

Henry Bustle appeared and the senior detective's first priority was to follow his usual habit of putting a piece of chalk to good use, by recording the basic details of the recent incident on a blackboard kept in his office. Rayner then grabbed his top hat and coat and made for the door.

"Right then Henry, let's go and see if we can find out some more about what brought about our man's unfortunate passing."

Chapter Two

Frederick Morgan owed an enormous debt of gratitude to Thomas Braker, the pharmacist in Princes Street, Westminster, or so he believed. The Pharmacist was the only one willing to supply a compound that brought some effective pain relief to the Chief Superintendent. The Welshman's salvation consisted of small sachets of white powder labelled, 'The Gold Remedy' and were handed over with a verbal warning not to take more than one a day. But, as the afflicted man had once said to, Mr. Braker, "When your arse is on fire, Tommy, you don't walk away from a bucket full of ice-cold water." So, the constant sufferer of inflamed haemorrhoids found himself taking one of those magical powders each time he felt the excruciating pain, which was virtually every couple of hours.

What Morgan failed to recognise, unlike every other police officer working at Scotland Yard, was that he had become less sympathetic when confronted with the slightest diversion from his normal daily routine. The tall, powerful looking former Major in the Coldstream Guards, had developed over recent weeks into an aggressive, impolite and impatient human being. One distinct factor was that his recent exhibitions of obnoxious traits coincided with his on-going addiction to his new-found pain relief and yet, to be without them, resulted in constant torment and debilitation.

The population of London had not yet fully recovered from the recent undetected spate of grotesque murders committed by the individual commonly known as 'Jack the Ripper'. Although two years had passed since the last of a series of grotesque atrocities, there still remained elements of fear instilled in people, women in particular. News of any murder in the capital naturally increased the already existing anxiety on the streets. When details of the recent slaying of the docker became known, the newspapers wasted little time in stoking up the public's sense of trepidation, by hinting that it could be the first of many others to follow, much to the denial and annoyance of Scotland Yard. Newspaper editors knew what garbage to feed their readers though and the biggest concern for the Metropolitan Police was if vigilantes would once again take to the streets, demanding their misguided view of justice. It therefore transpired that Scotland Yard's most prominent detective was charged with finding the person responsible for the most recent murder, quickly.

By the time Richard Rayner and Henry Bustle arrived at the mortuary, the post mortem undertaken by Doctor Critchley, had already been completed. They found the elderly pathologist seated in his small office adjacent to the examination room, completing his report through a pair of wire-rimmed spectacles perched on the end of his nose. The senior detective congratulated him on his speed and efficiency, before asking for a verbal account of the good doctor's findings. Rayner held the man in the highest esteem, always confident that whatever the outcome of his work represented, it would be of the utmost accuracy.

Critchley stood and led the way back into the examination room, shuffling through multiple scented herbs covering the floor. The corpse of Joseph Kelly was laid out on a slab, beneath a cotton shroud and the physician exposed the body, explaining that there were a number of unusual features involved in this particular case.

"As I mentioned earlier Richard, the victim received a nasty blow to the back of the head that resulted in a number of small fractures to the cranium, that could have very well been caused by that iron bar you asked me to compare. In fact, it matches the outer wound perfectly, but that was not the cause of death."

"Really, doctor?"

"There was water inside the lungs, indicating that he drowned after being beaten about the head and body. As you can see, there are multiple contusions and abrasions around the ribs and stomach areas, but what are most interesting are these." The doctor pointed to both the victim's kneecaps, that seemed to have what looked like, large puncture wounds in each.

"These were undoubtedly inflicted by some kind of drill or metal spike, about a quarter of an inch in diameter, that went completely through the patella on each leg."

"My God, was he still conscious when that happened," Rayner asked, wincing at the severity of the pain the victim would have suffered and surprised by the degree of violence inflicted on the unfortunate man.

"That's difficult to say, but I believe he was. He was certainly conscious when subjected to the blows to his body and would have lost consciousness as a result of the blow to the head."

"He was tortured then, before being drowned?"

"That does appear to be the sequence of events, yes."

The look on Henry Bustle's face was one of disbelief and he remarked that it was difficult to accept any logical reason why any individual would be subjected to such primitive violence.

"It doesn't seem logical that the unconscious man would have been thrown into the water to drown, then fished out again and carried into that shed to be later discovered," Richard Rayner argued.

"Can we be absolutely sure doctor that he wasn't drowned before being given a good kicking," Bustle enquired.

"That was not the case, I can assure you," the doctor confirmed.

The Chief Inspector continued, "From what you have told us, the only logical explanation is that our man was forcibly held down beneath the water, after being subjected to such unbelievable violence."

The pathologist was in full agreement with that scenario.

"I don't think I can remember ever coming across such an horrific and tortuous ordeal, previously."

Doctor Critchley, nodded.

"Certainly not in my experience, Richard," he confessed.

"Have we his clothing, doctor?" the Chief Inspector asked, and was directed to a small table near the exit door, upon which a bundle of the victim's clothing had been placed.

Rayner nodded to his Sergeant to carry out the usual search of the items, before asking the pathologist if there was any way they could differentiate between an individual being forcibly drowned and another just being thrown unconscious into the water. It was a point he needed to be clarified.

"Not from the quality of the water found in the lungs," Albert Critchley explained, "In both sets of circumstances, river sludge would be present, but I'm fairly confident your suggestion that his head was forcibly held beneath the water, is the most likely and I'll show you why."

The doctor then turned the corpse on to its side and pointed to some bruising to the back of the neck, suggesting physical pressure had been applied to the base of the skull to force the head down.

"A quite deliberate and intentional case of murder then doctor, that went beyond a confrontation between men."

"Yes, and I shall conclude with that hypothesis in my final report. From my findings, I would estimate death occurred at least three days ago, as I suggested earlier."

Only some loose change, a handkerchief and Port Authority work permit in the name of Joseph Kelly, was found in the items of clothing searched by Henry Bustle.

"Which tells us that the motive for the killing was not larceny, Henry."

"No sir, we have to find some other reason."

"My word, our Joseph Kelly must have really upset somebody," Rayner remarked.

Both detectives were about to leave when a young, attractive lady of West Indian origin, dressed in an ankle length white gown stepped into the examination room. Elizabeth Green had in the past, been Albert Critchley's apprentice assistant for a short period of time, before leaving to complete her medical studies at university.

Rayner greeted the woman warmly, enquiring if she had returned to the St. Mary's fold permanently.

"I certainly hope so, Mr. Rayner," she answered, articulately, "It is certainly good to see you again, and you, Sergeant Bustle."

The Chief Inspector's right-hand man blushed slightly, not being used to such a compliment being thrown his way, especially from such a learned young lady.

"It's Doctor Green now, Richard," the elderly pathologist confirmed, "Elizabeth has completed her studies and is now undergoing a further period of training in the main hospital building."

"Congratulations, Doctor Green," Rayner said, slightly bowing and displaying an infectious smile, "Hopefully, we shall be seeing more of you in the near future then?"

"I hope so, Chief Inspector," the recently appointed doctor answered.

"Please, call me Richard."

"And of course, I am Elizabeth, and how is Mr..." She paused, having forgotten the name of the Head of Rayner's Department.

"Frederick Morgan."

She nodded.

"He's much his normal self. He remains grumpy but alert and well."

"I am pleased to hear it, please give him my regards."

Rayner acknowledged he would, before finally leaving, followed closely behind by Henry Bustle.

Assisted by the eagerly distributed circulations of the daily bulletins, news of the callous murder committed in London's dockland quickly spread through the capital like a wild bushfire. When Rayner and Bustle returned to Scotland Yard, they found the front reception area filled with excited and vociferous newspaper reporters, all clambering for a story to prop up their headlines. Chief Superintendent Morgan was also present, but not to appease those seeking further information, but looking as though he was about to confront the whole assembly with a barrage of cannon fire.

There was an expression of vented anger on Morgan's face that surprised Richard Rayner, and the senior man was just threatening to lock each and every one of the intruders up in the cell block when the Chief Inspector appeared.

The journalists immediately turned to the more amenable senior detective for help, as soon as they became aware of his presence and he wasted little time in defusing the situation, by quietly confirming the briefest of details concerning the recent murder. Scotland Yard's most celebrated detective had always maintained a far better working relationship with the press than his senior had previously experienced and after sharing news of a male victim having been found murdered in the oldest part of London's dockland, a number of questions followed. They were dealt with in the Chief Inspector's usual patient and calm manner, justifying the respect afforded him by the local reporters.

After the satisfied herd of journalists had dispersed, much to the Desk Sergeant's relief, who had caught the brunt of the frenzied gathering, Morgan remained standing erect in his trouser bracers, not having moved a muscle from his original position. With both hands on his hips and a look of sheer disgust and anger masking his pale face, he continued to stare directly at Richard Rayner. His stance was a warning that thunder was about to descend on Scotland Yard's reception area. In fact, the Chief Superintendent looked ready to explode, reminding the Chief Inspector of a Gladiator standing in the Roman Colosseum, about to make his kill. Morgan's fiery eyes glared like two burning flames, leaving no doubt that Rayner was about to be subjected to all the vitriol the Welsh dragon could muster.

"I won't stand for it, do you hear me, you over dressed bleedin' peacock. What business was it of yours to interfere with the manner in which I was doing my job. You're not the bleedin' Head of Department yet Rayner, even if you act as if you were."

"I was only trying to..."

"Bollocks Rayner, you're getting too big for your boots mister and I'm the man to cut you down to size." Morgan's voice was booming out, in such a manner it would be difficult for the Commissioner on the top floor not to overhear his cutting and undignified attack.

The Desk Sergeant and a young constable, who was the front office assistant, turned away in embarrassment at witnessing the spectacle of one of Scotland Yard's most senior officer's over reacting and dressing down another senior detective, especially one who had achieved nothing but success.

At the same time, Henry Bustle disappeared, having muttered some feeble excuse about having to check something in the basement cell block.

Such was the anger displayed by Morgan, that Rayner thought at one stage, he was about to be spat at, but thankfully that didn't happen and the infuriated Head of Department turned and disappeared up the stairs, still snorting and mumbling under his breath.

The Chief Inspector was left standing there, utterly speechless at such an unexpected deluge of abuse, having only tried to help in dealing with what had been an awkward situation with the local press. He then found himself apologising for the Chief Superintendent's unacceptable behaviour to the seemingly confused and abashed uniform officers present, but what Richard Rayner knew for certain, the man who had just been throwing verbal insults his way, was not Frederick Morgan. Something was wrong and he needed to find out what it was, and quickly.

"Sorry sir, we didn't hear a word," the Desk Sergeant politely lied, apologetically offering some empathy to the detective, who smiled in response.

"Thank you, Sergeant," Rayner quietly answered, before following in Frederick Morgan's footsteps up the stairs to the first floor.

When he reached Morgan's office, the Chief Inspector didn't think the man was worthy of a knock on his door and ploughed straight in, to find his adversary sitting behind his desk, firing up his pipe. At least, what Richard Rayner was about to say, would be in private and would be far more dignified than the verbal lashing he'd just been subjected to.

"Don't you bleedin' well bother to knock now," Morgan bawled out, still being controlled by that Welsh temper of his.

The Chief Inspector stood on, facing the man, like a lion tamer confronting an unruly and dangerous big cat. Rayner's first demand was for an immediate apology for his friend's conduct, in particular the way in which Morgan had demeaned his character in the presence of other junior officers.

"Apology. I owe you an apology do I Rayner. You cheeky bastard, you should be thankful it's me that's saved your pompous arse so many times in the past." The Chief Superintendent looked different to when he usually chastised any of his officers. In contrast to his constantly flushed face, he was as pale as baking flour and his hair appeared to be ruffled, as though someone had just run a hand across the top of his head. Rayner also noticed a few beads of sweat on his brow and instantly made reference to his senior officer's health.

"You're not well, Frederick," he quietly and calmly announced, throwing all caution to the wind.

That was the trigger for Morgan to leap from his seat and fill his eyes with even more aggression.

"Why you bombastic self-opinionated, big-headed Judas, I'll not stand for any more of your false posturing Rayner, and you can stick your patronising bullshit up your arse, for what it's worth."

To continue the conversation would have inevitably resulted in a more hostile and irascible confrontation. The correct course to take, although demoralising, was for Richard Rayner to make an abrupt exit, until matters had settled down.

"Wait Richard," Morgan pleaded, suddenly sounding more genial, in total contrast to his behaviour seconds before.

Rayner did so, without losing his look of surprise and concern.

The truth was, in contrast to Morgan's allegations that he'd saved Rayner's career on numerous occasions, it had been Richard Rayner who had managed to lever Frederick Morgan out of various critical situations, virtually throughout most of their professional relationship. Whereby, as a young man, Morgan had been successful in the military, obtaining the rank of Major in the Guards, his friend had been an Oxford graduate who had declined a career in lecturing to seek more adventure and variety in the Metropolitan Police. And yet, their contrasting personalities had successfully gelled, for the majority of the time they had worked together. But now a gulf had appeared between them, that needed repairing with some urgency.

Morgan waved his Chief Inspector to take a seat, an offer that was declined in silence, before returning to his own.

"I apologise Richard," he offered, shaking his head, "It's just that these bleedin' piles of mine are giving me little respite. It's like having a swarm of wasps nesting up your arse and refusing to leave."

So that was it, but Rayner suspected it was more serious than the usual debilitating and painful attack that kept pushing Morgan so hard that he couldn't maintain his self-control.

"Between me and you mate, my back end is permanently on fire these days and it's starting to get me down. I don't know what's got into me."

"Then with the greatest of respect, for God's sake, why don't you see a physician and get something done about them, once and for all."

A look of painful anguish leapt to the other man's features and he shook his head once again.

"I'll not have them take a knife to me, Richard. They reckon it takes a year to recover once they've been to work with their scalpels and whatever else they shove up your two by two. That would just about kill me off and I don't fancy walking about like a stuffed ostrich for twelve months or more."

"I take it, pain relieving medication isn't sufficient then."

"The only thing that gives me some relief is what they call, 'The Gold Remedy' I pick up from Brakers Pharmacists, round in Princes Street, but he only lets me have one packet a week and I've usually run out after three days. When that's been used up, it's back to sitting on broken glass again, my old mucker."

"There must be a reason for that. As your friend, I can only advise you to put yourself in the hands of the physicians, Frederick."

"Out of the question."

"Have you any idea what's in these remedies you're taking."

"No, and I don't want to know, as long as they give me some relief and they do. Never mind that anyway, tell me more about the post mortem on that feller from the docks."

Whatever discomfort Morgan had been experiencing had obviously subsided and Rayner could only assume he'd taken one of those miracle powders before the Chief Inspector had entered his office. Without further ado, the celebrated detective gave Morgan an attenuated account of what Doctor Critchley had earlier shared with him, confirming that death was due to drowning. He also placed some emphasis on the fact the attack on Joseph Kelly had been a tortuous one, mentioning the victim's kneecaps had been pierced prior to his ending.

"Christ, and I thought my lot was painful enough."

"The motive does appear to be some kind of revenge act, to have been so brutal and callous as that."

"Or they needed to put him up as an example to silence others," Morgan suggested.

"Yes, that is a possibility."

The Chief Inspector needed to get back to his deliberations on the case and left Morgan, while he was still on top and whilst his relationship with his old friend was still intact. He could only hope that the remedial effect those white powders were having on the Chief Superintendent would become more prolonged in time. Until then, he had to be prepared for any other unexpected dramatic change in Morgan's character.

Chapter Three

According to Jack Robinson, the victim's wife, Mrs. Katherine Kelly, was naturally distraught at hearing of her husband's murder and too inconsolable to converse for any length of time. The young Detective Sergeant explained that he thought it best to leave her in the company of her two young daughters.

"But I did manage to find out that her husband was, in his wife's opinion, an honest hard-working man who never failed to put food on the table sir." Robinson continued, "When I asked if she had ever known him be involved in fights, she told me, never and that he wasn't the type."

"Which supports what Patrick Cronin told us down at the docks," Henry Bustle remarked.

Rayner looked at both his Sergeants and declared that revenge was the most favoured motive for the murder and they would have to take the Investigation forward on that basis.

"There is one other thing sir," Robinson said, "We found what looks like some tramp's sleeping arrangement in the dock next to the London Dock, where the body was found."

"St. Katharine Dock?"

"Yes sir, well actually it was Bartholomew Wright, the docks supervisor who pointed it out to us and I've told him to leave it well alone, thinking you might like to look at it yourself. It's only a few rags and some old bedding, but I thought the proximity of it to the murder might be of some interest. I also asked the lads who are still down there completing the searches to keep an eye on it."

"Well done Jack, I think we should all go and take a look."

Rayner's carriage was waiting for him in the backyard and within a few minutes, all three detectives were being conveyed back to London's dockland.

It was as Jack Robinson had described, a pile of rags partially concealed in between two separate warehouses, undoubtedly used by some individual to get their head down. The Chief Inspector was considering the possibility of the unknown itinerant having been the killer, when he came across an interesting object. A rickety handcart had been abandoned just at the back of one of the warehouses adjacent to where the bedding had been discovered. It contained mostly discarded rubbish, old pots and pans and rusted pieces of piping, certainly nothing of value.

"This lot probably belonged to the same geezer what got his head down here," Henry Bustle suggested.

"Very possibly Henry," Rayner answered, remembering what Frederick Morgan had mentioned about the youth his daughter, Estelle, had been concerned about. Raphael Dickens had been known to push a handcart through the streets in search of cast-off items he could sell on.

The senior detective turned to Jack Robinson and instructed him to see if there was any record at Scotland Yard of the same itinerant the Chief Superintendent had been interested in finding. He also told a bemused Henry Bustle to arrange for the handcart and everything contained inside it, to be taken back and stored at their headquarters building. Although, the discovery required further investigation, Richard Rayner doubted that a lad such as Dickens, as he had been described, would have been capable of committing the same atrocities against Joseph Kelly, but the reason for his disappearance might somehow be linked to the murder.

Following his most recent and unfortunate encounter with Frederick

Morgan, Richard Rayner quickly discovered he hadn't been the only recipient of the Welshman's fits of pique. A number of guarded complaints made by various members of the detective branch, regarding the Chief Superintendent's recent behaviour, came to his notice. In particular, it was said that the former Guards officer had acted excessively, when becoming upset by the slightest thing and on one occasion, had actually struck a young uniformed officer in the cellblock. The only misdemeanour committed by the lad was to omit calling Morgan, 'sir', when discussing some frivolous subject.

Rayner was well aware of the strength of character possessed by the majority of police officers he served with, knowing that not one of them would make a peep about the behaviour of a senior officer, unless the kind of conduct they had been subjected to, had been far more than just aggravating. He also became privy to another disturbing story told by the local Detective Inspector working at Cannon Row police station. Apparently, Morgan had randomly visited and found most of the detectives sitting at their desks dealing with paperwork. After vociferously bawling them all out, for not being on the streets chasing down criminals, he then kicked over a waste paper bin, before clubbing a couple of his subordinates to the floor, having to be restrained by others.

These were certainly not the actions of the same man Richard Rayner had worked with and got to know intimately over so many years and he was in no doubt, Frederick Morgan, had undergone some kind of dramatic and unpleasant change in his character. Of course, the Chief Superintendent had admitted to being subjected to a painful affliction, but his most successful detective was convinced there was more to his disturbing behavioural patterns, than just his personal battle with haemorrhoids. Morgan's mental problem had become a top priority for Rayner and he was determined to get to the bottom of it.

Sally-Anne Morgan, was the part-owner of a static circus in Bermondsey, from which she and her business partner, Emily Pratchett, had become extremely wealthy in recent years. She lived with her husband, Frederick Morgan and his daughter, Estelle, in a large house located in its own grounds in Richmond, just a mile from where Richard Rayner resided with his wife, Clarice. Unlike his colleague, who had married into money, the Chief Inspector had always been financially independent and both he and Clarice were able to employ domestic staff at the time they married.

On the afternoon following the discovery of the murder of Joseph Kelly, and knowing the Chief Superintendent was still engaged working at Scotland Yard, Richard Rayner went to pay Sally-Anne a visit. At the time, she was resting in between her circus performances that involved a sharp-shooting act with Emily Pratchett, the co-owner. It was one of the highlights of the circus programme.

The smartly dressed detective instantly apologised for disturbing Mrs. Morgan, who, in her normal manner welcomed her visitor warmly, inviting him to take refreshments, which he politely accepted. At the lady's suggestion, they walked together in the extensive gardens at the back of the house, admiring the golds and browns of the trees and hedgerows, enjoying the peaceful serenity whilst taking in the Autumnal air. Naturally, Sally-Anne was puzzled by Rayner's presence and eventually enquired if something had happened at work, causing him to appear on her doorstep.

"Not really Sal, it's just that recently, some of us have become concerned about Frederick's behaviour and I was hoping you might be able to throw some light on anything that has happened, which he might have mentioned to you. Some incident likely to have derailed him from his usual characteristic ways."

"My word, as bad as that, Richard."

"Well, it's just that he seems to have changed Sal. He tends to snap everybody's head off over the slightest thing and storms through the corridors on occasions, bawling and shouting at anyone who gets in his way, at times offering physical violence. I've never known him to be this way." He continued to explain, "Then he'll go quiet and remains as nice as pie for a few hours, before erupting again when some small or insignificant thing seems to get under his skin."

Sally-Anne listened intently to what was being said and when they reached a small alcove with a seating area, near to a summer house, offered Rayner a seat.

"I've asked James to bring our tea to us here, if that's suitable for you, Richard?" she confirmed, referring to the Morgans' butler.

Rayner just nodded and continued with his tale of woe.

"I want to help, Sal, if possible. People are beginning to talk, you know what they are like and if some of the stories and rumours being told reach the top floor, Frederick might just find himself being scrutinised by the wrong people."

She smiled nervously, or so the Chief Inspector thought, before describing how a couple of mornings beforehand, her husband had actually chastised his daughter Estelle, for having spilt milk on the breakfast table.

"It was only a minor accident, Richard, but you would have thought by Frederick's response the poor girl had just stolen the petty cash at the school where she works. He was like a wild bull in a China shop, which was more surprising as she is the love of his life and he would do anything for her. It was an incredible outburst, the likes of which we have never seen before and almost reduced poor Estelle to tears."

"That seems to fit in with his recent behaviour at work, Sal."

Having taken Richard Rayner into her confidence, the lady of the house continued to relate to other incidents where her husband had snapped her head off, for no apparent reason.

"But until now, I never really gave it much thought, except to suspect it was a passing phase probably the result of overwork."

"I understand from what he has told me, he still suffers greatly from haemorrhoids, has he ever spoken about that with you?"

"My God, Richard, he would never dare, he'd be too embarrassed to mention such a thing. Of course, I'm aware he has the occasional attack, but that's all I am privy to. Frederick is an extremely proud man, which I'm sure you already know."

"Yes, I do realise that." Rayner then asked if she was aware of any medication her husband was taking for his condition.

She confirmed that, apart from the usual medicinal concoctions intended to relieve pain, to her knowledge no other additional aids had been administered in recent weeks.

James the butler appeared, carrying a tray of tea and the necessary accessories. After pouring, the servant left the couple to continue their conversation.

"Has Frederick ever mentioned a remedy he is taking, known as the Gold Remedy?" Richard Rayner enquired.

She shook her head and referred to a bizarre incident she had just recalled.

"About a couple of weeks ago, in the early hours, I found his side of the bed was empty and from the bedroom window could vaguely see him walking through the shrubbery with a loaded shotgun."

"Did he say what he was doing?"

"Yes, he was still in his night clothes and told me he had spotted a tiger in the garden and was intending to shoot it. When I asked him where on earth he thought a tiger had come from, he suggested it might have escaped from our circus."

"And I take it, that hadn't been the case?"

"We have never had any tigers, Richard. I thought at the time, he'd just had a bad dream." She paused and then asked a fairly disturbing question.

"Do you think Frederick is going mad, Richard?"

It was a suggestion that had already gone through the Chief Inspector's mind, but he answered reassuringly, "No, I don't think so, Sal. I'm not sure what's causing this and can only suggest we both keep a quiet eye on him, until we have our answer. I need to find out what exactly is contained in that so-called Gold Remedy substance he's been taking."

Both then agreed to keep their meeting confidential, until at least they had got to the bottom of Morgan's recurring problems.

At the same time as Richard Rayner was delving into the current difficulties being experienced by Frederick Morgan, Henry Bustle was busying himself in the ground-floor detectives' office at Scotland Yard, having just returned with the handcart and its contents thought to belong to Raphael Dickens. The Sergeant was searching through some files to see if the murdered victim, Joseph Kelly, had any police record when he jumped with a start, after a hand was suddenly and unexpectedly placed on his shoulder. It was the Chief Superintendent.

"Do me a favour, Bustle, nip along to old man Braker at the pharmacists in Princes Street and pick up a parcel for me, my old mucker." Morgan had the look of a mischievous child and spoke almost in a whisper, as though parting with a state secret.

"Of course, sir, as soon as I've just finished..."

"Now, Bustle," the senior detective snapped, causing a few other heads to turn, before lowering his voice again and confirming, "There's nothing to pay, so don't worry about that but keep it to yourself, eh. I'll be in my office." Morgan's approach hadn't been in his usual boisterous manner, but more comparable with a school bully, attempting to persuade another child to do something extremely untoward.

By the time Richard Rayner returned to Scotland Yard, following his visit to the Morgans residence, he bumped into his Sergeant in the back yard, just about to deliver the Chief Superintendent's parcel, as directed.

When the Chief Inspector asked what it was, Bustle truthfully confessed to having just run an errand for the enigmatic Mr. Morgan.

"Any idea what it contains, Henry?"

"No sir, but I have a note here from Mr. Braker, addressed to the gaffer and to be handed to him together with the parcel." The Sergeant took it from his jacket pocket and handed it to Rayner. The note just confirmed that the package contained, what was referred to as, 'Gold Remedy' and that the recipient should administer the contents sparingly and as previously recommended.

"Very well, Henry. I'll take it up to him."

Bustle looked sheepishly at the Chief Inspector and begged that he should be allowed to complete the task, explaining that Morgan had requested the transaction be kept confidential.

That concerned Rayner, but he agreed not to cause any possible grief for his Sergeant and changed the subject, enquiring if more had become known about the murdered victim, Joseph Kelly.

"No sir, Jack has gone back to see the widow to try and find out more about his background and any known friends or associates he might have."

"So be it, Henry, you best get that package to Mr. Morgan before something happens to it."

Bartholomew Wright was the London Port Authority's officially appointed docks supervisor. He was a tall, slim man in his mid-forties, who spoke with a local accent and could easily be recognised amongst the workforce by his collar and tie, being the only employee wearing such attire. Owing to the incident involving Shed number nine where the dead man had been found, Wright explained to the detectives who had remained examining the scene at the request of Richard Rayner, that at present, chaos reigned. The closure by the police of the London Dock, meant a large proportion of the expected river traffic had been diverted temporarily to both the adjacent St. Katharine and the Royal Albert Docks. He was told by Detective Sergeant Claude Davey, in charge of the scene examination, that things could be returned to normal by the following day.

"We've virtually finished here now, Mr. Wright," the Sergeant explained.

"Thank the Lord for small mercies," the supervisor remarked, "It's been so bloody inconvenient having to move stuff around between the other docks."

"I appreciate that sir, but as I said, we're virtually finished here. There's just those two large barrels in the corner over there to be looked at and that's it, we'll all be off home."

Bartholomew Wright nodded and quickly explained the two remaining items that stood in the opposite corner to where the murdered victim had been found, were pickling barrels waiting to be disposed of at sea. When asked for the reason such items were got rid of in such a way, he told Davey that both barrels were filled with spent vinegar and had been standing there for a considerable length of time, waiting to be picked up.

"To be honest, Sergeant, I suspect there's little vinegar now left inside the bloody things and we usually move them out quicker than this but I must confess, I forgot all about them, knowing they wouldn't come to any harm. In fact, some of the men use the tops to put their victuals on when taking their lunch breaks."

Sergeant Davey asked how long the barrels had been there and Mr. Wright could only tell him, for as long as he'd been working as the supervisor there.

"I take it, they are both sealed then?"

"Oh yes. You'd soon know if they weren't by the stench that would come out of them. It has to be about near enough ten years, since they were moved into that corner."

"And I take it, they would have remained sealed during all that time then," Claude Davey suggested, looking for a reason for not having to look inside the heavy objects.

"Yes, as I said, about ten or more years ago I reckon but there'll be a record in the ledger we keep if you really need to know the date."

"Don't worry, I'll take your word for it, sir."

Davey then told his Detective Constable Raymond George, and Constable Granville Perkins, two officers he had been supervising, to begin to clear away their equipment, as he intended calling it a day.

"What about those monstrosities over there, sarge?" DC George asked, referring to the pickling barrels, "Shall I just mark them as having been checked?"

Davey hesitated, before having a change of heart. Turning to Bartholomew Wright, the Sergeant asked if the supervisor could unseal the barrels, having decided to search them after all.

"Of course, if that's what you want, but don't forget to hold your breath. I'll try and get them resealed as soon as you've dipped your nose inside them." The man chuckled at his own descriptive quirkiness.

"I think it best and then we can get out of your way."

The Sergeant turned to one of the uniformed constable's guarding the shed and told him to fetch a lamp, as the light was beginning to fade rapidly.

Just as the constable was returning with a Bulls Eye lantern, the dock supervisor was prising open the first of the two barrels with a crowbar, having called for a labourer to help with the resealing once the detectives had made their inspection. Suddenly the air was filled with the most obnoxious and putrid smell imaginable, forcing the five men in attendance to step back, each of them gasping and covering their noses and mouths with their hands. The stench was so penetrating and disgusting, young Constable Granville Perkins rushed out of the shed to throw up and the others blasphemed at such a foul smell unexpectedly attacking their nostrils.

"Close the bloody thing up again," Davey shouted across at Bartholomew Wright, who quickly nodded his compliance. But before resealing the lid, Wright glanced inside the first barrel and stepped back, pale faced and in total shock, almost stumbling over his own booted feet.

"I think Sergeant, you need to see what's inside here," he cried out, looking directly at Davey with a pair of eyes that resembled someone who had just awoken from their worst nightmare.

Davey grabbed the lantern brought in by one of his constables and cautiously approached the source of the obnoxious stench. Peering down into what was left of the ten-year old pickling vinegar, the Detective Sergeant could see the outline of a human body curled up at the bottom.

"My God, shift your arse and go and get hold of Rayner," he instructed his detective.

Chapter Four

Much to the detectives' surprise and astonishment, the message received at Scotland Yard was quite clear, another body had been found in Shed number nine and it was Frederick Morgan who led the way down to the docks, accompanied by Richard Rayner and Henry Bustle. The trio arrived fairly quickly and just a minute or two before the pathologist, by which time the foul odour coming from the occupied pickling barrel had dispersed a little. Not surprisingly, they found everyone present standing outside the large wooden structure and Sergeant Claude Davey, greeted them before relaying all he knew to the Chief Superintendent. By that time, it was early evening and darkness had already fallen, resulting in constables' providing lighting from burning lamps and lanterns. For once, a cold breeze coming off the water was welcome, helping to dissipate much of the stench that still lingered inside the shed.

Frederick Morgan's first enquiry was whether the second barrel contained yet another dead body, to which Davey had to confess they hadn't got round to opening that one.

"Then get on with it," the Chief Superintendent demanded.

"I'll go and fetch the supervisor, Mr. Wright sir."

"Stop acting the prat, Claude, and give me that crow bar."

Morgan then broke the seal of the second barrel and lifted the top off. Fortunately, the odour was nowhere near the potency of the first and was found to contain only a small amount of distilled spirit in the bottom.

When Doctors Critchley and Elizabeth Green arrived, the older of the two physicians immediately suggested, because of the partially decomposed condition of the body, it would be impracticable to perform a post mortem at St. Mary's. He was adamant the task required by law should be completed on site, to which Morgan agreed. In fact, the senior detective present would have agreed to any suggestion that avoided delay in escaping from the foul atmosphere still prominent. It did appear that for the time being the senior Scotland Yard man was his normal self, although watched closely by Richard Rayner, in case of any sudden impulsive and uncharacteristic outburst.

"You'll probably find that bleedin' thing inside that barrel is liquified by now doc," Morgan jested, inviting a look of disdain from the pathologist, who had always found the Chief Superintendent to be too coarse and flippant for his liking.

Ignoring the remark, Critchley requested a large tent be erected next to the shed and a table upon which he could conduct the necessary examination of the remains. Metal bowls, various surgical instruments and aprons were sent for from the mortuary and a short delay was necessary whilst preparations were made.

"How long as our pickle head been stuck inside that thing," Morgan asked.

"According to Claude Davey sir, the dock supervisor reckons both barrels have remained there sealed for at least nine or ten years," Rayner declared. The Chief Inspector then turned to Henry Bustle and instructed him to approach the dock supervisor, Bartholomew Wright, and find out exactly from his records when the items had been originally sealed.

A marquee type tent was erected soon enough and constables were deployed with the unenviable task of transferring the partially preserved human figure on a wooden board, each of them having tied handkerchiefs around their faces. Just as they were carrying out their instructions under the watchful eye of Albert Critchley, another item was recovered from inside that particular barrel. It was a gold pocket watch bearing the initials, L.C engraved on the back and was quickly handed to Richard Rayner, for closer inspection.

Henry Bustle re-appeared with the dock supervisor, having wasted little time in confirming the date on which the pickling barrels had been placed and sealed inside the shed.

"According to Mr. Wright's ledger sir, they were both first recorded on the 4th October 1881, nine years ago and have remained there ever since."

"Until today," Rayner remarked, before turning to Bartholomew Wright and asking the obvious question, as to why the items had been left in storage for all that time and from whence they had come.

"I've already explained to Sergeant Davey, Chief Inspector," the supervisor answered.

"Then explain to me, if you will sir."

Mr. Wright did so, confessing that he had inadvertently forgotten they existed and should have arranged for their disposal long before now. His concerns that he might face some kind of admonishment for having failed to carry out his duties properly, were put aside when Rayner suggested that it was a good thing he had been neglectful, otherwise the remains might never have been discovered.

"Is it possible someone could have opened the barrel and resealed it," the Chief Inspector enquired.

The supervisor shook his head and confirmed that if the original seal had been broken, it would have been visible. Wright also confirmed that at the time both barrels were received for storage, no record had been made of their source, explaining that they could have been delivered by any factory or shop that used the substance contained within them.

"And I assume there is no record of the person who would have received them."

"No, it could have been any of the workers here at the time."

Although aberrant in Rayner's view, Bartholomew Wright's

forgetfulness was sufficiently bizarre to be believed and he handed the pocket watch recovered from where the deceased had been found to Henry Bustle for further investigation later.

"I take it those initials, L.C do not mean anything to you Mr. Wright?" he asked the supervisor.

The Port Authority's employee glanced at the timepiece and initially shook his head. Then he asked to take a closer look before outwardly showing some recognition.

"I could be wrong Chief Inspector, but those initials could stand for Leonard Crockett."

"Who was Leonard Crockett, Mr. Wright?" Richard Rayner enquired.

"He used to be a Stevedore who worked here at the time I took up my present position and from what I can remember, he spent most of his time employed in St. Katharine Dock next door."

"I recall he was also murdered by his wife sir," Claude Davey announced, having remained close by, listening to the verbal exchanges.

"Do you remember much about the case, Claude?" Rayner asked.

"Oh yes sir, I was a young detective at the time and it was the first murder I was involved in. Leonard Crockett was stabbed to death by his wife who was convicted of his murder but the body was never found."

"How do we know he was stabbed to death, if the body was never found?"

"Because the murder weapon was found at the scene; a large kitchen knife covered in blood, I remember sir."

"I take it she was hanged?"

"No, she wasn't. There was some kind of mitigating circumstances I think and she was saved from the hangman. The woman should still be serving a life sentence in Holloway, unless I'm mistaken. I shall have to look at the papers back at Scotland Yard to be sure."

"Where was the murder supposed to have happened, Claude?"

"Where they lived sir, in Denmar Street, Whitechapel."

"It looks cut and dried then, Rayner," Frederick Morgan suggested.

"We shall see sir. Henry, go back and see if you can lay your hands on the file."

Bustle needed no second invitation to leave the scene and scurried away to fulfil the Chief Inspector's request.

"I shall go back with him, Rayner," Morgan announced, finally finding a valid reason for leaving the stink that was becoming unbearable for the Welshman, "Let me know about the post mortem in the morning."

An eerie silence prevailed over the whole scene, with Albert Critchley spending the next couple of hours conducting his examination of the human remains, ably assisted by Elizabeth Green, who had accompanied him to gain more experience. When the pathologist had finally completed his work, he reported his findings to Richard Rayner, who had been standing inside the temporary shelter, watching from a distance.

"Step over here, Richard, and let me show you," the elderly physician invited, which Rayner did so, without giving the pathologist's request a second thought.

"He was fully clothed, as you can see, wearing a jacket, shirt and trousers." Everything about the corpse was blackened as a result of partial decomposition and having been subjected to the substance it had remained in for such a lengthy period of time.

"There can be no doubt he died from three stab wounds to the chest, here, here and here, the latter having penetrated the heart, so death would have been virtually instant. There are also some wounds inflicted to the right lower arm and palm of the right hand." The doctor pointed to the marks he was referring to that were just barely visible.

"Defence marks, I should imagine," Rayner commented.

"Yes, no doubt. Unfortunately, there isn't much more we can determine because of the time it's taken to recover the body."

"No other wounds visible then doctor?"

"No, with Doctor Green's assistance, I need to clear up and get these samples off to the laboratory and then might I suggest an undertaker be called for a burial that is obviously well overdue."

When Richard Rayner stepped back outside he found Jack Robinson standing with Claude Davey and quickly asked the older Sergeant for the name of the woman who had been convicted of the murder.

"As I said sir, it was the man's wife, Annie Crockett. A waif of a lass if I remember correctly. I wouldn't be surprised if she's already expired in prison. She certainly wasn't the strongest of women you'd ever come across."

"Can you recall the number of the house where they lived in Denmar Street?"

"I can't I'm afraid sir, but I could take you to it. I remember it was thought she'd killed her husband in the kitchen and we found the murder weapon in the back garden."

"Did they have any children can you recollect, Claude?" Rayner enquired further.

"Now you come to mention it, there was a young daughter who I think witnessed the murder or saw something that helped to convict her mother." The Sergeant paused, trying hard to remember more about the incident, before continuing, "That was it, the girl saw her mother cleaning up the blood off the kitchen floor, it'll all be in the file sir."

"Can you remember the daughter's name?"

"No, sorry, but I think she was only about eight or nine years of age at the time. I know it knocked her about a bit, as you can imagine."

"Yes, thank you Sergeant. Get yourself home and if I need any further information, I'll send for you."

When Rayner and Robinson finally returned to Scotland Yard, they found Henry Bustle going through the various papers connected with the case, having retrieved the file on the Leonard Crockett murder from the basement.

"It's as Mr. Morgan said sir, it appears to be cut and dried," the Sergeant declared, "The murder weapon was a kitchen knife found in the back garden of number 73 Denmar Street, Whitechapel, where the couple lived with their nine-year old daughter, Priscilla Crockett."

"Who would now be an eighteen-year-old young lady," Rayner remarked.

Bustle continued to read from the file, confirming that the convicted woman, Annie Crockett, had initially confessed to the murder but had then retracted her statement, pleading not guilty at her subsequent trial.

"It appears that, because no actual body had been found at the time of her conviction, she was spared the noose and is currently serving a life sentence in Holloway, as Claude Davey mentioned."

Rayner then suggested that whoever had put the dead man inside the pickling barrel had no intention of it ever being found, to which both his Sergeants agreed. The Chief Inspector then posed the question as to how, if the murder took place in Denmar Street, it was moved to the London Dock.

"Perhaps it was placed in the barrel of picking vinegar at the house, before being transported to the dock," Jack Robinson suggested.

Rayner smiled and responded to that notion by confessing he would have found it impossible to have moved a large oak barrel, filled with liquid as well as a human body, just a few feet, never mind a mile or so to the docks, even if a horse drawn carriage was used. It was a mystery that must have been looked at by the investigating officers at the time, or so Henry Bustle believed.

"Not so, Henry, they wouldn't have known at that time the victim had been taken in a barrel down to the docks."

"No, of course not sir, but I wonder if the killing of Joseph Kelly is connected in some way with the Crockett murder." the older of the two Sergeants offered.

"We don't know that yet, Henry, but let's keep an open mind."

"I have a feeling you are doubting this woman's guilt, Chief Inspector," Bustle suggested, once more trying to read his Chief Inspector's thoughts.

"I appreciate the lady in question made an initial confession to the killing, Henry, but I think we need to dig further, as on the surface, everything seems to have been far too pat for my liking. Does it make any mention in those papers of what her defence was at the trial?"

"From what I've read so far, sir, it seems she never had a defence."

"Then I think we need to re-open the case and see where it leads us to."

"You do believe then that she was innocent?"

"I'm not saying that, Henry. We need to approach this Investigation believing she was innocent and if we find that was the case, then an injustice has been committed and the real killer has been walking about free for the past nine years or so."

"Or, if we fail to find that was the case, it will show she was guilty of that for which she is serving her sentence."

"Exactly, Henry."

The house in Denmar Street, where the Crockett family once lived was now a small terraced property, void of any occupants. Claude Davey had managed to obtain the keys for the dwelling from the Whitechapel Housing Department, before accompanying Richard Rayner to inspect where the murder of Leonard Crockett was believed to have taken place. The Sergeant's recollection of his first murder was a lot clearer by that time and as soon as they stepped inside the narrow hallway, Davey began to recall when he was there as a young inexperienced detective. He confirmed that very little appeared to have changed, except for the fact there was no longer any furniture present.

Rayner was particularly interested in the back kitchen where it had been alleged the atrocity had taken place and made that his first location to visit.

"Young Priscilla, their daughter, gave evidence at the trial outlining how she had looked into the kitchen from the hallway on that particular evening and saw her mother crouching down, cleaning the floor with a cloth," the Sergeant explained.

"Did she say what exactly it was her mother was cleaning up off the floor."

"No sir, but we assumed it would have been blood."

"Did the girl say anything about how her mother looked at that particular time, anxious or perhaps concentrated on what she was doing."

"I remember she did tell the court she thought her mother looked worried, sir."

"Was any trace of blood found here, Claude?"

"No sir, we just thought that Annie had made a good job of cleaning it up."

Rayner looked sceptical and then asked Davey to show him exactly where the kitchen knife had been found in the back garden.

It was a small patch of overgrown turf with a path running down one side and the Sergeant stood about halfway down, near to the centre of the garden.

"The grass was much shorter then, obviously sir and the kitchen knife was found lying just here, covered to its hilt in blood."

"Not concealed or hidden from view then."

"No sir, we thought at the time she had just thrown it or dropped it here after committing the dirty deed on her husband."

"So, I take it, apart from the blood on the knife, there were no other helpful signs anywhere else?"

"No sir."

"Did you ever recover the cloth Mrs. Crockett was using to clean the floor with, Claude?"

"No sir."

"Was any consideration given to what she might have done with the body?"

"It was thought she might have buried it somewhere local or perhaps further away. We did make a search of the area but of course, got nowhere with that enquiry." Davey paused, as if remembering something else of importance, before continuing, "I recall there was a woman living next door at number seventy-one, who heard the couple fighting earlier on the same evening."

"Yes, a Mrs. Rose Pendry," Rayner suggested, having read the lady's statement in the file before leaving Scotland Yard earlier that morning.

"I think that was her name sir."

"Then let's go and see if she still lives there."

Mrs. Pendry was a blonde woman who answered the door wearing a pink housecoat, the front of which was covered in rolls of lace. Most noticeable was her face had been subjected to a layer of heavy make-up, as if she was about to attend a ball. After Rayner had introduced himself, she invited both detectives' inside, where they were taken into a lounge that appeared to have been recently decorated. It was obvious that the woman was extremely house proud and believed in keeping up with appearances. There wasn't a sign of a single hair out of place on her head, or a solitary cushion having been sat on. So fastidiously tidy was the room they occupied Rayner thought the interior resembled a doctor's clinic, rather than somewhere in which people actually lived their lives.

He verbally took her back to the night of the alleged murder and asked what exactly she had heard coming from next door.

"They were arguing Chief Inspector, quite loudly. The walls are only thin and I could hear two voices going hammer and tongue at one another."

"Mr. and Mrs. Crockett?"

"I presumed it was them, yes. I couldn't be absolutely certain as the voices were muffled, but it was definitely a man and a woman."

"Arguing or fighting, Mrs. Pendry?"

"Definitely arguing."

"How did you get on with Mrs. Crockett?"

"I didn't really know her. She wasn't my kind of person, if you know what I mean."

"What about her husband, did you know him at all?"

"Yes, Len Crockett was a nice man, often spoke whenever I came across him. He occasionally drank in the same pub as my husband."

"What's your husband's name by the way?" Rayner asked.

"Charlie."

"Did he overhear the argument as well?"

"No, he was in The Bushell at the time, which is at the bottom of the street and didn't get back until after closing time, about half past ten I think."

Richard Rayner had one more question for the lady.

"Do you know of any male friend or male callers Mrs. Crockett might have had around that time?"

"Plenty, she had more than one who used to call when her husband was at work, but I didn't know any of them personally."

"So, you would describe her as being a loose woman."

She smirked when answering. "Very loose, Chief Inspector and take it from me, she deserved all she got."

Those last few words caused Rayner to look across at Claude Davey, who just shook his head. There was definitely a hint of jealousy or something similar to resentment in the woman's voice.

Chapter Five

Spotty Finkel had just finished cleaning out the spittoons in the empty bar room of the Canal Bargee public house; a daily job he cherished in return for a miserly glass or two of black ale from the landlord. When the diminutive itinerant saw Henry Bustle appear, he spontaneously made for the door leading into the backyard, attempting to avoid another thick ear that was the usual greeting he received from the Sergeant.

Bustle leapt across the room, managing to grab hold of the shabbily dressed little man's mop of unkempt hair, just before his regular informant escaped through the open door. A sharp slap across the head with an open palm followed, before Mr. Finkel was dragged out of the public house on to the street.

"One of these days, you slimy little toad, I'm going to let you go and then broadcast to the world what a traitorous squealer you are," the Scotland Yard detective threatened. In truth, he was the only friend the small-time villain possessed.

"I don't mean no harm, Mr. Bustle, it's just that every time I see you, I cop for a clout across the head."

"That's just to wake you up, Spotty, and to raise that twisted brain of yours out of the swamp it sits in, inside that mass of bone you call a skull."

"I'm a working man, Mr. Bustle, and I've got rights."

"The only rights you've got my little cock sparrow, are those I give to you. Now listen carefully, if you can concentrate for more than a couple of seconds without a bucketful of booze inside yer."

"I'm listening," the objectionable little man confirmed, resulting in Bustle releasing his grip.

Spotty's playground was the Whitechapel district, adjacent to the docks and he usually got to know about most things that went on, especially the kind of recent gossip that was circulating around the corner public houses and soup kitchens, which Henry Bustle was interested in. What the ferret-faced wanderer didn't know about, wasn't worth picking up on.

"Joseph Kelly was the name of the geezer found beaten to death in the London Dock. So, tell me, my smelly little wretch, what's being said about it on the streets."

"You have a way with words Mr. Bustle, that don't encourage somebody like me to be an upright citizen and I ain't favouring having personal insults thrown down my throat all the bleedin' time."

The Sergeant shoved a one-pound note in the man's grubby palm that quickly disappeared into the pocket of his well-worn flannel trousers, held up by a piece of hemp.

"How encouraged are you now, Spotty?"

The man grinned, showing a set of blackened teeth, a couple which were missing and quickly flashed his ferret like eyes around where they were standing, to ensure they were alone.

"Just a bit of respect goes a long way, Mr. Bustle," he mumbled.

"Time to cut out the bullshit mate and tell me what you know about this Kelly geezer."

"Honest enough bloke from what's they're saying and lives with his missus up in Mary Ann Street."

"I already know that. So, what's the quid I've just given you worth?"

"He ain't your normal villain from all accounts and drinks in The Lantern on the corner of where he lives."

"Spotty, this is like drawing teeth, not that you've got many left to pull. Now take a deep breath and come out with it or so help me, I'll start digging into those cabbage patches on either side of your head with a spike."

"Ain't that worth a quid, Mr. Bustle."

"Spotty?"

"Okay, okay. If he was found in the London Dock, people says he was probably involved in the smuggling that's going on there."

"What smuggling?"

The informant stood for a moment in silence, with a wry smile on his face and looking at Henry Bustle in expectation. A ten-shilling note was produced, that rapidly followed the same path as the previous payment.

"They reckons all kind of stuff is brought in, mostly at night, booze and baccy and all that kind of merchandise. It comes off the boats that tie up down there."

"Who's behind it?"

"Now if I knew that, I'd be asking for ten quid, Mr. Bustle."

"Then tell me, who did you hear this from?"

"Everybody with a pint of ale in front of them. It's general knowledge around here, but I can try and find out some more for you, Mr. Bustle."

"You do that Spotty, and you might just yet earn that tenner you mentioned."

For a number of years now, Frederick Morgan, had always been the first to arrive each morning at Scotland Yard. However, Richard Rayner had noticed over recent weeks the Chief Superintendent wasn't surfacing in his office until closer to midday. At first, he paid little attention to his senior's change of habit but having given more consideration to Morgan's apparent change in attitude and behaviour, began to wonder if being late for work was part of that same problem. The Chief Inspector calculated there was another hour to go, before the Head of Department would show up and decided to slip along the corridor to the adjoining office. He knocked and having received no answer, stepped inside.

The odour of tobacco smoked from Morgan's pipe the night before remained in the air and Rayner quickly went to the man's desk. He found the top right-hand drawer locked and worked quickly with his penknife to open it. The item he was looking for was there, a small package marked, 'Gold Remedy'. It had been already opened but just as Richard Rayner was about to delve into the contents, he heard footsteps approaching the door from the outside corridor. The last thing he needed was for his Chief Superintendent to find him rifling through his desk without a reasonable excuse and at that very moment, he couldn't think of one.

His heart leapt into his mouth and the package quickly went back inside the drawer. Rayner stepped away, just in time to see the office door opening. He breathed a sigh of relief when he saw it was Jack Robinson.

"You look like you've just seen a ghost, sir, if you don't mind…"

"Never you mind, Jack, what are you doing here?"

"I was looking for you sir," the young man confessed, "I have some news about Annie Crockett's daughter, Priscilla."

"Very well Jack, wait for me in my office, I won't be long."

The Sergeant disappeared and Rayner stood for a moment recomposing himself. Frederick Morgan was no fool and if he caught his Chief Inspector, or anybody else for that matter, delving into his personal business, he'd bring thunder and lightning down upon their heads. Most likely, in his present mood, he could just physically attack any intrusion on his privacy, no matter who it was.

Quickly, he returned to the desk and recovered the package. Inside, he found small caches of what looked like a white powdered substance and took one, concealing it in his jacket pocket. Having returned the item back to its original location, he closed the drawer, ensuring it was locked before hastily making his way back to his own office to converse with Jack Robinson, arriving just a little breathless.

"I spoke to one of the solicitors that was a member of Annie Crockett's defence team," the Sergeant explained, "I was trying to find out more about what was offered to the court to prove her innocence at the trial, sir."

"I understand, Jack."

"Well, the subject of his client's daughter came up and Mr. Wetland, that was the name of her solicitor, explained that after Mrs. Crockett had been sentenced, Priscilla was moved to an orphanage in Kentish Town."

"She won't be there now, Jack, that's for sure."

"I know sir, but this is the real surprise, according to Mr. Wetland, the last he heard of her, Priscilla had changed her name and was going under the name of Yvonne Petroni."

"She's married then?"

"I'm not sure, but she's working as a trapeze artist for a group calling themselves, 'The Flying Petroni's', at the Pratchett and Longfellow Circus."

Both detectives were well aware that Sally-Anne Morgan's name before she was married to their Chief Superintendent, was Longfellow and the circus referred to by Robinson was in fact, the one she was part owner of, located in Bermondsey.

"Well done, Jack, we need to speak to the former Miss Crockett as a matter of urgency, but first I have a small errand to do."

Jack Robinson watched the Chief Inspector reach for his top hat and coat and then asked if the senior detective really believed that Annie Crockett had been innocent of murdering her husband and hiding his body in a pickling barrel.

Rayner smiled and calmly explained, "To be honest Jack, I'm not sure but what I don't believe is that the original Investigation was conducted with sufficient guile."

"I was just wondering sir, only there seems to have been a lot of evidence piled up against her."

"I think there appears to have been a lot of assumption, but let's just keep an open mind, Jack."

Instead of having his driver take the two detectives' directly to Bermondsey, Richard Rayner instructed him to stop off at St. Mary's

Hospital first, specifically at the mortuary, which was located in its own building within the hospital grounds. When they arrived, he then instructed the young Sergeant to wait for him inside the carriage before making his way down the steps leading to the only entrance to where the post mortems and other probing assessments were carried out.

Rayner found Elizabeth Green, alone inside the examination room looking as if she was about to leave. The lady physician welcomed him with a broad smile and confirmed that Doctor Critchley had gone out for lunch.

"He should be back shortly though, Richard, unless there's something I can do to help."

"Actually, Elizabeth, it's you I wanted to see." He produced the small cache of white powder taken from Frederick Morgan's desk and enquired if it was possible she could analyse it to see what exactly it contained.

"Of course, I can do that this afternoon for you."

"Thank you, and if I might ask that you don't make any mention of this to anyone else."

She nodded, looking a little mystified by such a strange request, but knowing you didn't question a man of Richard Rayner's reputation.

It was nearing lunchtime when Rayner and Robinson finally arrived at the circus site in Bermondsey. A low-lying mist had failed to lift during the morning and the numerous caravans, mobile homes and tents, clustered together inside a perimeter fence, was similar to some ghostly apparition beneath a grey sky, which an artist would give a lot to capture on canvas. Nearest to the main gates through which the paying public were allowed access, stood the Big Top, impressive even in the greyness of the day with the usual Pratchett and Longfellow pendant remaining limp at the top of the large canvas structure, in the absence of any breeze.

The Chief Inspector's carriage passed through the gates before stopping outside the entrance to where the entertainment was provided. Once inside, they found the centre arena occupied by various circus employee's rehearsing their individual acts, with a number of high wire performers practicing certain manoeuvres in the roof of the Big Top above a widely spread-out safety net. There were two more hours to go before the matinee performance was due to take place and Richard Rayner, looked for and found both Sally-Anne Morgan, and her business partner, Emily Pratchett, standing to one side, conversing with a third lady who was holding the reins of one of the show ponies.

They called over to the flamboyantly dressed detective and his Sergeant in greeting, as soon as they first caught sight of their friend. Both lady owners had known the Chief Inspector for as long as they had been acquainted with Frederick Morgan, and in fact, Rayner had previously helped Miss Pratchett in finding her niece who had been kidnapped up in Cumbria, from where she originated.

Emily welcomed him warmly by kissing him on the cheek and Sally-Anne immediately asked if there was further news regarding her husband's recent odd behaviour.

Rayner chuckled and explained his visit had nothing to do with the Chief Superintendent, although he did enquire if there had been any incidents since the last time the couple had discussed her husband.

"Well, he's still like a cork bobbing up and down in the water, Richard," Sally-Anne submitted, "Nice as pie one minute and bawling his head off the next."

The Chief Inspector thought it was only fair to tell his friend's wife of what steps he'd taken towards getting to the bottom of her husband's problem and did so, having purposefully manoeuvred the lady out of earshot of Jack Robinson. It wasn't as though he didn't trust his Sergeant, he most certainly did, but a degree of reverence had to be maintained when discussing the affairs of a senior officer.

"You think then, he could be doping himself?" she asked.

"I'm not sure Sal, but I need to know what's in those powders he's been taking, it just seems too coincidental. But that's not the reason I'm here, I understand you have a troupe calling themselves, The Flying Petroni's working for you?"

"Yes, they're up there on the high wire, preparing for the matinee that's due to take place this afternoon."

Rayner further explained that he was interested in speaking with one of the group, in particular a Miss Yvonne Petroni, who would now be an eighteen or nineteen-year-old young lady.

"Of course, I'll bring her down for you."

"What kind of a girl is she Sal," Rayner quietly asked.

Sally-Anne couldn't give the detective much information, explaining that the trapeze artists comprised of a father, mother and son, and that Yvonne Petroni had joined them about two years earlier, adopting their surname. She did however, describe the girl as being quiet and unassuming, never causing any problems and certainly very skilled at what she did as a trapeze artist.

Both Rayner and Robinson watched as the slip of a girl descended to the floor of the arena down a rope ladder. She was petite with fair hair tied up in a bun on top of her head and certainly looked younger than her age. In fact, the Sergeant remarked surreptitiously that the girl they had come to see, still looked as though she was of schooling age.

After introducing himself and his Sergeant to the young lady, Richard Rayner asked if there was some where they could go to talk in private and Sally-Anne, handed him the key to her private caravan, located away from the Big Tent.

"Might I ask what this is about sir," Miss Petroni enquired, looking a little sheepish.

"Yes, it's about your mother, miss, but I shall explain more shortly."

Chapter Six

It came as no surprise to Richard Rayner, when at first, the former Priscilla Crockett was reluctant to acknowledge her real name, timidly giving her reasons in an apprehensive manner. The young girl explained just how difficult it had been for her to accept and become widely regarded as the daughter of a murderess. She professed to hating her mother, knowing what she had done and for wrecking her life when so young, in addition to taking her father from her, who she had loved dearly. The pale faced girl, dressed in her circus costume of bright sparkling pink sequins sat in front of the Chief Inspector, looking a pitiful sight indeed and attracting a great deal of sympathy from the celebrated detective.

"Why are you asking about my mother, Chief Inspector?" she finally asked, sitting with her upper body in a posture similar to that of a young ballerina, "I do not wish to discuss what happened all those years ago and prefer it to be left buried in the past."

Rayner leant forward and in a quiet, calm voice explained, "We are trying to unravel the truth about what happened during, what must have been a terrible ordeal for you miss." He paused for a moment, before continuing, "Is it better to know the truth, no matter how long ago the incident happened, rather than allow a wrongful deception to remain festering, where there could have been a possible injustice, especially where your own mother was involved."

"Are you telling me that my mother is innocent, sir?"

"No, I cannot say that at this time but I believe there is a need to establish the reality of certain aspects of the case."

The girl maintained her rigid bearing, but nodded her acquiescence of what she was being offered as a reason for the interview.

"Tell me," Rayner continued, "Did your mother ever confess to you that she murdered your father?" It was a pointed question that had to be asked and the senior detective wanted to get it out of the way sooner, rather than later.

"No, but she didn't have to. I found her washing away his blood on the kitchen floor and the knife she used was found in the back garden."

"How did you know it was your father's blood she was cleaning up?"

"Because one of the policemen told me."

The senior detective sat back in his chair and then begged, "Please, if you can, tell me exactly what you saw and heard on that dreadful night."

Priscilla Crockett quietly and slowly described how she was a mere child of tender years and was awakened by a scream she believed was her mother. She overheard voices arguing downstairs, assuming they belonged to her parents. So disturbed was the little girl, she left her bed carrying a small teddy bear and silently crept down the stairs until reaching the narrow hallway inside the house in Whitechapel, the same dwelling Richard Rayner had already visited. It was then she looked through into the kitchen and could see her mother crouching down on her hands and knees, wiping the kitchen floor with a piece of rag.

Richard Rayner quickly made some notes before continuing his questioning by asking, "Did you see your father at all, at that specific time?"

She shook her head, obviously distressed by having to once again recall her own personal nightmare, one that had lived with her throughout the years that had followed. A daunting look remained on her face throughout the time she spent inside Sally-Anne Morgan's caravan.

"When did you last see your father, can you recall?"

"Yes, it was much earlier that same evening when he returned home from work. He had something to eat and then left the house." She wasn't sure where he went to, but believed it was to go to The Bushell public house, on the corner of Denmar Street.

"Was your mother at home, when he came from work?"

She shook her head, claiming she only remembered her mother putting her to bed earlier that night, until the time of the incident in the kitchen. The young lady added that everything had become hazy.

"Are you absolutely certain it was your mother and father you overheard arguing that night?"

"They were always arguing, Chief Inspector."

"But on that particular evening?"

Again, she shook her head, confessing she only thought it was but that the voices she heard were muffled.

Rayner then asked if she actually saw the kitchen knife recovered from the back garden and she denied she had, having been told it was the weapon used to kill her father by detectives visiting the house at the time.

Until then, the Chief Inspector had been reluctant to tell Priscilla Crockett of the discovery of her father's body, but now felt compelled to do so before the young woman read about it in the local newspapers. After sharing the details with her, he noticed her eyes beginning to well up and immediately apologised for having put her through the same traumatic experience of ten years previously.

In a trembling voice, she then told him that she owed a great deal to Mr. and Mrs. Petroni for having treated her like their own daughter.

"I have my own life now, sir," she said, trying hard to remain composed, "A life, which has been normal and brought me much happiness. As far as my mother is concerned she might as well be dead and needs to remain in the past."

Richard Rayner didn't offer any verbal response to that announcement and just nodded.

"I shall be seeing your mother in the near future Priscilla, is there anything you wish me to tell her?"

"No."

Realising he had probably put the girl through enough torment on that occasion, he offered to walk Priscilla Crockett back to the Big Top tent explaining that, although difficult, it was important if she remembered anything else that took place on that fateful night, he needed to know. He left her with one of his personal contact cards before he and Jack Robinson made their way back to Scotland Yard.

Blackie Jennings was a giant of a man with a full beard and flushed face. Being a former mariner, the colossus was proud of a number of sketches of seafaring galleons tattooed on both muscular forearms and earned enough money to keep himself and his elderly mother with whom he lived, by working as a loader in St Katharine Dock. The likeable man was also indebted to Henry Bustle for once having paid his landlord, at a time when Jennings and his mother were about to be evicted from their hovel, having insufficient funds to pay the rent. Occasionally, the labourer would meet the detective in some quiet corner public house but was never one to disclose any on-going villainy at the docks.

The big man became nervous when he first saw Bustle walking along the quayside, heading directly towards where he was working with other labourers and could only hope he wasn't the subject of the Sergeant's visit, unless something had happened to his mother. It hadn't, but his anxiety increased when he was led to one side by the Scotland Yard man.

"This is not the place to meet up, Mr. Bustle," he whispered, looking back to see how many of his workmates would have noticed the association.

"I wouldn't be here unless it was urgent, Blackie," Bustle explained, "But I need to know more about this smuggling that I understand is going on down here, especially at night."

The informant glanced across at three other dockers, who had stopped carrying parcels into the warehouse where he'd been working and were now showing a great deal of interest in the two-man meeting taking place.

"I can't talk to you here, Mr. Bustle, there's too many watching."

"Then what time does your shift finish, Blackie, and I'll meet you in the snug at The Peacock."

Jennings told him and nervously advised his friend to leave, quickly.

The Sergeant agreed and turned to walk away but as he did so, the three other interested parties were already walking in their direction, looking extremely hostile and each grasping iron bars. There was no way in which Richard Rayner's right-hand man was going to avoid a physical confrontation and he would certainly never walk away from one.

"What's your business down here, copper?" one of the men demanded to know, in a gruff and threatening voice.

"Why, I've come to enquire what the rest of you Raven's shit have done with all the parcels you've been nicking from here," Bustle answered, smiling and inviting his assailants to come on to him. The man had never felt fear since a teacher once used the cane on him when a mere infant. It would take more than three hard looking labourers to unnerve Henry Bustle, who had been born and raised in the slums of Whitechapel himself and had the scars to evidence that.

The same man looked affronted and without hesitation pounced, stepping forward with his iron bar held high in readiness to bring it down on top of the detective's head and obviously intent on turning it into a canoe.

Henry Bustle's vast experience in street brawling instantly came to the fore and he moved with the agility of a panther, managing to avoid the first attempt to dissect his head, before bending his knees and forcibly wrapping his truncheon across the knees of the self-appointed leader. The man collapsed to the cobbled stones, screaming out in agony and grasping his heavily bruised kneecaps. A violent confrontation to Richard Rayner's right-hand man was like having an enjoyable breakfast at a riverside café and the Sergeant grinned, as his other two assailants came charging in.

Until then, Blackie Jennings had naturally hesitated before deciding which side to take and then, having made that decision grabbed the nearest of the assailants, wrapping his muscular arms around the surprised man and holding on to him in a vice-like grip, threatening to squeeze the life out of him. That left Bustle with the easy task of putting the third hostile docker out of the game, but in his hurry to inflict some pain, unfortunately slipped, losing his footing and joined the man he'd already put down, on the cobbles. Such an unexpected mistake resulted in bruised ribs, as a pair of hob-nailed boots dug into his side, causing him to groan and remain helpless in the prone position.

"Throw the bastard into the water Syd," the first man called out, still nursing his bruised knees.

Two gnarled hands reached down to grip Bustle by his collar, but before the incapacitated detective could be lifted off the ground the shrill of a high-pitched whistle could be heard being blown in the near distance and they all knew what that represented.

The third man turned and ran towards the entrance to the warehouse, only to be brought down by one of the two patrolling constables who had come to Henry Bustle's assistance.

The Sergeant regained his feet and seeing red, shouted to Blackie Jennings to release the man in his clutches, before clobbering him across the head with his truncheon. And just for good measure, he also struck the man with the throbbing kneecaps over his head, to ensure he was going nowhere. It was over and the need for Henry Bustle's fighting spirit was no longer required. He quickly instructed the constables who had come to his assistance to commandeer a carriage to convey the three prisoners back to the cells at Scotland Yard. Blackie Jennings was to make up a fourth apprehended docker, just for the sake of appearances.

"Are you alright, Sarge?" the one young constable asked.

"I was, until I slipped on those bleedin' cobbles," the detective answered.

The three bravados who had been responsible for attacking Henry Bustle, were locked up inside the cell block in the basement of Scotland Yard, all looking the worst for wear and nursing their individual reminders of their failed efforts. But before being interrogated by the detectives' investigating the murder of the Stevedore, Joseph Kelly, Blackie Jennings was spoken to surreptitiously by the Sergeant he had come to trust and in the company of Richard Rayner. What the big man shared with them in a series of whispers came as a surprise, casting a different light entirely over the incident they were enquiring into.

The labourer, who still regarded Henry Bustle as his saviour, appreciating the help given him and his aged mother in the past, described how in recent months there had been an increase in violence, committed against a number of employees at the docks. Jennings pointed the finger directly at the on-going evolvement of an organisation within the workforce that was supposedly representing the rights of individuals, specifically those employed with the loading and unloading burdens at the warehouses that fronted the quaysides.

"We all have to pay weekly subs towards, what they term, are running costs incurred when looking after the interests of the workers, but in reality," the man explained, "It's nothing more than a bullying protection racket."

"Do you yourself pay towards these people, Blackie?" Henry Bustle asked.

Jennings nodded and explained, "If I didn't, I'd just end up like the rest of them."

"In what way?" Richard Rayner enquired.

"By being badly beaten one dark night by jaspers carrying iron bars and risking another thrashing if I refused to leave my employment."

Rayner glanced across at his Sergeant, both men wondering if they had stumbled across the motive behind the killing of Joseph Kelly. The Chief Inspector asked Blackie Jennings if he had known the dead man personally and was told he had, but didn't think that Kelly had been murdered by, what he was describing as being, 'the union men'.

"What makes you so sure?"

"Because, he always paid his dues like the rest of us."

"Is there a ringleader behind this organisation, Blackie?"

The man lowered his eyes to the floor and the detectives had to wait, while he considered whether or not he should answer the question. He was obviously in fear of saying too much and told them so.

"My life wouldn't be worth a farthing, Mr. Bustle, if they ever found out I'd been talking to you," he anxiously announced, with genuine trepidation in his voice.

"We assure you, Blackie, what you tell us will be in the strictest confidence," Rayner explained, "You have my word on that."

"Whatever you tell us now my old mate, will stay within these four walls," Henry Bustle added.

"His name is, Tom Herrick, and he's one of the loading supervisors in St Katharine Dock. He always goes about with a couple of heavies at his side and he's the geezer that controls all the money they take off the dockers."

"What does he look like, apart from the two horns sticking out the top of his head?" Henry Bustle asked, not even tickling the other man's sense of humour.

"He's a little shit, but a dangerous one, Mr. Bustle."

"But what does he look like, Blackie."

"He's a small, whisper of a geezer with a trimmed moustache and a pair of eyes that look right through you. I'd say he's in his mid-thirties and believe me, there's not a docker who ain't frightened half to death by the little bastard. It's usually some new kid who gets taken on and then refuses to pay his subs that cops for the beatings."

Henry Bustle then asked what his informant knew about the claims made by Spotty Finkel, regarding smuggling activities going on at the docks and was told that such practices were very likely.

"I've never been involved in that sort of thing but it's widely accepted that stuff comes in off the boats when the docks are quiet, mostly at night." Jennings then went on to explain that he had never worked a nightshift, owing to his infirm mother's requirements, but wouldn't be surprised if the man Herrick, was involved in that sort of thing.

"Listen, I can't afford to be out of work, Mr. Bustle," he then continued to plead, "But once they hear that I was released and the others kept inside here, I can't see how I'll be able to carry on working at the docks."

Richard Rayner immediately provided the answer to the man's anxiety and dilemma.

The Chief Inspector looked across at Henry Bustle and asked if he'd suffered any kind of injury as a result of the attack on him.

Bustle smiled and shook his head, knowing what was about to be suggested.

Rayner then told Blackie Jennings that the others would be released as well as himself, on the grounds that there was insufficient evidence to prove they were aware that the Sergeant was a police officer.

The man's eyes lit up and his confidence was quickly restored. He thanked Rayner, but was told there would be a condition to the charity afforded him, which was to keep Henry Bustle informed of any kind of criminal activity going on, in particular, any incident involving Tom Herrick.

Jennings agreed, before being ushered out through the back door of Scotland Yard and with the Sergeant being appreciative of the course of action his Chief Inspector had taken.

Sidney Chatham, Arthur Redding and Callum O'Brien, were also all questioned by the two detectives about their assault on the Detective Sergeant, and as anticipated, refused to speak a word to their interrogators. All three were eventually released after being warned that should they come to the notice of the police in the future, they would be dealt with far more harshly.

When finally returning to Rayner's office, Bustle thanked his senior detective for having protected his informant, knowing there weren't many at Scotland Yard who would have done the same.

"It's you who should be thanked Henry," Rayner quipped, "After all, it was you they had a go at, but I think we should be having a word with this man, Thomas Herrick, after things have returned to normal down there," he suggested, referring to the docks.

After Jack Robinson had joined his two colleagues, the Chief Inspector returned to his blackboard, noting down everything they had so far discovered about the dead man, Joseph Kelly.

Richard Rayner suggested that, having accepted the killing had been motivated by some kind of criminal involvement by Kelly, the allegations made of smuggling at St Katharine Dock in particular, should be looked at more closely. Both Bustle and Robinson were then instructed to conduct night-time observations on the dock, just to see if anything untoward did take place.

"Starting tonight, so you best get off and get some rest while you can. I'll arrange for some constables to join you later."

Chapter Seven

The Bushell public house was situated no more than a couple of hundred yards from where Annie Crockett had lived with her husband, Leonard, in Denmar Street. It was a typical red-bricked terracotta building, small but sufficient for the socialising requirements of that part of the local Whitechapel community. According to the name over the door allowing access to the saloon, Thomas Peterson was the licensee and having just opened his doors to conduct business, the landlord was standing behind the bar when Richard Rayner entered, looking as pristine as ever in his top hat and tails. There was no other person present, except for an old swamper who was collecting glasses off the tables from the night before.

"Might I take a glass of your best black ale, landlord," the former Oxford graduate politely requested, the soles of his boots tending to stick to the ale covered floorboards, "And some information if you please."

"We don't serve no toffs in 'ere mister," the landlord snapped back, looking a little irritable from beneath a pair of thick bushy eyebrows, "And we certainly don't dish out information willy nilly."

"How long have you held the licence to this place, Mr. Peterson?"

"I just told yer…"

"At the moment landlord, I am asking, but if you prefer I should use other means to communicate…"

"Who wants to know?"

Rayner smiled and explained that Mr. Peterson would be best advised to co-operate if he wished to renew his liquor licence next time he was up in front of the justices.

"I am Chief Inspector Rayner from Scotland Yard and I just happen to be making enquiries into a man who used to use this establishment about ten years ago. So, I repeat, how long have you been here, Mr. Peterson?"

The landlord immediately looked disgruntled and somewhat defiant but answered the question, albeit reluctantly.

"Me and the missus have been here for the past fifteen years or so, who is it you're interested in?"

Rayner quietly mentioned the name of, Leonard Crockett.

The man whose thick walrus moustache made up for a lack of hair on top of his head, placed the drink on the counter whilst trying to recollect the name given him, eventually conceding that it did ring a bell. He couldn't put a face to the individual at first but then, as if struck by some pearl of wisdom, spurted out the words, "Hang on, wasn't he the geezer who was done in by his missus down the street somewhere."

The detective nodded and then continued, "Can you ever remember him coming in here?"

The man shook his head and confessed, "Can't say as I can, it's been a while back when that happened and I remember it was the talk of the district."

"Can you remember the night it was supposed to have happened," Rayner asked, inquisitively.

"I remember having to furnish a couple of your blokes with drinks then and the scrounging bastards kept me up half the night, if that's any use to yer."

Rayner took a gulp of his drink before congratulating Thomas Peterson on keeping a decent drop of ale. He then asked if the man knew another of the locals, Charlie Pendry, who lived next door to where Leonard Crockett resided in Denmar Street.

"Charlie gets in here most nights. A cheerful kind of a bloke."

"Do you know his wife?"

The landlord shook his head and answered confidently, "No, never seen her and from all accounts she's one who keeps a tight rein on him, but never been in here as far as I know. I can ask the missus."

"Do you recall if Charlie Pendry was in here on that same night the murder was committed?" Richard Rayner knew he had to remain persistent if he hoped to get any kind of response from these people who lived their lives beneath a cloak of tight lips and suspicion.

"Yes, he was and I can remember clearly because he came in with another bloke." The landlord stopped talking for a moment or two and then declared, "You know, I reckon that bloke's name was Len, I remember Charlie calling him by that tag."

"What did he look like, this other bloke with Charlie?"

"That much, I couldn't tell you. I reckon I've done well remembering what I have, mate."

"Can you remember what time they left here that night?"

"Hang on, I'll fetch the missus." As he turned to step into the back, another two customers appeared and Thomas Peterson bawled out, "Dot, come and speak to this copper," before returning to the bar to serve the newcomers, who he was evidently acquainted with.

Dorothy Peterson was a small but rounded woman, who spoke with a Glaswegian accent. There was no doubt from her demeanour and the manner in which she spoke, she was a lot brighter than her husband and in all probability, the driving force behind the running of their establishment. After Richard Rayner had identified himself, she instantly remembered the night he was interested in, speaking concisely and without hesitation.

"I do remember Charlie Pendry and his friend, Lennie Crockett, very well Chief Inspector," she openly confessed.

"Had you seen them both in here before that night Mrs. Peterson?"

"Occasionally they'd come in together, but Charlie is in here most nights and I suppose Lennie Crockett might have popped in a couple of times on his own before that awful night."

"Did you notice how each of the men reacted to one another."

The lady shrugged her shoulders and confirmed, "Friendly, they were both friendly enough or so it appeared from where I was standing. It's a long time ago."

"This is very important, Mrs. Peterson, can you remember the time they left here?"

"Not the exact time, but..." she paused to give the question more thought and then continued, "I'm fairly sure they didn't leave together. Now let me think, Charlie Pendry left earlier than usual. We put the towels on at ten o'clock and I'm sure his friend was still here then because I had to tell him to drink up. I was taken aback when I found out it was him who was done in by his missus."

"How long before that time, did Pendry leave?"

"It must have been at least a good hour before time was called, so I would say, about nine o'clock."

"Thank you, you have been a great help."

"I felt sorry for that wretched woman who killed him. I used to see her in the street now and again, a waif of a girl and they had a young daughter you know."

"Did you ever speak with her?"

"No, she wasn't the type, always kept herself to herself but a sorrowful looking lass, not an ounce of confidence in her."

Rayner finished his drink and left. As he journeyed back to Scotland Yard, he pondered over the conversation he'd had with Dorothy Peterson. Rose Pendry had lied to him about the time she had said her husband returned home that night from the public house. The woman had been quite clear that Charlie Pendry hadn't arrived home until half past ten and well after closing time. So, where had the man been for that missing hour and a half and more importantly, what had he been doing. These were questions that the initial investigating detectives' should have been asking, but there was no reference to Pendry or Crockett's movements that night in the file. By the time the Chief Inspector arrived back at Scotland Yard, he felt that Mr. Pendry needed to be spoken to as a matter of urgency and perhaps his wife be given the opportunity to change her story.

It was much later that same day when Richard Rayner received an unexpected visitor to his office, the ever-pleasant Doctor Elizabeth Green. He thanked her for coming, explaining that he was intending visiting the lady at St Mary's at the next possible opportunity.

"I appreciate that, Richard," the young doctor told him, "But I thought you should know the result of my analysis of that sample you gave me, as a matter of urgency."

After inviting the female physician to take a seat and offering her refreshments, which she politely refused, he listened with the utmost interest in her findings.

"The sample you gave me contained some harmless substance, but ninety percent of it was made up of Morphine, which would undoubtedly relieve pain but such a quantity could certainly be highly addictive, even if administered under supervision and certainly in my professional opinion, should never be made available to the public in such extensive amounts."

"A danger to an individual's health then, in your view, Elizabeth?"

"It's more than my view, Richard, frequent administering of such a highly toxic substance would most definitely produce some hallucinatory effect and as I said, be highly addictive to the recipient. I take it you are not the subject of this remedy?"

Rayner explained he had given her the sample on behalf of Frederick Morgan, and briefly described the Chief Superintendent's recent inconsistent and aggressive behaviour, that had been giving some concern in various quarters.

"That certainly supports my professional conclusion that it would be habit-forming and would have a noticeable effect on the individual's character, Richard."

"So, what's the cure doctor," he asked, already pre-empting what the suggested remedy would be.

"Have you any knowledge of the reason why he is taking the drug?" she genuinely asked.

"I believe, as a pain killer." Rayner didn't want to disclose too much about Morgan's personal affliction, without him knowing.

"Well, there's only one way in which Mr. Morgan can be helped, he must stop taking the drug immediately and then subject himself to isolation and rehabilitation as quickly as possible. There are a few establishments that facilitate what is needed, but I can try and find one that would be suitable, if you wish?"

Rayner told her that he was appreciative of her assistance and that he would get back to her if he needed more help. Firstly, he had a responsibility to share her diagnosis with Frederick Morgan, a task he wasn't looking forward to undertaking.

Clarice Rayner was in her office at Kings College, studying a number of sketches of the human skull when her husband unexpectedly appeared. In addition to her study of facial reconstruction, for which she had become a world-renowned expert, the Chief Inspector's wife lectured on the same subject to undergraduates and was currently in the middle of preparing for her next demonstration. Clarice was always overjoyed to see her detective husband and immediately embraced him in a warm greeting.

"And pray tell me the reason for such a wonderful surprise visit," she asked the man she had loved since first meeting him, when Rayner was lodging with her mother as a young detective. She was an art student in Brighton at the time, visiting her mother for a few days and their feelings for each other blossomed when Clarice assisted the young Richard Rayner with a fairly complex case he was engaged with.

He told her about his concerns relating to Frederick Morgan, emphasising the change in the Chief Superintendent's behavioural patterns and mentioning the pain killing treatment he was self-administering.

"How awful, Richard," she answered in response.

Rayner then gave her brief details of what Elizabeth Green had reported back to him, suggesting the Chief Superintendent might well have become addicted to Morphine.

"My God, Sally-Anne will be mortified. Have you told her yet?"

"No dear, at the moment there is just myself and Elizabeth Green, aware of the circumstances."

"She needs to be told, so she can support her husband," his wife suggested.

"I know what you're saying Clarice, but I haven't told him yet and the reason why I am here is to do with what Doctor Green recommended, that Frederick needs to spend some time in isolated rehabilitation in order to cast aside his addiction."

"I'm sure he won't be very happy when he does hear. Are you sure you have done the right thing, I mean going behind his back, dear?" Clarice was making a valid point, one that had left Rayner feeling a little guilty when taking such unilateral action.

"It's not something I relish but I did it as a friend, knowing that he wouldn't even recognise he had a problem."

"Of course, dear, I know just how stubborn Frederick can be."

Rayner sat astride one corner of her desk and his wife asked how she could help.

"I remember you mentioning some time back a professor working here at Kings, who was researching drug addiction," he pointed out, removing some fluff from the lapel of his tailored jacket.

"Yes, Cuthbert, Professor Cuthbert Paris. I understand he's been studying the detrimental effects of opium on human beings."

"Would he possibly be aware of a reputable institution where addicts are treated, do you think?"

"I could ask him dear. Unfortunately, I have a lecture in ten minutes, but I can have a word with him after I've finished. Perhaps I could invite him to dinner this evening."

"Would he come do you think?"

"Of course, how could he refuse and you'll find he's excellent company, Richard. I can leave early after the lecture and warn cook we shall have a visitor for dinner."

"Marvellous, thank you dear, I can ask no more." Rayner kissed his wife, before making his exit.

Richard Rayner was well aware that, if Elizabeth Green was correct in her assumption, Morgan was in need of help then the sooner the man received that support, the better. Of course, he had to talk to the Chief Superintendent first but needed to recommend a suitable institution at the same time, one where he could begin his therapy. He was intending to converse with his friend after speaking with Professor Paris over dinner later that evening, but when he returned to Scotland Yard, he was surprised to find his friend sitting in his office.

"Ah, Rayner, I hear that our Henry Bustle has been beating up a few dockers recently," Morgan enquired.

"Not exactly sir, in fact, he was lucky to come out of a skirmish with his whole skin intact." Rayner then briefly described the incident involving his Sergeant and gave an attenuated account of what Blackie Jennings had disclosed regarding the ongoing protection racket organised by the loading supervisor, Tom Herrick. He felt a twinge of embarrassment when having to confess the reason for releasing Bustle's attackers from custody, but his explanation appeared to go straight over Morgan's head. However, the Head of Department did suggest a quick solution to the problem surrounding the alleged existence of a protection racket.

In his usual boisterous manner, Morgan declared, "There's only one way to deal with scum like that, Rayner; hit 'em hard and flush 'em out. Take a dozen men with you, each armed with a pickaxe handle and cave a few heads in before carting them back here. That will quickly put an end to their little scheme, trust me."

"I'm not so sure sir, such a course of action might also result in retribution and endanger the lives of other innocent dockers," Rayner suggested, "And the problem we have at the moment is, we don't know the identities of those men who are siding with this Thomas Herrick."

Morgan gave that comment some consideration, before asking his Chief Inspector how, in that case, he intended progressing the matter.

"We need more intelligence I might suggest sir and I was thinking about planting one of our own men, purporting to be a docker at St. Katharine Dock. He should then be able to give us a better assessment of how the land lies."

"Anybody in mind?"

"Not yet sir, no."

"Then let me know, once you've decided who it is you need."

Morgan stood to leave, but before reaching the door, Richard Rayner commented on how well the Chief Superintendent was looking.

The senior man remarked that he'd just took a powder, which had eased his 'aches and pains'.

It was the time Richard Rayner had been dreading. The time when, in trying to help his friend and colleague, he might just be about to fall on his own sword. But he could no longer delay and felt duty bound to share with Morgan what he and Elizabeth Green had recently discovered, or so the Chief Inspector thought. He did so, avoiding initially any mention of how he had obtained a sample of the senior man's miracle remedy in the first place.

Morgan stood there listening and after the most highly reputed detective at Scotland Yard had finished, having placed a great deal of emphasis on the fact that the Gold Remedy contained no less than ninety percent of the highly addictive Morphine, he released the kind of verbal explosion Rayner had been fearing.

"I can't believe what I'm hearing, you bloody Toad in the Hole. You've had the bleedin' audacity to go behind my back and stick your powdered nose into my personal affairs."

"It wasn't like…"

"I cannot believe you of all people, Rayner, would commit such a traitorous act of sedition."

"I don't think you could call it sedition. I was only…"

"It was bleedin' sedition against me. Well, I'm totally bombed out."

"That's exactly the reason behind my actions, sir. According to Elizabeth Green, you…"

"And you had the bleedin' nerve to discuss my personal business with a stranger. You absolute shithole."

"Doctor Green is hardly a stranger, Frederick. She's trying to help, in the same way as…"

"It's 'sir' to you, Rayner; we are no longer on first name terms you grovelling toad. Pack your bags mister and piss off. Your time in this department is at an end, do you hear me. You're finished here. I need men around me I can trust and you have just lost that privilege."

Morgan then turned and left, slamming the door behind him, causing the walls to shake. There might just as well have been an earthquake hit the building.

Both men had previously crossed swords on many numerous confrontational occasions, but Richard Rayner had never before seen such fire and venom in Frederick Morgan's eyes and had to accept, his career as a detective might well be at an end… And yet, if he could turn the clock back in time, he would do exactly the same thing again.

Chapter Eight

If Frederick Morgan's meaningful threat to end Richard Rayner's career had been made with genuine and determined intention, the Chief Inspector would have had no hesitation in making a dignified exit from his profession, without further prompting. Unlike others, his priority in life was not that of earning money to feed his family, Rayner was already a wealthy man in his own right. There would have been no argument or appeal to the Commissioner and the renowned detective would have packed his bags, as had been suggested and disappeared, no matter how much he loved the job he was doing. However, the former Army Major was reputed for having made similar threats on previous occasions and was widely known for blowing hot and cold. Only time would reveal just how sincere he had been in his last 'off the cuff' demand.

By the time the Chief Inspector reached home that evening he felt like a man walking a tight rope, not really knowing his fate. Of course, he was aware of the Head of Department's recent erratic behaviour, but Rayner believed that at the time of their recent conflict, Morgan had all his wits about him and the anger he displayed was quite unfeigned. His efforts to read the other man's sincerity had dominated his concentration for the remainder of that day, causing him to forget about the dinner guest he and Clarice were expecting. After being welcomed home by his butler, Albert, the master of the house was immediately informed that his wife and their guest were in the lounge taking sherry.

Professor Cuthbert Paris was a man in his fifties, extremely tall and thin, wearing a light grey suit and satin cravat to match. He spoke with a broad Gloucestershire accent and looked smart, apart from a pair of brown moccasin shoes on his feet that were in vivid contrast to the rest of his attire. But the two prominent features about the man that surprised Richard Rayner, was the professor's shoulder length grey hair and a nose that resembled an eagle's beak, pointed and leading the way where ever he went. Balanced on the very tip, were a pair of rimless spectacles, hardly noticeable at first glance.

Clarice was looking radiant and quickly introduced her colleague to her husband, encouraging Rayner to thank their guest for attending.

The professor reciprocated by sharing with the couple his admiration for the work Mrs. Rayner conducted at the college, clearly stating that he had always held some distant interest in the scientific study of facial reconstruction.

"How can anyone not be captivated by the creation of human features from the application of mathematical equations and whatever other effective tools she uses, to obtain such impressive accuracy," he told Richard Rayner.

"It's less difficult when the subject is a horse or dog, as I have been commissioned with doing on occasions, professor," Clarice made clear, at the same time chuckling at her own confession.

Having received many similar plaudits in the past, she felt no embarrassment from Cuthbert Paris's praise, but immediately moved the conversation towards the reason why her colleague was there, prompting her husband to explain his unenviable situation.

"Ah now, I find by discussing the true business of the evening before dinner, always stimulates the appetite, Richard, if I might call you Richard?" the learned professor suggested.

"Of course."

"Then do me the honour of addressing me as Cuthbert. I understand you are interested in seeking out some suitable accommodation for an unfortunate close friend who has fallen foul to some addictive substance?"

Rayner agreed that was the reason for the meeting, but firstly, wished to change for dinner and apologised before leaving the company to go upstairs. He was surprised when his wife followed him up to their bedroom and stood watching as her husband quickly washed himself down before getting changed.

"My thoughts have been very much on what you told me earlier Richard, about Frederick Morgan's current problem," she remarked, "And I find it all very distressing."

Rayner told her of the conversation he'd previously had with Sally-Anne, mentioning the Chief Superintendent's unusual and bizarre behaviour, even having strongly and unreasonably chastised his daughter Estelle and having chased a fictional tiger around the gardens in the middle of the night.

"I wonder Richard, if that has anything to do with Estelle meeting that black boy I saw her with earlier today and yesterday."

The Chief Inspector looked genuinely interested and asked his wife when and where that had taken place.

"Outside the school gates in the Strand. After leaving college, I saw them together yesterday afternoon and again today. He seemed to be a poor wretch of a lad who was in dire need of sustenance."

"And you're sure it was Estelle, Clarice."

"Of course, how could I possibly mistake such a lovely looking young lady for anyone else. We'd better not leave the professor waiting much longer Richard."

The Chief Inspector made a mental note of what his wife had told him and hastily escorted her back downstairs. They found the learned man seated in the dining room with Albert the butler in attendance.

Clarice quickly apologised and both college academics were soon wrapped up in conversation concerning each other's specialised subjects.

The hostess was her usual charming self over the meal and the cook, Mrs. Uddlestone, served a pot roast in person as Tilly the maid had been given the evening off. The affair was delightful with most of the conversation centred on the work conducted by their guest, who surprised his two hosts when indicating the vast number of opium dens contained within the London boundaries. Richard Rayner admired the man when learning how hard working and committed he was towards discovering a cure for opium addiction and was fascinated by some of his descriptions of those he was trying to help.

"As you are most likely aware Richard, the drug plays an important role in medical science," the professor explained, "It's only in circumstances when abuse takes control that it proves just how devastatingly harmful it can be in the wrong hands when taken clandestinely."

When Rayner thought the time was right to resurrect the reason for wanting to meet the professor, he was reluctant to identify Morgan as being the subject of his enquiry. He did however, give the professor a brief outline of the circumstances supporting his and Elizabeth Green's reasons for suspecting addiction.

"You will usually find Richard, that most addicts remain in denial, which inevitably makes curing them far more difficult. Is your man in the same state of mind?"

"I'm not sure," Rayner answered, truthfully, "But his character tells me he probably is."

Cuthbert Paris then continued highlighting the signs that most drug addicts holding high professional positions, tend to display and Rayner listened intently, becoming more and more enlightened and suspecting any lecture given by their guest on his specialised subject would have been fascinating to have attended.

The front door bell sounded, which was Albert the butler's cue to leave the dining room. When he returned, he informed his master that two more visitors had arrived unexpectedly, Mr. and Mrs. Morgan. Rayner wondered if his moment of truth had arrived at such an inopportune moment.

The meal had finished and Clarice suggested that their two friends be shown into the lounge and offered drinks, instructing the butler to tell them they would be joined shortly.

Albert bowed and left.

Of course, any opportunity Richard Rayner might have had to tell his wife of the Chief Superintendent's recent loss of control, had been naturally deferred by the presence of the professor. For that reason, he was also reluctant to disclose to Clarice that the reason for the Morgans' visit might just be connected with his friend's request for him to leave Scotland Yard. He was also wary of mentioning to Cuthbert Paris, that he was about to meet the subject of his concerns and hoped that matters would be unravelled through the natural course of conversation.

All three found Sally-Anne and Frederick Morgan sitting drinking brandy and Clarice warmly greeted them both, before introducing her colleague from Kings College. It was with some pride that she explained to the professor that her closest friend was indeed the part owner of the Pratchett and Longfellow Circus and was a highly skilled sharp shooter to boot. That news instantly guaranteed her colleague's interest in the lady visitor and the conversation quickly concentrated on Sally-Anne's professional lifestyle.

"I have seen you dear lady and your most talented partner, Miss Pratchett, on many occasions," the professor confessed. "Forgive me, but I am an avid follower of the circus and retain the fascination of a child."

Clarice chuckled, thrilled by the excitement stirred by the presence of one of her closest friends and neighbour, whilst her husband sat opposite his Scotland Yard senior, cautiously smiling politely and waiting for whatever remarkable verbal statement Frederick Morgan would eventually make.

As for Morgan, he continued to look like a youngster who had just seen his pet dog unexpectedly put down. The butler stood close at hand, knowing the Chief Superintendent's drinking habits and ready to recharge his glass when a mere nod of the head came his way. Finally, the Welshman's true character came to the fore and he could no longer play the role of the observing subservient, there to make up the numbers.

"Damn it, Richard, I am here to apologise for my outburst this afternoon," he bawled out, ignoring the others present, "I appreciate you have only been trying to help and acted like a mad squirrel in turmoil. Please accept my sincerest apologies."

The room fell into a hush as Rayner quickly reached across and offered his hand in friendship. It had all been so childish and unnecessary, but the Chief Inspector recognised it might also be the right time to explain the true purpose of Professor Paris's visit.

"I beg of you not to take offence, Frederick, but it just so happens..." A description of the learned visitor's specialised subject was quickly uttered and at first, Rayner wondered if he'd just derailed Morgan from his current good behaviour, watching the man's face drop as if being betrayed yet again. His fears were soon proven to be unfounded.

The professor immediately took control of the conversation, realising that Morgan was the man his host had been referring to earlier. He sensitively asked the Chief Superintendent for what affliction he was taking drugs containing Morphine, a well-known pain killer.

Spurred on by Sally-Anne, Morgan reluctantly told him.

Richard Rayner then reiterated the findings of Elizabeth Green, emphasising that the powder being administered to Morgan, contained ninety percent of the addictive drug.

"Then if I might be so bold as to tell you sir, to continue on such a course can only result in ruination," Paris pointedly declared.

Morgan just sat there, nursing his glass of brandy without making any response. His manner was now similar to a sedated rabid dog facing its end of life, where anger and defiance had once reined there was total submissive compliance. Clarice Rayner in particular, felt her heart go out to the man, but remained silent.

It was Sally-Anne who confessed to having engineered their visit to the Rayners' home, after hearing her husband describe the confrontation between himself and their host.

"We both accept what you say, professor," she said, speaking to Cuthbert Paris, who remained in awe of her presence, "Don't we, Frederick?"

Frederick just grunted, obviously unhappy with having a part of his personal situation being discussed by others, but having little other choice. In reality, this was the former Major's crossroads. The stage reached, whereby he could no longer step back and hide, when there was a necessity to confess to all.

Clarice Rayner looked on sympathetically and the professor kept his own counsel for a short period, waiting for the future patient to verbally respond more positively.

"So, what would you suggest prof," Morgan finally asked.

"I can only recommend what any physician would tell you, sir. A period of isolated rehabilitation, with perhaps a change of medicinal application, one that contains drugs that are not so addictive."

Morgan's eyes found his wife's and he sat back, leaving Sally-Anne to ask the same question put to the professor earlier by Richard Rayner. Where could her husband obtain such a restricted course of therapeutical remedy.

"There is a clinic in Mayfair dear lady, that facilitates what would be necessary for your husband's recovery, but might I suggest another perhaps more suitable alternative."

Both Sally-Anne and her husband nodded their willingness to listen.

"Forgive me for being intrusive, but do you possess sufficient funds to afford the employment of a private nurse?"

"Our friends are two of the wealthiest people in London, Cuthbert," Clarice Rayner confirmed.

"In that case, I would recommend a course of treatment at home," the specialist in drug addiction continued to suggest, "With the support of a good physician and a lady who I can highly recommend, who specialises in this kind of therapy."

At least such an idea would be preferable to being imprisoned within strange surroundings alien to Morgan and where he could be subjected to the whim of others. Both visitors to the Rayner household nodded in appreciation. Finally, it appeared that progress was about to be achieved.

Both Henry Bustle and Jack Robinson were sat in Richard Rayner's office when the Chief Inspector arrived back at work the following morning. His committed Sergeants were grey faced and resembling a pair of phantoms, having worked throughout the previous two nights lying in wait for any possible smugglers and subjected to the damp atmosphere of rolling mists coming off the river. As was the usual case, there was nothing to report and Rayner suggested they both went home and got some sleep.

It was Bustle who enquired how long the senior detective intended to maintain the all-night vigil on St. Katharine Dock, only to be told, until further notice. That was the easy answer for Rayner, but he knew it was also unfair on his detectives who both had families to consider. He therefore reconsidered and told them to give it until the end of the week and the operation would be terminated then, should nothing untoward happen.

"Has there been any further development on the Leonard Crockett murder sir?" Jack Robinson asked, "Or are we satisfied his wife was responsible after all?"

"Far from it, Jack, I strongly believe that Investigation and the conviction of Annie Crockett was driven more by assumption than actual facts. There are a number of features that just don't add up and I shall be interested to find out what the lady has to say, some ten years after the event for which she was sentenced."

After the couple had left, Richard Rayner walked down the corridor to Frederick Morgan's empty office and collected a number of papers the Chief Superintendent had failed to deal with. His loyal senior detective would see to them, after updating the Commissioner of Morgan's plight, but it seemed somehow strangely quiet and in a bizarre way, abnormal, with the usual bawling and shouting having been replaced by an extraordinary period of silence.

Professor Paris had eventually managed to convince the man addicted to Morphine, to remain a prisoner inside his own home for at least three months, under the strict supervision of a specialist nurse. Of course, any officer holding a lesser rank would have most probably lost their job in such circumstances, but the Head of the Detective Branch was virtually guaranteed the full support of the Commissioner, or so both he and Richard Rayner hoped.

In fact, when standing in front of Sir Edward Bradford later that morning, the Head of the Metropolitan Police was extremely sympathetic, after the Chief Inspector had made his representations on behalf of Frederick Morgan.

"Drug addiction is a ghastly affliction," the Commissioner remarked, "Is there anything he requires, Mr. Rayner?"

"No sir, just lots of nursing and support from his wife and closest friends."

"Quite so, well give him my regards and best wishes for a speedy recovery and I shall expect you to keep me updated on Mr. Morgan's progress. In the meantime, I shall still require my daily briefings, which will now fall on your shoulders until our gallant but unfortunate Chief Superintendent returns."

"Of course, sir." Rayner turned to leave, but was stopped in his tracks by an exaggerated cough coming from the most powerful man at Scotland Yard.

"What about today's briefing Mr. Rayner," the top man enquired.

The Chief Inspector apologised and immediately gave an attenuated account of those enquiries made following the murder of Joseph Kelly, outlining his vague suspicions that the killing was ritualistic and could be connected with either a smuggling operation ongoing in the docks, or a suspected protection racket being conducted at the same location.

"Is it possible the two could be linked; the same people responsible for making the workers lives a misery, also being involved in the smuggling racket," Sir Edward suggested.

"Yes, we are bearing that in mind sir."

Rayner then made mention of the discovery of Leonard Crockett's body in the pickling barrel, close to where Kelly had been found, but suggesting there was no connection between the two murders. When he explained that the victim's wife had been tried and convicted for her husband's murder ten years previously, adding that he was sceptical of the manner in which the original Inquiry had been handled, the Commissioner instantly became protectively resistive.

"It would not be in our interests to delve too deeply Mr. Rayner, into a case for which a conviction was achieved. Do I make myself clear?" It was a telling warning for the Chief Inspector to drop whatever enquiries he was making in the Crockett case.

"Perfectly clear, sir."

"Just imagine what the press would print, should it be even hinted we had got the wrong person, even ten years ago. They would have a field day with us."

"Yes sir."

"Very well, then I suggest you have your hands full, delving into the murder of Mr. Kelly."

The message was loud and clear. Rayner was to concentrate solely on the Kelly murder and ignore his own concerns regarding Annie Crockett's possible misfortune.

After leaving the Commissioner's office, the Chief Inspector was feeling a little rankled by the obvious concern the top man had openly portrayed, relevant to the media. Why on earth did it matter how the police were seen in the public eye, if in the end it was discovered that an injustice against an individual had been committed and the truth had eventually been revealed. No matter how much he risked the Commissioner's wrath, he had no intention of walking away from his own suspicions that there had been a perversion of truth. Of course, if he was wrong, then he had no doubt the consequences would be severe. What the senior detective was certain of, it was time to speak directly with the woman who had been either, wrongfully accused or justifiably convicted and incarcerated. But first, he had one more necessary obligation to delegate.

Chapter Nine

Lombard Jones, more commonly known as Lonnie to his associates, was a colossus of a man, the kind whose height and build normally cast a shadow over most people he came into contact with. The former guardsman who once served under Major Frederick Morgan, was now a farrier, working at a stable in John Street, close to the New Blackfriars Bridge.

When Richard Rayner unexpectedly appeared in the open cobbled yard where Jones was busy crouched over an anvil and banging away with a hammer, the man he had called to see hadn't changed much from the last time he'd clapped eyes on him, with Frederick Morgan. He was well aware of the vast amount of admiration and loyalty the farrier had for the Chief Superintendent and was about to put that to the test.

As soon as the former soldier recognised his visitor, he dropped the hammer and hugged him in a friendly way, just as though Rayner was a long-lost brother who had just returned from the front.

"Mr. Rayner, it's good to see you," the giant blurted out, excitedly, "How is the Major keeping these days my friend."

"He's fine, just fine, Lonnie," the detective gasped in reply, reluctant to encourage a lengthy conversation regarding Morgan's current personal problems.

"It seems to me, you've lost some weight, isn't the missus feeding you properly?"

"We are all fine and well, Lonnie. I've come to ask a favour of you."

"Then you shall have it," the farrier announced in his deep, gruff voice, "Come inside and warm your cockles."

The visitor knew exactly what possible consequences could result from the invitation and the last thing Richard Rayner needed at that time of day, was any kind of alcoholic beverage. However, his host had made the offer and he couldn't really refuse. So, with Lonnie's muscular and powerful arm around the back of his shoulders, the man from Scotland Yard was ushered into a large shed, in which there was a burning red-hot furnace.

From out of a cupboard in one corner came a bottle of clear fiery liquid, the contents of which were used to quickly fill two crock tumblers. One was handed to the detective, after being shown to a wooden bench and his host raised his small vessel and toasted, 'absent friends'. It was all so repetitive of the last occasion Rayner had visited the same yard and he played his part, knowing that to fainaigue would be an affront to his host.

The illicit Irish spirit, known as Poitin, or 'the Devil's spittle', brought tears to the Chief Inspector's eyes and after his second tumbler, he thought he'd suffered enough in the name of companionship. Just as good old Lonnie was about to begin reminiscing about a particular skirmish he and Major Morgan had experienced during their service in Africa, Rayner quickly diverted the conversation to the reason he was there, acting like a sacrificial lamb to the slaughter.

"How well do you know the docks, Lonnie?" he asked, his greatest wish at that moment being for a gallon of ice-cold water to douse the flames occupying his chest cavity.

The farrier instantly adopted a serious look on his face and sat down, almost tipping the bench over. At first, Richard Rayner thought the colossus was about to object to having had his humorous wartime tale interrupted, but was wrong.

"The Major's in trouble?" Lonnie Jones woefully but wrongfully acknowledged.

"No, nothing like that, but Mr. Morgan has asked me to approach you for a big favour."

"Tell me more, my friend."

Richard Rayner then explained how he and the Major, required Lonnie to seek employment as a labourer at St Katharine Dock, if only for a week and to report back anything he learned that might be out of the ordinary. He briefly described how it was thought one of the loading supervisors, Tommy Herrick, was running a protection racket amongst the dock workers and they needed to confirm if that was true.

"If you are agreeable, Lonnie, we will cover more than a week's wages for you."

"And you want me to batter this, Tommy Herrick?"

"No, no, nothing like that, just report back to me what you see and hear, that's all."

"An undercover poleece then?" he suggested, "I have my mother to think about."

"Oh, I see."

The big man suddenly burst out in raucous laughter, slapping Rayner across his back and propelling him to the dirt floor.

"When do I start?"

"Whenever your mother agrees to let you go," Rayner answered, joining in with Lonnie's jesting.

After more boisterous exchanges and another tumbler of fiery liquid, the detective was wondering if he should cancel his visit to the prison. But he had to persevere and forcibly but jocularly fought his way out of the yard in John Street, back to his carriage and driver, after receiving more robust slaps on the back from Lonnie Jones. At least he'd achieved the purpose of his visit, even if it had left his head swimming.

By the time he'd reached Holloway, two tankards of water had gone down Richard Rayner's throat, provided by Constable Samuel Brown, who was the Chief Inspector's long standing and trustworthy driver. When approaching the large and foreboding gates of the prison, the visiting detective had almost restored himself back to something like normality and was once more thinking clearly.

A mental portrait of what Annie Crockett looked like had been formulated in his mind from how people had described her and he was wondering what the woman looked like having spent so much time away from the outside world. The majority had told him she was frail and fragile; a waif of a girl who could easily be blown away by a breeze. Such had been a common enough portrayal and those who remembered her believed prison life would by now, have seen her dead and buried.

His first sighting of the individual he had come to visit, was when she was escorted into the visitor's room with both hands shackled by heavy chains. In his mental portrait, Annie Crockett looked far better than she did in reality, standing there before him. The wretched woman appeared withdrawn and emancipated, pale with both eyes sunken and a hard-set mouth below what had once been a quaint nose slightly pointing upwards at the end. Her prison clothing hung in tatters from her skinny shoulders and consisted of a drab grey cotton dress, beneath a well-worn pinafore and head covering of the same material. Her eyes depicted nothing more than total detachment.

"Are those chains necessary officer?" he asked the escorting guard, with genuine concern.

"'Fraid so, suh, it's the same for all lifers when out of their cells," the man answered, allowing his charge to sit at a small table opposite Rayner, before stepping back to remain near to the door.

The Chief Inspector did notice a slight sparkle come to the woman's eyes at the same time he had asked the question, as if for the first time in ten years, she had recognised a hint of genuine caring from another human being.

He introduced himself and explained that he was conducting an internal

Investigation into the death of her late husband, a death for which she had been held responsible by a court of law. Rayner immediately regretted having sounded so rigidly official with his opening words, but could find no other way in which he could express himself or explain his presence.

"Of course, you are not in any way committed to talking to me Annie," he continued in a subdued voice and still trying hard to avoid any hint of authority, "But I beg that you hear what I have to tell you."

She just sat there, looking across at him with pathetic eyes. If there was such a thing as a truly wretched individual, this lady was a prime example, which in fairness he had anticipated.

Rayner watched her closely as he unravelled the details of recent events, looking for any sign of recognition or awareness of what he was saying. When he mentioned that her former husband's body had been found in a pickling barrel at the docks, he studied the woman closely, but there was nothing. He might just as well have been discussing the weather with her and assumed that any enthusiastic claim of innocence she might have possessed, had been diluted as a result of spending so much time incarcerated.

He then reminded her of the circumstances in which she had been seen cleaning the floor of her kitchen and of the kitchen knife covered in blood, discovered in the back garden of the house in Denmar Street, Whitechapel. Still there was no spark; not the slightest flicker of acknowledgement by Annie Crockett.

Rayner played one more leading card, still hoping to encourage a two-way conversation by mentioning the name of her daughter, Priscilla. That was a most effective manoeuvre, sufficient to melt the ice and the look of impassiveness immediately began to subside. It was a start, which was all he had hoped for during this first initial visit.

"She sends her regards," the Chief Inspector lied, but trying to offer some encouragement.

"How is she?" Annie enquired, retaining an indifferent expression.

Those were the first words she had spoken since entering the room, probably the first words for a very long period of time.

Rayner described how she was now working as a trapeze artist for a family named, Petroni, at the Pratchett and Longfellow Circus in Bermondsey.

"Cilla still lives here in London, then?"

"Yes, and she is with a good family who love her dearly. I take it, you and your daughter were very close to each other?"

"She was very young."

"From what I have discovered thus far, Annie, I have been left in some doubt as to your guilt." Rayner deliberately stopped talking at that conjecture, inviting the woman to come back at him with pleas of innocence, but she didn't and just remained silent, her eyes dropping to the floor.

"From my own enquiries, I suspect that there was someone else involved on that particular night, when your husband's life was taken."

Only another vacant look followed that supposition.

It was time to put the most poignant and meaningful question to her and Rayner quietly asked, "Annie, did you kill your husband?" He sat back, waiting for her reply and for a good minute the room remained in silence, apart from the occasional grunt from the official standing near the door.

Finally, the quietude was interrupted by the sound of the chains around her wrists dragging across the table, as the prisoner clasped her skeletal hands together.

"No," was all she whispered, and at that moment, her eyes filled with honesty.

"Very well and for what it's worth, I believe you," Rayner continued, "So tell me, what exactly happened that night, Annie?"

The woman appeared to have been stunned by her own declaration of innocence and instantly retreated back into her self-imposed reticence. For a moment, just one single blip in time, she glanced across at him and he detected a look of mournful dismay, even a small tear in one eye. He might just as well have been the hangman about to place the noose around her neck. Rayner knew at that very moment, having gained her interest for that tiny glitch, he'd now lost her.

"I can help you, but I need to know everything that happened," the detective persisted in a quiet, calm voice, "What was it you were seen cleaning off the kitchen floor? Was it blood?"

She turned her head to one side, to avoid any eye contact with the visitor and remained silent. The doors barring the way into her inner most thoughts had been well and truly shut tight. Even knowing any further attempt to draw her nearer to him would be futile, he patiently pursued her recollections.

"Did you see who it was that killed your husband?"

Still nothing; no response.

More questions followed, soliciting only further quiescence and leaving Richard Rayner confused and puzzled why an innocent woman, would wish to conceal anything from someone who was trying to offer her freedom and justice.

Finally, he asked if it was possible to visit and speak with her again in the future and she shrugged her shoulders in an uncaring manner. He smiled at her, before producing a small bottle of expensive perfume from the palm of his hand and placing it in hers, unseen by the guard.

She looked at him and shook her head in defiance, although the gift remained where Richard Rayner had placed it.

"Only to remind you of what freedom can mean," he whispered, before nodding for the guard to remove her back to whatever hovel of confinement she was living out her life.

Richard Rayner left Holloway Prison with mixed emotions following that first encounter with Annie Crockett. The lady had a secret, of that he had no doubt. The kind of mysterious paradox that was deeply embedded within her inner-self and which, for some reason she refused to divulge, even if such guarded intimacy meant spending the remainder of her life behind bars. But what kind of influential secrecy created such determined reluctance. Rayner asked the question of himself. Was it fear or shame, or perhaps even love that was demanding she continued with her punitive way of life? Whatever telling emotion existed deep inside the corridors of her mind, it was the key to finding the truth behind whoever it was who had actually so brutally murdered Leonard Crockett, and concealed his body in the callous hope it would never be discovered. Many investigators would have walked away at that point. After all, why should anyone bother to help an individual not prepared to help themselves. And yet, Rayner thought it fortuitous that he had been the one who had accepted the responsibility of identifying and coming to terms with, what he truly believed had been a severe miscalculation by the Judiciary.

In a bizarre way, the pitiful woman he had just visited brought to mind, Clarice, his wife. There was little doubt that Annie Crockett had been an attractive lady prior to the scars of the last ten years distorting her features and reducing her physique to skeletal proportions. For a fleeting moment, he wondered how Clarice would have coped if placed in the same situation, before dismissing such comparison from his mind. He would persevere in his quest to ensure justice was fulfilled without fear or favour, no matter what the consequences, should he fail.

There was no moon that night and St Katharine Dock was blanketed in total darkness. Both Henry Bustle and Jack Robinson were crouched behind a pile of empty wooden crates left on the quayside, overlooking the sheltered water of the port. Two uniformed constables were invisible on the opposite side and a carriage containing five additional men remained within calling distance, close by in Saint Katharine Street.

A number of non-descript vessels were moored around the basin, waiting to be loaded with merchandise the following morning, but until the dawn arrived, the vast expansion would remain deserted. A cold breeze was lifting off the water, causing both watching detectives to pull up the collars of their overcoats and for Jack Robinson to comment, this was a part of investigative work he loathed. The sound of Big Ben striking two o'clock reverberated around the city and the stillness and silence remained.

Henry Bustle dozed and Jack Robinson yawned, thinking only of a warm bed and the good night's sleep he was missing. Then the first sign of activity came. A medium sized sailing craft silently skimmed across the black water, heading directly towards that part of the quay where the two Sergeants were concealed. The younger Sergeant nudged the older and both watched as the vessel drew nearer. Finally, a sense of optimism gripped them, realising their prolonged test of patience was about to be rewarded.

The boat edged its way along the quayside and two dark figures could be seen leaping from its deck onto the concrete walkway. Others could be seen moving about inside the vessel, until it had been secured with ropes. One man from the boat then approached the doors of a small warehouse, just to the left of where Bustle and Robinson were crouched down and within seconds, had yanked open two sliding doors.

The Scotland Yard men continued to watch what looked like wooden crates being carried by some of the men into the building and Bustle counted a total of five participants in all. Nine crates had been transferred from the boat, when a sixth man suddenly appeared, seemingly from nowhere. He was wearing a cloth cap and stood watching the labour with both hands tucked inside his overcoat pockets, resulting in Henry Bustle whispering that he would be the main target to grab hold of.

After the delivery had been made, the group of men stood together, quietly conversing with the individual in the cap and that was the time for the detectives to strike. Bustle blew hard on his whistle, sparking an explosion of activity.

Most of the smugglers fled back to the launch that was being hastily untied from the quayside, as police officers suddenly appeared from everywhere. The man in the cap turned to make his escape down an alleyway separating two of the warehouses, only to be brought down by the nimble Jack Robinson, before his arms were pinioned behind his back and secured by handcuffs. The target vessel managed to move away from the quayside with just three of the men having managed to get back, but was immediately confronted by the River Police, who had also been put on standby. No one escaped and when the two Sergeants inspected the crates now resting inside the warehouse, they found them to contain contraband tobacco and whiskey. The operation had been a total success and Richard Rayner's insistence that they continued with their vigil had paid dividends, much to the detectives' joy and delight.

Chapter Ten

The achievements of the previous night could be seen in the cell block at Scotland Yard, where Richard Rayner was delighted to find the complete crew from the smugglers' boat occupying that part of the basement. The first thing the Chief Inspector did was to congratulate his two Sergeants on a job well done, before emphasising the importance of the next stage of that operation. It was now a priority to discover whether or not the murder of Joseph Kelly, was connected in anyway with the night time goings on at the docks.

"We netted more than just a few sprats though sir," Henry Bustle remarked, looking pleased with himself, "Both the agitator, Tommy Herrick and one of his men, Callum O'Brien, were there to greet the boat when it arrived at the dock."

"Wasn't O'Brien one of the men we had in here earlier for assaulting you, Henry."

"That he was sir, and I had to clobber him again when he was trying to run off last night. We didn't notice him or Mr. Herrick, until all hell broke loose."

"How unfortunate, for the man I mean. I can only hope he's fit enough to be interviewed."

"Of course, sir. The name of the boat they were using is the 'Juliette hors de Calais'..." the Sergeant explained, reading from his notes and encouraging Rayner to translate.

"The Juliette out of Calais."

"If you say so sir and her crew consisted of four Frenchmen, one in particular has given us his name as being, Jean Popet. He appears to have been the skipper but they are all claiming none of them can speak English."

Bustle then went on to describe the illicit merchandise the prisoners were attempting to bring into the country.

"Their cargo consisted of tobacco and a mixture of spirits, mostly rum and whiskey, which we've left in the care of the customs officers."

"Have you spoken to any of them yet, in particular our Mr. Herrick," Rayner enquired.

Bustle nodded and explained that the man who had recently come to their notice in relation to the protection racket ongoing at the docks, had claimed he was only visiting there because he'd lost his wallet the day before and had returned to find it.

"According to Herrick, he'd earlier asked his friend, Callum O'Brien, to accompany him, just in case there were some undesirables lurking about at that time of night." Bustle added, with a grin and hint of sarcasm.

"Well Henry, that certainly sounds like a story concocted between them. Can we prove they are lying?"

"It seems too absurd to be believed and from what me and Jack saw, they were both very chatty with the frogs once the baccy and booze had been transferred into the warehouse."

"All the plans of mice and men, eh. They'll probably tell us they were just asking the French if they had seen Herrick's wallet lying around," Rayner joked, "Who was it that gave the French access to the warehouse?"

"One of their own had a key."

"Who owns the building?"

"I suspect it belongs to the Port Authority, as it's derelict."

Richard Rayner then walked across to the large window of his office and spent a moment staring out across the rooftops towards the impressive dome of St. Pauls Cathedral. It seemed that every pigeon in London was having a meeting on his window sill and there was a flurry of feathers, as he tapped the pane of glass. His mind was actively trying to apply a wider perspective to the events that had taken place, attempting to identify a possible connection between the smugglers and the murdered, Joseph Kelly. Of course, there existed a distinct possibility but why would the dead victim be subjected to the tortuous act of spiking his kneecaps. It somehow didn't make sense. From an evidential point of view, the four French men were already convicted as far as Rayner was concerned. From what Henry Bustle and the others would testify, there could be no escape from justice for them, but he was concerned about the position of the two English speaking men who had been arrested in their company. He turned to face his senior Sergeant.

"You look tired Henry, get yourself home and come back later," he sympathetically suggested, already knowing what the response would be.

"I'm just fine sir, I'd much rather see this out if that's okay by you."

"Where's Jack?"

"I've sent him home to get some sleep and he'll be back this afternoon."

"Very well, I think we'll start by having a word or two with this French skipper, what's his name again."

"Jean Popet, but he doesn't speak any English sir."

"Then it's fortunate I have a little French. We shall see."

The French skipper of the Juliette hors de Calais, was a heavily built man with a full dark beard. He was wearing a woollen mariner's short overcoat and a peaked cap with the insignia of an anchor embossed on the front. The man's eyebrows were quite distinctive; similar to a couple of strips of matting joined together in the centre of his brow.

Rayner introduced himself in English, before asking, "Parlez-vous anglais monsieur."

"No," the man answered to the question; as to whether or not he spoke in English was unclear but seemed surprised when Richard Rayner continued the conversation in the best French he could muster, at times struggling to find the correct words and having to concentrate hard on interpreting those spoken by the prisoner - not that many were offered in response.

"How long have you known Mr. Herrick?"

"Who?" the skipper asked, raising his shoulders and forcing a look of confusion.

"Tommy Herrick, the man you conduct your business with at St. Katharine Dock."

The man shook his head, claiming that he had never heard the name before.

"And Mr. O'Brien, Callum O'Brien, how long have you known him?"

The question was again met with total negativity and insincere bemusement.

"It looks as if we are going to have to go the long way around, Henry," Rayner told his Sergeant, reverting back to English.

"Perhaps he will understand better if I give him a few hard taps on his head, sir."

Rayner smiled and sarcastically thanked Bustle for his suggestion, but declined the offer.

"Our Monsieur Popet here, is already a convicted man Henry, as he well knows," he explained, before asking the prisoner who it was, he had intended selling his smuggled merchandise to.

The skipper just shrugged his shoulders and defiantly refused to divulge that particular information.

"Who owns the boat in which you crossed the channel last night?"

"I do, me."

"Very well, monsieur, you and your crew will be charged with smuggling offences and will be staying with us for a long time to come. You most certainly won't be seeing Paris again for a number of years and I have no doubt your boat will be confiscated by the British Customs."

Before Jean Popet could raise any objections, Rayner instructed his

Sergeant to return the skipper back to his cell, not having any inclination to continue verbally jousting with the man, albeit the conversation had been mostly one-way.

When Bustle joined him in his office he asked his Chief Inspector what he intended doing with the two men, Tommy Herrick and Callum O'Brien.

"Let them stew for a bit longer, Henry, before we go down that path."

"What path would that be sir?"

"To find out what they know about the murder of Joseph Kelly."

Frederick Morgan was only two days into his mandatory rehabilitation period, having already taken an intense disliking to the woman who had been hired to take charge of his long road back to recovery. Martha Longfeet was a lady specially trained and well experienced in dealing with drug addicts and difficult men. She wasn't attractive, far from it and boasted a figure similar to a wrestler at a fairground booth. The nurse's dark brown hair was permanently tied in a bun at the back of her neck and her cold, staring eyes and protruding chin, inaccurately portrayed a person who lacked compassion or mercy, even though in reality, she had a heart as big as a bucket. She also had the ability to make others instantly become wary and fearful with one long stare and if it wasn't for her ankle length black dress, beneath a white cotton pinafore and a small nurse's cap perched on top of her head, she could have been mistaken for being a gargoyle. No, Morgan didn't like her one bit, but thanks to Sally-Anne and the family doctor, he'd had no say in the woman's appointment.

At the same time as Richard Rayner was interviewing the French mariner, Jean Popet, the Chief Superintendent was sitting relaxed in his spacious lounge, enjoying the company of his wife and his first glass of sherry of the day. Without warning, a large hand swept down from behind where he was seated and skilfully snatched the cut glass tumbler from his hand, including the contents.

"What the bleedin' hell is going on," he painfully yelped out, as if having just been bitten by one of the many stray dogs that roamed the streets of London.

"No alcohol, Mr. Morgan," the heavy-handed nurse directed, looking back at him as she made her way towards the exit, as though he was the Devil's serpent.

Morgan shot up from his seat and demanded to know, "Who said so."

"I said so," she snapped back, "No alcohol at any time during your period of rehabilitation and that's not for debate Mr. Morgan."

Morgan looked down at Sally-Anne, who appeared to find the episode amusing and with a look of distress on his shocked face held up both palms, pleading for his wife's support.

"You must do as nurse has instructed, Frederick," his wife suggested, much to his disgust, "She is only trying to help you."

"By taking away the only pleasure I have left under my own roof," he despairingly protested.

"Five minutes, Mr. Morgan, and I want you stripped off ready for your morning shower," Miss Longfeet insisted, before leaving and closing the door behind her, taking Morgan's sherry with her.

"I'll be blown apart first Sal, if I'm to put up with this. That bleedin' woman is half man and I'll not stand for being dominated in my own house."

Sally-Anne chuckled and stood from her chair, before trying to appease her afflicted husband by placing a gentle hand on his shoulder.

"Now you know what Doctor Collins said dear, you must have patience and follow Nurse Longfeet's advice to the letter, if you are to cure your addiction." She was referring to the same family doctor, Richard Rayner had known most of his life and who had been recommended to the Morgans' by the Chief Inspector, well before the Chief Superintendent had his recent medical problems.

"So, I'm to take off all my clothes in front of the domestics and allow this abominable apparition to continue taking the piss out of me. Never Sal, that's not going to happen. I want her bloated posterior out of here now."

"Then go back to your white powders Frederick and ruin our lives. You will never escape this addiction if you fail to succeed now. The doctor said there would be times when it would be difficult and you just had to be patient and allow nature to take its course."

"Bollocks to nature and its course, Sal, I'll not take off one single garment for that domineering female despotic."

Ten minutes later, Frederick Morgan was standing completely naked in his back garden, watched over by his wife as his nemesis stood close by putting a high-pressure hose to good use, spraying him from head to toe with icy cold water. The air immediately turned blue, so did the patient's private parts, as he twirled and cussed, blasphemed and screamed at all humanity, under the influence of the tortuous freeze that was enveloping him. Fortunately, only James the butler was allowed to be within sight of the unusual and grotesque scene, every female member of the domestic staff having been ordered to remain downstairs during their master's remedial open-air shower.

One thing was certain, following his confrontation with nature, Morgan would either recognise the benefits of his punitive therapy and proceed willingly with the treatment inflicted upon him by the determined nurse, or he would sack her on the spot. His wife, Sally-Anne, waited in anticipation, fearing at one stage that he might strike out and plant the nurse in the cabbage patch.

The small, thin faced man boasting a pencil line moustache across his upper lip, sat in the interview room facing Richard Rayner and Henry Bustle. The image reflected by the prisoner was one of anger, a false portrayal that Rayner had seen many times previously when dealing with individuals of such dubious character. Even before the Chief Inspector had introduced himself, Thomas Herrick demanded to know when he was to be released, giving sworn testimony of his intention to take legal action against the Metropolitan Police as soon as it was practical for him to do so.

The threat was ignored and Richard Rayner remained unperturbed, calmly announcing, "As far as I am concerned Mr. Herrick, my sincerest hope is that you will remain behind bars until your hair turns white and you are no longer physically capable of beating and bullying your work colleagues." That short introductory statement, momentarily but effectively set the loading supervisor aback, before he recovered and retaliated.

"By what right have you to say that?" he demanded to know, in a voice that trembled with anger and was a little high-pitched, "I've already told this skivvy here of yours, I had nothing to do with those frogs you laid your hands-on last night. I was only there..."

"Yes, I know what you have said but we are not fools Mr. Herrick, so treat us with some respect please or you might find we will respond in a similar manner."

"Respect, for you, after what you've just said to me. You can go and piss in the wind."

"You are not here just for your illicit smuggling activities my friend, I am more interested in the part you played in the horrific torture and murder of one of your work colleagues, the unfortunate Joseph Kelly."

That particular allegation visibly shook the dock supervisor, who looked instantly and genuinely stunned.

"Joey Kelly! I had nothing to do with that," he anxiously claimed, the one side of his face twitching as he spoke.

"The man must have done something really terrible to have you pierce both his kneecaps before killing him," Rayner said, ignoring the words of denial and remaining his usual calm self, "Pray tell me, what kind of a demented monster are you, Mr. Herrick."

The prisoner looked veritably shocked by the accusation and shook his head, repeating his previous answer but with a nervous tremour in his voice. Smuggling was one thing, but the mention of murder had shaken him to his very core, replacing his bumptiousness with subservience.

"I had nothing to do with killing or torturing Joey Kelly, if what you say is true."

"You, Mr. Herrick, have a reputation for bullying and making men's lives a misery and the time has come for your recompense. Your oppressive behaviour won't be tolerated here I can assure you."

Herrick sat back in his chair and folded both arms across his chest, continuing to shake his head in defiance.

"So, tell us, you weasel, how much do you pocket from your protection racket?" Rayner then asked, persisting in riling the man as much as he could.

The prisoner glared across the table at him and it was then that Henry Bustle decided to move around the room, positioning himself immediately at the back of the docker in such a way his threat to inflict imminent physical injury was obvious. It was a tactic the Sergeant had used many times before to unsettle a subject, especially one he had taken an instant disliking to. It would only take one nod of the head from his Chief Inspector and Tom Herrick would be thrown against a wall and pummelled.

"Look," the man said, leaning forward and grasping both hands on the table in front of him, aware of the peril coming from behind, "Some of the dockers pay subscriptions towards the cost of representing their interests, so what's wrong with that? It's not a protection racket and I can assure you, completely voluntary."

"You sir, are a liar," Richard Rayner snapped back, before pausing to watch the look of disdain fill the other man's eyes. The anger and cockiness had by then disappeared and he was beginning to resemble a rat cornered in some sewer.

"Let me tell you the kind of man I believe you are, Mr. Herrick," the Chief Inspector continued, "You are as I have said, a bully; a little man who promotes fear in others through a gang of heavies you employ to do your dirty business. You don't give a hoot about your work colleagues and are happy to leave them in peace, as long as they continue to line your pockets. And when they refuse, you have them so badly beaten they find themselves physically incapable of doing their jobs."

The prisoner sat back, exhaling loudly and forgetting momentarily about the man standing behind him.

Henry Bustle could no longer resist temptation and spontaneously planted the knuckles of his right fist into the top of Tom Herrick's head, causing him to cry out in pain and covering the sore spot with both hands.

"Sorry about that," Bustle said, apologetically, although insincerely, "But I couldn't help myself, knowing the kind of shithouse you are."

"And he hasn't warmed up yet, Mr. Herrick," Rayner added, "Perhaps you would like to reconsider your unco-operative approach towards us."

The docker held up a palm in submission and pleaded for his tormentors to hear him out.

"Look, okay so I cream off a few untaxed goods coming into the docks now and then, whenever an opportunity comes my way. I admit that, but I swear on all the Bibles I have never laid a finger on Joey Kelly and I've certainly not murdered anybody, even if from time to time I do have to use a little force to secure payments, I admit that. And that's the God's honest truth."

"You must realise, with both you and your crony, Callum O'Brien, locked up in here and out of harm's way men will be quite willing to come forward and tell us all about your activities, so much so, you could be facing the noose."

The man's blood pressure began to rise and his face reddened, "I've admitted to what you've said haven't I, but I have never tortured or murdered anybody. How in God's name can I convince you of that?"

Richard Rayner had always been a good judge of character, being a weapon in his personal armoury he frequently put to effective good use. But from what he could see of the man sitting opposite him, he strangely believed he was telling the truth. Of course, he would have been capable of ordering any of the dockers to be beaten unmercifully, but to commit murder didn't really fit with the man's character. It did appear that this individual was driven by money and not revenge and the methods used to torture Kelly, in Rayner's view, went beyond what was acceptable to even this self-confessed bullyboy.

It appeared the Investigation was back to square one.

Chapter Eleven

Richard Rayner was amazed to see his Chief Superintendent looking so rosy red cheeked and healthy, after being shown into the lounge by James the butler. Sally-Anne had left for the circus, to perform in that afternoon's matinee and the recovering drug addict was more than happy to receive another visit from his friend and confidante.

"I'm afraid I can't offer you a drink, Richard, because the house is now under the control of Apate, the Greek Goddess of Darkness, who's hidden all the bleedin' whiskey and brandy."

"I don't follow, sir."

"I'm referring to Miss bleedin' Longfeet, who I reckon at birth was refused the teat by her mother and has been complaining ever since and who in reality, is a disciple of the Devil in disguise, no less. A harsher and crueller woman you will never wish to meet."

Morgan then went on to describe how every morning he's made to stand under the hosepipe in the back garden, as naked as a jaybird.

"And then, I'm forced to freeze my bollocks off before running at least three times around the outside of the garden and once backwards, would you believe. It's not the done thing for a man of my standing and I can't see me taking much more of this bleedin' insane purgatory."

"Well, I must confess I've never seen you looking so well for a long time," Rayner remarked.

"Bollocks to looking well, my old mucker. If I keep this up, I'll be under the sod within a week."

Rayner then went on to update Morgan on the most recent events, preferring to change the subject of the Chief Superintendent's nurse and offering the antics of Tommy Herrick as a more suitable diversionary discussion.

"He admits to virtually everything he's been guilty of, except the murder of Joseph Kelly, which he denies emphatically."

"Do you believe him?"

"Yes, I think I do."

"Then, now you've got the worm on the end of your spade, use him," Morgan suggested, just as the Goddess of Darkness entered the room and demanded her patient took a large swallow from a medicine bottle, explaining it would help to settle his taut nervous system.

Morgan's eyes rolled but he succumbed to the woman's insistence before she made herself scarce, leaving Richard Rayner feeling a little embarrassed at not having been introduced to the lady.

"By getting Herrick to help us, you mean I should persuade him to take up the spy down at the docks?" Rayner enquired, returning to their previous conversation.

"Yes, if anybody could pick anything up about that murder, I reckon he could from what you've told me about him."

The Chief Inspector then mentioned, Lonnie Jones, explaining how the farrier had agreed to work for him at the docks and report back anything overheard that might be of some interest.

"You know, he's got a heart as big as a horse's rump but our Lonnie's not the brightest star in the night sky my old mucker and he's more likely to miss more than he actually learns. No, my money would be on Herrick, provided he thinks by helping us, he might get his sentence reduced."

Richard Rayner then brought up the subject of the discovery of Leonard Crockett in the pickle barrel, which Morgan was already aware of, having initially visited the scene with the Chief Inspector. The interview with

Annie Crockett was discussed and Rayner made it quite clear he believed in the woman's innocence.

"What happened on the night of her husband's murder had to have been committed or cajoled by a man, of that I am certain. How else would that barrel be transferred to the docks from the scene of the murder, or alternatively I cannot see how a woman as fragile looking as Annie Crockett, could have possibly carried a dead weight all that way to where it was eventually discovered."

Morgan was thoroughly enjoying his senior detective's solicitation for professional advice and opinion, reminding him that he was still a part of Scotland Yard. It went a long way towards stimulating the Chief Superintendent's feelings of importance and usefulness, and it showed in his eye contact with Richard Rayner.

"You make some good points, Richard," he said, "But how many times have I heard you say how important motive is. If some other man was involved, then that could take the reason for the murder away from a mere fight between husband and wife, don't you think."

"Yes, I agree and if our lady had a jealous lover who for some reason lost control, I would agree yet again, but I think there's more to it than that. Whatever the reason is for Annie Crockett to remain silent about what actually took place that night, she is gripped totally by fear, the kind of foreboding that goes well beyond a desire to protect a lover."

"A woman with a secret then," Morgan remarked, "It must be some bloody secret to have thrown herself into the bear-pit and be willing to spend the rest of her life in that hovel, Holloway Prison."

"Yes, and what concerns me, is..."

"What concerns you Richard is that, she has already served ten years in the jug, protecting that little secret of hers, so it seems very unlikely she is ever going to tell you what you want to hear. Am I correct?"

Rayner nodded, sitting there opposite Frederick Morgan, feeling a little strange without having a glass in his hand.

"Well then, you will just have to get to the bottom of it by wearing some leather off your boots and start asking the right questions of the right people, knowing you won't be getting any assistance from the woman you are trying to help. It makes you wonder Rayner, if she ever went to confession, eh."

That last remark, although said in jest, gave the Chief Inspector an idea. He stood, suddenly anxious to return to Scotland Yard and apologetically told Morgan he would return to keep him updated on what was happening, as soon as he had more news.

"Look 'ere, my old mucker, take that bleedin Goddess of Darkness with you, why don't you and see if you can manage to throw her fat carcass into the Thames," the Chief Superintendent blurted out.

"I'm sure when this is all over, you will appreciate everything Miss Longfoot has done for you."

"It's Longfeet, or hadn't you noticed?"

Rayner left him laughing his head off at his own joke.

Although Richard Rayner's long list of successes was second to none, earning the respect and admiration of everybody working at Scotland Yard from the Commissioner downwards, somehow his inner self-confidence had always been subservient to a fear of failure. Such an emotional weakness was a constant encumbrance to him, in similar fashion to a coalman carrying a ton weight of fuel on his back. The celebrated detective was the only human being on the planet who failed to acknowledge his own professional analytical skills and often doubted himself, in the belief he never truly deserved many of the accolades thrown his way. The mystery with which he'd been confronted by the circumstances surrounding Annie Crockett had increased that self-doubt, until now. Morgan's adlib comment regarding the woman's possible religious beliefs had resurrected the possibility of progressing his Investigation further.

When he returned to his office, Rayner found Jack Robinson sitting at a table scrutinising a pile of papers, obviously taken from the filing room in the basement.

"What have you Jack?" the senior detective enquired.

"Nothing yet, sir. I was just trying to find out more about the background of our Mr. Kelly, but it appears he's lived the life of a Trappist Monk."

"That's unusual Jack, but tell me, are we aware of Annie Crockett's religious denomination?"

"She's a Catholic sir, or was a Catholic who attended her church most Sundays."

"How do we know that?"

"I read it in her file sir. A Father Michael Day, was her local priest and gave evidence of character at Annie Crockett's trial."

Rayner could have kicked himself for having missed that particular piece of information and was appreciative that Sergeant Robinson hadn't.

"Well done, Jack, and do we know which church that was."

"St Patrick's in Upper East Smithfield, close to the Mint. You don't think the church was involved in the murder do you sir."

"Not in the murder Jack, no, but perhaps this Father Day might know something that we don't and which could be of use to us, that's of course if he's still there. Grab your coat, you can come with me to find out."

It was a young curate they found attending the altar inside St. Patrick's Roman Catholic Church, a place of worship in which, the interior had been designed in a rather unorthodox manner. The rows of pews faced inwards with a central aisle separating them, similar to how meeting houses used by Quakers were designed. Such a rare interior design for a Catholic church gave testimony to the historical age of the building and Richard Rayner was also impressed by an arched ceiling supported by wooden beams that reminded him of a church in Oxford, where he worshipped during his years as a student.

The man dressed in a black Cossack quietly introduced himself as Father Nicholas Ground, and when asked by the senior detective how long it had been since he'd replaced Father Day, he smiled and explained that he was a mere assistant doing God's work and that Father Michael Day, was still the parish priest at St. Patrick's.

"Is it possible I might have a word with him, Father?" Rayner requested.

"Of course, Chief Inspector, Father Michael is always available."

The young priest then escorted the two visitors to a door at the side of where the altar stood and which gave access to the vestry. After knocking, he stood back to allow the detectives to enter.

The man they had come to see was seated at a cluttered desk: a tall, thin but imposing individual with combed back silver hair and a pleasant smile of welcome. Surprisingly, he spoke with what the Chief Inspector believed was a slight Canadian accent.

After the usual introductions, Rayner asked the elderly priest if he remembered the lady who once lived in Denmar Street with her husband, naming Annie Crockett and explaining that he understood she used to be a regular attendant at the church.

Father Michael spoke softly, giving the impression he was a man at peace with himself and confirming he remembered the woman well, expressing his sadness at the course of events that had resulted in Annie's fall from grace.

"She never missed a Sunday morning service, Chief Inspector," he quietly explained, "And often came to confession prior to taking communion, which was fairly frequent."

"Can you tell me, in your opinion Father, what kind of lady she was."

"A quiet, unassuming fragile looking woman, I recall, devoted to her religious beliefs, but a devotee who never mixed much with other members of the congregation. I do confess, when first hearing about what took place, I was shocked and have prayed for her soul ever since. I was relieved when hearing she had escaped the hangman."

"Did her husband, Leonard Crockett, ever accompany her on the occasions she attended mass."

"No, I never met the man, but I understood he was of the Anglican denomination and didn't practice his religion. Might I be so bold as to ask the reason you are showing this interest after all these years, sir."

Rayner explained that Mr. Crockett's body had only recently been discovered and that he felt obliged to review the way in which the original Investigation was conducted.

"I see, well if I can be of any further help..."

"You might very well be, Father. I was wondering if you were aware at that time, of any unusual event that might have happened to Annie Crockett, prior to the unfortunate demise of her husband."

The priest looked at Richard Rayner with a blank expression, before confessing he still had some difficulty in accepting she had committed the foul act of murder.

The Chief Inspector sensed Father Michael wasn't being completely open with him. He persisted by asking if the woman had ever disclosed anything in confession that might have led him to believe she was troubled. Rayner anticipated the answer before the pastor briefly explained that whatever was said in the confessional box, was between the confessor and God.

The senior detective then decided to confide further in this impressive ecclesiastic and informed him of his own beliefs, that Annie Crockett was innocent of the crime for which she had been convicted ten years previously.

"But I suspect something happened to her," he continued, "Prior to her husband's untimely death. Something for which she is so fearful even now, she refuses to disclose the details. I was hoping Father, she might have made mention of whatever that was to your good self."

The priest stood from his chair, holding a large book beneath one arm and explained that he had to prepare himself for that evening's sermon. He apologised for having to cut the interview short but insisted on now being left alone to deliberate on what he intended preaching to his flock. It was obvious Father Michael did not wish to continue with the conversation, for reasons that were different to the explanation offered.

In response, Richard Rayner spoke deferentially, retaining his usual articulate manner.

"It is I who should apologise Father, for having interrupted your work unannounced but all we are trying to do is discover whether there has been a gross miscarriage of justice committed against the lady in question. I'm sure you understand that."

Father Michael hesitated and then explained, "I am bound by my holy office Chief Inspector, not to divulge any information shared with both myself and God, by any individual. I cannot break my sacred oath of confidentiality."

"I am aware of that Father, but was hoping that Annie Crockett might have revealed something to you that might not have fallen within the boundaries of that sacred oath you speak of."

Again, the priest hesitated before finally and quietly admitting that, in his opinion, the woman in question was a troubled soul. He spoke cautiously, selecting his words carefully and with the greatest of consideration.

"Can you elaborate further, Father." Rayner felt like some backstreet newspaper reporter, seeking his next story, but was compelled to find out as much as he possibly could that might unlock that which was trapped inside the deepest recesses of Annie Crockett's mind.

"Only to say this. The poor woman was the subject of a great deal of personal difficulty and distress at that time, but not the kind that would have caused her to commit the heinous crime of murder. I'm afraid Chief Inspector, I cannot say any more on the subject. You must now excuse me."

Richard Rayner bowed and thanked Father Michael for his time, but before actually departing, asked one last question of the priest.

"After she had been convicted and sent to prison, Father, did you ever visit her in Holloway Prison."

"Yes, I felt duty bound to try and offer the troubled soul a way of coming to terms with her predicament through God, but alas, she refused to see me, which was of course, her right."

"Most probably as a result of the burden of shame she was feeling at the time."

"Only Annie Crocket can tell you that Chief Inspector."

The Priest was aware of Annie Crockett's secret, of that Richard Rayner was convinced, but he also knew that no further help or assistance would be forthcoming from that direction. At least he had learned that, prior to the murder she had evidently been a troubled soul and Father Michael had described her concerns as being difficult and distressing, which could have meant one of a thousand different burdens troubling her.

"Am I right in saying Jack, our lady has no known relatives," Rayner asked the Sergeant, as they were leaving the church.

"None that we know of sir."

"Then dig deeper. We need to know her birth name and try and identify any individual by the same surname that might have been related to her. All we know at present is the fact she was married to Leonard Crockett, and it would be interesting to find out what kind of life she led before their marriage. And Jack, leave no stone unturned, because I suspect the answer to this riddle lies somewhere in Annie's past."

"Her daughter, Priscilla, should be able to help us with that, sir."

"Yes, but I have no intention of bothering that young lady, just at this time. Perhaps later."

It was dark by the time Estelle Roland reached the outer gates of the school. All the children had left, together with most of the other teachers and Frederick Morgan's daughter knew that her father's carriage and driver would be waiting for her, just around the corner off the Strand. A downpour of rain had just turned to sleet as she slowly walked along the glistening pavement in the direction of Kings College, where ironically, Clarice Rayner worked. The young lady's head continued to turn until suddenly, there he was, standing in front of her, having just stepped out from a side alley.

"We need to talk some more about this trouble you are in Ralphie," she told the youth, "I need to know everything about what you saw."

The tall, dangly youth was wearing a large floppy cap that covered the top half of his ears and immediately apologised for being such a pest to the teacher.

"You're not a pest, Ralphie, I want to help you."

"I'll tell you all about it, Miss Estelle, but is there somewhere safe we can go to talk," he begged.

"I know just the place, Mr. Dickens," a gentleman wearing a top hat said, who had just appeared to one side of the young man.

Raphael quickly turned in the opposite direction to where the stranger was standing, only to face another human obstruction barring his way.

"Don't make me have to belt you son," Henry Bustle warned.

The youth looked back towards the first man and stared into the eyes of Richard Rayner. He sighed and both shoulders slumped, realising there was nowhere to go. He felt like a wild animal caught in a hunter's trap with no means of escape. Raphael Dickens's life of freedom was at an end.

Chapter Twelve

"Richard, what are you doing here," Estelle gasped, with a hint of desperation in her voice and her eyes portraying those of a frightened child having just been caught with her hand in the cookie jar.

"Hello my dear," Rayner said, tipping his hat with a gloved hand and not taking his eyes off the young itinerant standing in front of him, "I just thought it likely that our Mr. Dickens would try and make contact with you Estelle, and we need to ask a few questions of this young gentleman." He then told Estelle's friend, he was taking him to Scotland Yard for questioning in connection with the murder of one Joseph Kelly, to which the youth nervously denied having any knowledge.

Bustle grasped his arm tightly and pulled him towards a waiting carriage standing just a few feet away.

"Then I'm coming with you, Richard," Estelle demanded, quite convincingly.

"The best thing you can do miss, is to go home. No harm will come to your friend, provided he's honest with us."

"I'm coming with you, Richard," she repeated, "He will tell me a lot more than he will share with you."

Rayner could see her father in her; that look of utter determination and obstinacy that was very much similar to how Frederick Morgan behaved from time to time.

"Very well, then you had better come in our carriage, but I warn you, your father will not be best pleased."

"This has got nothing to do with my father and I have my own carriage nearby."

"Then wait in the front entrance at Scotland Yard for me, once you get there."

Estelle turned to Raphael Dickens and promised she would make sure he would be treated fairly and that she wouldn't rest until she had spoken with him.

"That might very much depend on what your father says, Estelle," Richard Rayner advised, but knowing she would be beyond the control of her papa.

On the journey to Scotland Yard, Rayner noticed how the lad constantly manipulated the fingers of both hands, staring out of the carriage window with a petrified look on his face. In a way, the Chief Inspector felt sorry for this young tramp of the streets, one of many who had no roof over their heads and more importantly, seemingly no future on the horizon. Something had caused the youngster to appear so terrifyingly disturbed, that much was obvious and when they finally arrived at their destination, rather than place the lad in a cell, the Chief Inspector instructed Henry Bustle to escort Mr. Dickens up to his office on the first floor.

In legal terms, the young man of West Indian origin had been arrested and it was not exactly in keeping with the correct procedures to offer a prisoner in custody, alcohol. But that was exactly what Richard Rayner did, filling three glasses of malt whiskey and handing two of them to his Sergeant and Raphael Dickens. Such an act of generosity surprised both Bustle and their young prisoner, but the lad needed something to calm him down, or so the senior detective thought.

The troubled youth gulped his drink down and was sitting in front of a blazing fire when the Chief Inspector asked when it was he had last eaten.

He just shrugged his fragile shoulders and claimed he couldn't remember, resulting in Rayner instructing Henry Bustle to go and fetch the heartiest meal he could lay his hands on.

Dickens looked surprised when hearing those last words, looking across the room at his benefactor, like a scarecrow dressed in a badly worn flannel shirt and trousers that had more holes in them than a piece of Swiss cheese. He also had a glint of suspicion in his eyes, never before having been the subject of such charity.

After the Sergeant had left, Rayner tested the lad's honesty by making mention of the bedding found at St. Katharine Dock, enquiring if Raphael had any knowledge of that.

The lad spoke quietly, almost inaudibly, acknowledging that he'd been sleeping rough there for a number of weeks.

"Then I take it that cart we found close by, belongs to you?"

"Yeah, that's everything I own, mister."

"So, tell me son, what was it that made you abandon everything you own in such a hurry."

The youth finished his drink and stared directly into the fire. His upper body began to tremble and he muttered something beneath his breath, Rayner couldn't quite understand.

"Ralphie, I give you my word that everything you say within these four walls will remain here. Do you believe me?"

The young man nodded, but not convincingly.

Rayner then quietly went on to suggest that, whatever was disturbing the itinerant had taken place at the docks, most probably having occurred late at night when Dickens had settled down for the night.

"It's quite obvious you left your hand-cart close to where you were sleeping, but what was it Ralphie that caused you to suddenly run away, abandoning everything you ever owned."

The lad continued to shake his head in silence.

"Was it something you heard, or even saw."

Still, the youth remained resilient and continued to tremble and stare into the flames.

The detective then repeated what Frederick Morgan's daughter, Estelle, had told him, that Dickens had claimed there were some men after him.

"Who exactly do you think is after you, Ralphie. I can help you, protect you, but not if I don't know what it is you're afraid of and the reason why."

Finally, the young man looked up and his lower lip began to tremble. The fear in his eyes became more exaggerated.

"Take your time son," Rayner suggested, taking a gulp of his own drink.

Then, as if trying hard to lift some heavy millstone hanging from his neck; some terrifying encounter of nightmare proportions, the youth began to disclose that he'd actually bedded down for the night at St. Katharine Dock. According to what he told the Chief Inspector, Dickens had only just closed his eyes when he was disturbed by the sound of loud screams coming from the adjacent dock. They were the screams of a man and he left his pathetic campsite to surreptitiously discover the reason for the commotion.

"It was horrible to see," he continued, mumbling as if he was afraid that Richard Rayner would hear his words.

"Go on, Ralphie, take your time," the detective prompted.

"Some geezers were dragging another geezer covered in blood, towards the water. The screams coming from him were unearthly Mr. Rayner." Dickens abruptly stopped talking and covered his face with both hands.

"Take a deep breath, Ralphie," Rayner said, "Where were you standing when you saw all of this?"

"In the dark, on that stretch that separates St Katharine with the London Dock."

"Did you see where they dragged the injured man from."

He nodded and told the detective the men had physically forced their victim out of one of the warehouses.

"How many were there?"

"Three and the woman."

"A woman?"

Again, he nodded, before continuing, "He was still screaming when one of them hit him over the head with something to quieten him and then I heard the woman say something to them and two of them stuck his head under the water."

Rayner then asked Raphael to describe the woman and he confessed he could only see her outline in the darkness. He said the same about the men involved, in answer to another similar question.

"What happened then, Ralphie?"

"They carried him back inside the warehouse and the woman stayed outside. I was shitting myself Mr. Rayner and turned to get away."

"And they saw you?"

"No, but they must have heard my boots on the gravel; any roads the woman did, because she called out to the geezers to get me. I took off and they came chasing after me like a pack of mad dogs."

The lad then described how he fled through various alleyways, making his way towards the network of yards and side alleys in Whitechapel, until he managed to lose his pursuers by hiding in the open cellar of a derelict house.

"I've never been so scared in all my life. As I was running away, I heard the same woman shout after them to do me in."

"So, they wouldn't have known who you were."

"It wouldn't take much to work it out though, as I'm the only sleep out at the docks."

"When you heard the woman shout after them, what did her voice sound like. I mean, did she have a local accent, or any kind of accent at all?"

"I don't know, I was too busy running to save my skin."

"And you didn't recognise any of them?"

The youth shook his head, explaining that it was too dark.

"They won't stop looking for me though Mr. Rayner, I know that much and I'd stake my life they already know who they're looking for."

Rayner sat back in deep concentration. The fact a woman had been present at the murder placed everything into a different and confusing light. Raphael Dickens's mannerisms gave testimony to his honesty and the detective was in no doubt the youth's fears were genuine enough. He truly believed the lad's life was in imminent danger from whoever those men were, including the mystery woman.

Henry Bustle returned with a large crock jug of steaming faggots and peas obtained from a local public house, together with three dishes and spoons.

Rayner declined the meal and watched as his Sergeant dished out the contents of the jug, before handing a dish to the young man and indulging himself in one of his favourite meals.

Mr. Dickens ate hungrily and soon cleared the dish, even before Henry Bustle was halfway through his meal.

The short break gave the Chief Inspector time to once again go over in his mind, all that the lad had told him. One thing had now become apparent, Joseph Kelly's murder was in all probability, unconnected with the business run by Thomas Herrick. He was beginning to surmise that illegal importation of drugs could have possibly been responsible for the killing.

Once satisfied that Raphael Dickens had eaten his fill, Rayner repeated his question regarding the chances of the lad giving them any kind of a description of the men and woman. But no matter how hard he tried to think back, apart from telling the senior detective they were three heavily built 'geezers', Estelle's friend couldn't offer any further assistance.

"Except they were wearing hobnailed boots from the sounds I could hear when they were chasing me, but who doesn't wear them down at the docks."

"Very well," the Chief Inspector said, moving from behind his desk, "Henry, our friend here will be staying with me for a few days, or until at least we have got to the bottom of this."

Bustle swallowed his food down the wrong way, when attempting to come to terms with what he'd just been told and took a moment to violently cough.

Richard Rayner paused, before requesting, "And Henry, when you're ready, could you pop down to reception and make sure that Miss Estelle gets home safely. Tell her I'll explain everything to her at a later time."

A red-faced Bustle nodded, unable to speak at that moment.

The senior detective then turned to the young itinerant and explained that the lad was about to sleep in a real bed for at least a few nights and would have the benefit of indulging himself in hot meals. They both left the Sergeant still struggling to finish off his supper.

Raphael Dickens remained a confused and nervous young man, as their carriage passed through the wrought iron gates and approached the front door steps leading to the Rayner house. Never before had the young man been invited to stay in such a palatial residence and matters didn't improve when he was met by a stare of concerning disbelief from the butler, Albert.

The old man's anxiety was quickly dispelled by the authority in his master's voice.

"Mr. Dickens will be staying with us for a short time Albert," Richard Rayner directed, "So, if you would be so good as to arrange for one of the spare rooms upstairs to be made up and ask Tilly to prepare a hot bath for our guest, if you please." He then turned to the street muffin and explained, "Rest assured, Ralphie, you will be safe here until I have tracked down those men you made mention of. Oh, and Albert, find him a change of clothes from somewhere."

The butler muttered something under his breath before leading the young visitor down towards the servants' quarters.

When Clarice first heard of the human specimen her husband had brought home with him, her first thought turned to the safety of the valuables they kept inside the house. When Rayner explained the circumstances in which he felt a need to protect Estelle's friend and shared details of the dangers imposed on young Raphael, she could only agree and admire her spouse's charitable behaviour.

"He must not be allowed to leave the house, Clarice, under any circumstances until I am absolutely sure it will be safe for him to do so."

"I shall make sure the staff are aware dear and have no fear, he will be treated as if he was a member of the family."

The unusual guest was allocated a bedroom only two doors away from where the master and mistress slept and spent the remainder of that evening in Richard and Clarice Rayner's company, although remaining distant from the couple. In fact, it was the mistress of the house who eventually escorted a seemingly exhausted young itinerant to his room, continually reassuring him.

The Chief Inspector slept uneasily that night, tormented by what his most recent houseguest had told him, having witnessed the murder of Joseph Kelly. The mystery woman who appeared to have been giving the orders to the thugs was of prime interest to the senior detective. Her presence clouded any attempt to discover the motive for the act of barbarism and it was almost dawn when Rayner finally found sleep.

The next surprise to come from this particular saga was when, Tilly the maid, entered Raphael Dickens room early the next morning to wake the lad up. She found the bed had been slept in but the room was empty. The youngster had fled, undoubtedly back to the streets.

Such behaviour that was completely mystifying to Richard Rayner might well have been better understood by the likes of Henry Bustle, or any other individual who was better acquainted with the way in which these homeless street vagabonds thought and acted. In fact, when the Chief Inspector had left Scotland Yard the previous evening, the Sergeant had wondered for how long his senior detective would have been capable of keeping the young itinerant under wraps.

"He's wearing the same clothes Mr. Winkle gave him last night sir," Tilly confirmed, referring to the butler.

Rayner was both disappointed and concerned for the young man's safety and Clarice tried to offer her husband some reassurance by suggesting there was nothing more he could have done to help the absconder. That made little difference however, to his feeling of self-incrimination. The youngster would now have to take his chances alone, using the vast network of decaying buildings, courtyards and alleyways in his efforts to survive.

After arriving back at Scotland Yard, the first thing Richard Rayner did was to circulate Dickens's description to every patrolling constable in London. He then thought about approaching Morgan's daughter to find out if the lad had been in touch with her, but didn't think that would be a realistic option, considering the last time the young man had gone to see that young lady was when he'd been apprehended. 'Ralphie' had elected to go it alone and it would be no surprise to the senior detective if his dead body was found in the near future.

The Eagle and Tun was a small corner public house in Cartwright Street, just a couple of hundred yards from St Katharine Dock, and where Richard Rayner had arranged to meet Lonnie Jones. The man purporting to be the most recently employed labourer at the docks, arrived looking fairly jovial and when the Chief Inspector asked how he had coped with his first few days working on the loading decks, his informant responded with a display of blackened teeth behind a wide grin.

"The work itself Mr. Rayner, is like putty in the hand. It's the blokes I have to work with that's the problem."

"Why is that?" the detective asked, nodding towards the pint of ale he'd purchased for Jones, prior to his arrival.

"Nobody speaks to yer," he answered, before taking his first large gulp of his drink, "They all seem to be suspicious of each other and keep themselves to themselves."

"That's not surprising Lonnie, so, I take it there's nothing to report then."

The human colossus shook his head and wiped the foam from around his mouth with the back of his shovel-sized hand.

"Nothing," he said, "And believe me, I've had my eyes wide open."

"Give it until the end of the week, it might be that once they get used to that amazing characteristic face of yours, some of them might feel more like talking to you." Rayner was being sensitive, not wanting to describe his helper as being ugly, as that might have hurt his feelings.

The door to the snug unexpectedly sprung open, bringing a look of surprise to the faces of the two men. That surprise turned to one of concern, when they saw standing there in the doorway none other than the docks supervisor, Tommy Herrick.

"The bastard must have followed me," Lonnie Jones gasped.

The threat posed by the figure standing there was instantly obvious to Richard Rayner and his informant. Herrick, boasted a look of self-righteous gratification on his face, reminding the Scotland Yard detective of an individual who had just burst in on an illicit game of poker. The man was savouring every second of silent embarrassment that passed by, until the detective made the first move, finding it difficult to conceal his astonishment. Totally ignoring Lonnie Jones, the Chief Inspector verbally expressed his surprise at seeing the unexpected caller's appearance and quickly offered to buy him a drink.

"I wondered if you or any of your workmates used this place," Richard Rayner lied, trying hard to look untroubled and reassured.

"We don't, I was just interested in the copper's nark you've got sitting there," the smaller man answered, provoking Lonnie Jones to get to his feet with a look of hostility on his face and both fists clenched. Mr. Herrick was a brave man, realising that the farrier could have used him as a toothpick if he so desired and he was certainly sending out an invitation for that to happen.

"Is that all that concerns you, Tommy?" Rayner asked, maintaining his posture of authority.

The man seemed to relax, still grinning and directed his next words at Lonnie Jones.

"Take it easy feller, I followed you from the docks guessing you were up to something and I know you wouldn't have anything worth telling our Mr. Rayner here. You can't fool those blokes working at St Katharine's, and you certainly couldn't fool me."

"Calm yourself, Lonnie," the Chief Inspector suggested, before asking the intruder, yet again, what he'd like to drink.

"I'll have a large whiskey with you Mr. Rayner. I think you owe me that much."

"I owe you nothing Mr. Herrick," Rayner retorted.

"I think you'll change your mind, once you've listened to what I've got to tell you."

Rayner then told Lonnie to finish his drink and return to his own yard in John Street, inferring that his undercover work was now at an end.

The farrier nodded, but couldn't resist snarling as he stepped past the dock supervisor on his way out. What Lonnie Jones wouldn't have given to be able to lift the obnoxious little man off the floorboards and bang his head on the ceiling... However, he turned his back on the room and quietly left.

Chapter Thirteen

Rayner replenished his own glass and supplied the drink he'd promised to Tommy Herrick. Once the two men were sitting facing each other, the detective decided to wait for the other to speak.

"I've been asking a few questions about Joey Kelly, but before I say any more I want some assurance you'll be on my side when I go up in front of the beak," the docker explained.,

"I'm surprised you are still in a job, Tommy," Rayner said, remembering Frederick Morgan's words of advice, to use the man as best he could.

"That's only because the guvnors know nothing about it yet, but have no fear, I'll be shoved out quickly enough once it gets in the papers."

Rayner still found the man and everything he stood for, despicable but knew only too well, to allow personal feelings to interfere with the manner in which he needed to continue the conversation, would be unprofessional. He took a swallow of his drink and sat back, looking as calm and as unruffled as he usually did before explaining, "The only people who have lost out from your smuggling activities so far Tommy, are the taxmen and of course those who have physically suffered at your hands quite badly."

"I'm finished with all of that now, Mr. Rayner, they can get some other mug to look after their interests. In any case, they're more likely to take the piss than part with their money from now on, thanks to you and your blokes."

"I'm sure there will be a lot of men relieved to hear that."

"So, will you be putting a good word in with the judge or not."

"Let's hear what you have to say first."

The grin returned to Herrick's face and he drank half the whiskey in his glass in one hasty swallow, before telling the detective what he'd found out.

"Joey Kelly was a philanderer, Mr. Rayner, a geezer who didn't give a shit about his missus or kids."

"I'm listening, Tommy."

"According to the blokes at the docks and I must admit, I didn't know anything about this going on, Kelly was seeing a woman who, after he'd finished his work would pick him up in some fancy carriage before they'd take off somewhere."

"Did he ever tell anybody who this woman was?"

"Naw, he wasn't stupid, but apparently when one or two mentioned her to him, he took the piss and used to smile. Not a nice man from all accounts, but one of the blokes once heard him call her by a foreign name, Natalia, or something like that, Russian sounding."

"Or Polish, are there any Poles working on the docks?"

"One or two but they don't mix with any of the others."

"Did anybody tell you what this fancy carriage looked like?"

"It was all black with a gold trim, but according to one or two of them, she always stayed inside it and had a driver up top. It seems she was a woman of means and most of them just thought Joey had landed on his feet."

Obviously, from what he'd just been told and provided Tommy Herrick wasn't trying to hoodwink him with some fairy tale, which Rayner doubted, the Scotland Yard man surmised there was more to this Joseph Kelly than they knew about. Whether or not he was in a relationship with this Natalia, remained to be seen though.

"Tell me Tommy, did Kelly ever mix much with the others on the docks?"

"I never saw him but according to a couple, he used to go for a drink after work with them, but that was before this wench of his came on the scene."

"Was he ever known to spend much money?"

"Not that I'm aware of. He wasn't exactly on top hole, but he'd have been earning enough to get by on."

"And I take it she hasn't been seen since his murder."

"I'm not the detective Mr. Rayner, you are. I can ask around some more if you want."

Rayner sat in silence for a short time, digesting everything he'd just been told. Undoubtedly, the news of another woman being on the scene had a bearing on the way in which he had been looking into Kelly's murder. There was also the mention by Raphael Dickens that a woman was present when the atrocity was committed. Could it be possible they were the same person? The Chief Inspector believed it was a big coincidence if they weren't.

"So, what about it, Mr. Rayner. Are you going to help me or not?"

The docks weren't the kind of place for the faint hearted and Richard Rayner knew only too well, many of the labourers working down there were the hardest men in London. Fights between them was common place, but as long as they did their work without causing any problems, turning a blind eye was preferable to getting rid of men. Tommy Herrick was just an example of the kind of character that survived amongst the dockland community and having broken up the man's smuggling activities, only with a view to throwing more light on the Joseph Kelly murder, Rayner's ploy had succeeded.

"I need you to find out more about this woman, Tommy. The time of day she picked up Kelly and more of a description of that carriage she was always inside, and anything known about her driver."

The man nodded, still waiting for the Chief Inspector's reassurance that he would put a good word in for him at court.

"If you can help me find that woman," Rayner continued, "I'll drop all the charges against you Tommy, provided you stop your protection racket and desist from beating up half the labour force."

The man's face brightened and he nodded his full agreement.

"I need more information though," Rayner insisted.

"And you shall have it, Mr. Rayner. If anybody can find her, it's me." The docker had been promised much more than he'd anticipated and was elated. His offer of further help was completely genuine.

It was a cold and wet gusty night, when the Chief Inspector's carriage turned into Mary Ann Street, Whitechapel. His destination was a small house in one of many backyards, displaying the number three on the door at the back of twenty-five, where his transport came to a stop. Knowing the reputation that area of London had during the hours of darkness, his driver, Constable Brown, offered to accompany Rayner, but was told to stay with the horse and carriage. Even at that late hour, it was quite possible for the transport to disappear if left unattended for a minute.

When approaching the terraced three-storey house, which included an attic, the first thing the senior detective noticed was the drawn curtains in the front room. Instead of being the usual paper-thin drab and well-worn material, they looked refreshingly new, bright and colourful.

A pale-faced, feeble looking woman answered his knock and looked surprised when seeing how the gentleman standing on her doorstep, was dressed. The Chief Inspector looked more like a member of the House of Lords, than a Scotland Yard detective. Not surprisingly, she was dressed in black and obviously still in mourning, or so her visitor assumed.

Rayner tipped his top hat and enquired if he was addressing Mrs. Kelly.

She nodded and the detective introduced himself before asking if he could step inside as there were a few questions he wished to put to her, outside the hearing of her neighbours.

She stepped back and Rayner found himself standing in a front room with walls that had recently been decorated with heavily embossed paper. There was an expensive looking orange velvet lamp cover hanging from the centre of the ceiling. A fire was burning brightly inside a small but ornamental fire surround and the whole of the interior reflected opulence. When offered a seat, he chose a brown leather sofa covered in lace throws and gazed for a moment at an array of gold-gilt framed pictures on the walls, mostly of country scenes. The room was a far cry from the usual décor in which the inhabitants of Whitechapel lived. There was even a walnut drinks cabinet standing in one corner, which again was the kind of furniture that just wasn't found in that part of London, unless it had been stolen and there was no reason for Richard Rayner to suspect that.

"Please accept my deepest condolences for this intrusion at a time of your grieving, Mrs. Kelly," he politely offered.

She nodded and perched herself on a chair nearest the fire with both spindly hands grasped together on her lap. The dress she was wearing hadn't come from a pawn broker and was obviously new. In fact, apart from her mournful facial features, the lady's appearance was similar to what he would have expected from the wife of some wealthy Parliamentarian or successful businessman. He assumed from the lateness of the hour the children would have been upstairs in their beds.

"I wanted to let you know we haven't yet identified the killer of your husband, but I assure you we will, eventually."

She just smiled, giving the impression of not being one hundred percent attentive.

"Did your husband have any relatives, could you tell me?"

Finally, she spoke in a nervous, weak voice, reminding the detective of the demeanour of Annie Crockett, the wretched woman he'd recently visited in Holloway.

"No sir, not that I am aware."

"Then forgive me, I have been misinformed."

"In what way sir."

"It's nothing Mrs. Kelly, a mistake on our behalf. I was told your departed husband had recently come into some money, possibly left him by some aunt or other relative," he lied.

Again, she shook her head and was adamant her husband had not received any inheritance. As if noticing the detective's curious regard towards the affluent interior of her house, she qualified her last answer by explaining that her late departed had been a hard-working man.

"Joseph spent a great deal of his time at work, sir," she said, "Working many hours overtime and not getting home until late at night. He put all of his hard-earned coppers into this house."

"Did he ever work a nightshift at the docks, Mrs. Kelly?"

"No, but he always worked until very late in the evenings."

"I have no doubt Mrs. Kelly he was a devoted husband, which makes it even more imperative we find his killer. How are you coping, financially I mean?"

"He left me fairly comfortable Chief Inspector. We'll manage to get through this."

"Of course, madam," Rayner quickly answered, "Then I shall not intrude on your privacy any further."

As he stood from the sofa, she asked if he knew when her husband's body would be released for burial and he confessed that wasn't his decision.

"I see no reason why it shouldn't be released now Mrs. Kelly," he conceded, "Allow me to make some enquiries so you can make the necessary arrangements."

As the lady showed him to the door, Rayner suddenly turned and asked if she had ever heard her husband mention the name, Natalia.

"No, never sir," she genuinely answered, "Is it important."

"Not really Mrs. Kelly, only it's connected with something completely different."

The Chief Inspector left, having succeeded in achieving the purpose of his visit. As he walked through the darkness, back towards his waiting carriage, Rayner's analytical mind was in overdrive. He knew from what Tommy Herrick had told him, Joseph Kelly had worked little overtime at the docks and yet the man had come into a lot of money based on his own observations and from what Mrs. Kelly had told him. He needed to find out who the woman, Natalia, was and what exactly had been the nature of her relationship with the dead man. The fact that Kelly had been given access to what must have been a fairly large amount of cash at the same time as he had been associating with the woman in the black carriage, could not have been a coincidence. It was vital that she was traced as quickly as possible and Rayner had no doubt, she could have somehow been connected with the manner in which the murdered man had acquired his recent good fortune. That being the case, it was also reasonable to suspect she might also have some knowledge of the people who had committed such a barbaric and tortuous killing, the details of which had been withheld from the widow for obvious reasons. By the time he reached his carriage he was convinced the woman seen at the docks by the young street muffin, and Joseph Kelly's mysterious female associate, were the same.

When arriving at Scotland Yard the following morning, Richard Rayner's first priority was to communicate the urgent need to trace the woman known as, Natalia, beginning with his two Sergeants. She had become a central figure in the Investigation and putting chalk to slate, he wrote the name in large letters across the top of the blackboard followed by everything they knew about her, which was very little.

"I believe she is foreign to these shores, possibly from Russia or Poland or some other Baltic country," he explained, watching both Bustle and Robinson make notes as he spoke.

"We know she is a woman of wealth or has access to wealth, from the description given by Herrick of the carriage she travels in, black with a gold trim and apparently always accompanied by her own or a hired coachman."

"Are we sure we have the right name sir?" Jack Robinson asked, "Is it possible someone misheard the name?"

"Yes, that's possible Jack, but at the moment we can only progress with what we have been given."

"It's knowing where to start looking," Bustle remarked.

"Yes, but there can't be many women by that name in London, that's if she lives here, Henry. The main thing we do know about her is that Natalia most definitely had some kind of liaison with Joseph Kelly, prior to his murder. She was a frequent visitor to the docks, St. Katharine's in particular, but where did the couple go to after meeting."

"It might have been anywhere in the country."

"No, not anywhere. I suspect whatever they got up to, took place somewhere in the city, as according to Mrs. Kelly, her husband always arrived home late at night, but was never absent overnight."

"I'll check the usual places as a matter of urgency," Henry Bustle offered.

"Thank you, Henry, and Jack, I want you to look deeper into Kelly's background. Any known associates or places frequented that might throw some light on who this woman is."

Rayner then explained that he didn't believe the relationship between Natalia and the docker was of an intimate nature. In his opinion, it was an alliance, one that profited both parties, probably in ready cash and lots of it.

"Try and put yourself in her shoes, Jack and ask yourself, why would you require the services of a docker."

"In similar fashion to those smugglers we captured the other night sir, to help bring unlawful goods into the country."

"Exactly, and most importantly, why choose Joseph Kelly, from all the dockers who work there?"

That query was more difficult for the younger of the two Sergeants to answer and he quickly reverted to the enquiries he'd been making about Annie Crockett's background.

"Her maiden name was Arrowsmith sir and she originated from Smithfield."

"Well done, Jack, has that been progressed further?"

"Not yet sir, I'm still working on it."

The Chief Inspector nodded his satisfaction and left the two Sergeants to carry on with their allotted tasks.

The Commissioner's office was the most spacious and impressively furnished at Scotland Yard but Richard Rayner sensed all was not well, when stepping inside. The time had arrived for yet another daily briefing and yet the atmosphere was hostile and from the angered look on Sir Edward Bradford's face, the Chief Inspector was the source of the antagonism.

"Good morning sir," Rayner said, attempting to keep the conversation that was to follow at an amicable level, "I'm pleased to say, we have made some progress in the docks murder."

"Never mind that, Rayner," the words came out of a strained mouth embedded in a flushed face, "I understand you have recently visited the convicted woman, Annie Crockett, at Holloway Prison, after I distinctly told you to leave well alone."

The Chief Inspector couldn't deny the allegation. He was without excuse or mitigation and instantly recognised there was no way out of his predicament. All he could do was to confess his sin and await whatever punitive measures the most powerful man at Scotland Yard wished to bestow upon him. Unfortunately, Richard Rayner didn't hold a position as elevated and as close to the Commissioner as did Frederick Morgan, and was well aware his current position was sufficiently fragile to be in jeopardy.

"To say I am disappointed is insufficient to describe my true feelings, Chief Inspector, I am absolutely furious that you chose to so blatantly disobey my orders."

It was obvious that whatever action the Commissioner was about to subject him to, had already been decided and the best thing Richard Rayner could do was tell the truth and defend his own course of action by arguing his belief in the female convict's innocence.

"It is my opinion..." he began, before being abruptly interrupted.

"Blast your opinion sir, you are not employed by me to offer any opinion on what I have so clearly instructed."

"I truly believe that a woman has wrongfully served ten years imprisonment for a crime she was not guilty of having committed and feel strongly that I have a duty..."

"Don't cloud the issue with your impudence sir, I will not have any of my senior officers acting unilaterally and against my directives. If that is not sufficiently clear to you, I suggest you should consider resigning your position."

This wasn't Frederick Morgan the Chief Inspector was arguing with; this was a man who could decide Rayner's future by a snap of his fingers and the renowned detective felt as if he was treading on glass. This was one battle he could not possibly win and to save his position, there was a need to manoeuvre extremely cautiously. To inflame the Commissioner's vexation even more so, would be committing professional suicide. He had to roll over and concede, like a pet dog having just attracted the annoyance of its master.

"I can only apologise sir," he finally offered, in complete capitulation, "Please accept I meant no insult or disparagement to yourself." To apologise was an admission of guilt, but Rayner had no other choice.

The Commissioner sat back and huffed and puffed for a short time, before looking up from his desk and enquiring as to what progress his Chief Inspector had referred to in relation to the Kelly murder. At least Sir Edward hadn't followed up with a killer blow that would have ended Richard Rayner's career at Scotland Yard, much to the detective's relief.

Rayner explained briefly the results of the enquiries made so far, placing some emphasis on the woman, Natalia, known to be an acquaintance of the dead man.

"Who is she?" Sir Edward asked, making a note of the name mentioned and showing genuine interest, although still speaking precipitously.

"We haven't yet traced her sir, but we will." Rayner then spoke of the carriage used to convey the lady when frequently visiting the docks and of his suspicions that the murdered victim had, in his view, received a great deal of money as a result of whatever the relationship he'd had with the same woman.

Although the manner in which Richard Rayner was speaking to the Head of the Metropolitan Police, was as articulate as ever, this was still an ordeal he could very well have done without. His discomfort was increased further by the nature in which Sir Edward turned sideways in his seat and remained staring at a wall throughout the Chief Inspector's narrative, giving the impression he wasn't completely absorbing every word being said. When Rayner had finished, he was pleasantly surprised when the Commissioner unexpectedly made a suggestion, confirming he had in fact been listening intently.

"Natalia is an unusual name Mr. Rayner." He then paused, allowing the Chief Inspector to acknowledge that fact, his large face having by then restored some of its natural, healthier looking colour.

"Bolak Baranski is the Polish representative in London," he continued, "They have no embassy as such and the man usually stays at the Dorchester when staying here on diplomatic business. He has two daughters who usually accompany him, Lena and Natalia Baranski. Perhaps you find that of some interest."

Chapter Fourteen

Even after discussing the Joseph Kelly murder, Rayner was still reeling from the admonishment he'd just been subjected to and stared back at the man sitting behind the desk, reluctant to make any suggestion on how to approach either of the Polish ladies identified. He feared that one word spoken out of turn or carelessly, could incur Sir Edward's wrath, but the senior man continued with his suggestions in a relaxed manner, as if having forgotten about the earlier confrontation.

"If it suits Mr. Rayner, I know Bolak very well and could arrange for his daughter, Natalia, to be seen by yourself, here at Scotland Yard, if you think that would help. It might very well be, we are barking up the wrong tree but as I have said, the name isn't a common one."

"No sir and yes, I would appreciate that."

"Very well, leave that with me and Rayner, I would appreciate being kept informed of your Investigation into this woman, Annie Crockett." He then dismissed the detective with a wave of his hand.

That last request was certainly a turn around by the Commissioner and Richard Rayner smiled and nodded, relieved that one of the most powerful men in the capital hadn't placed further restrictions on his enthusiasm relative to Annie Crockett's predicament. In fact, as he made his way back to his own office the senior detective was confounded by the way Sir Edward Bradford had brought down the whip for having continued enquiring into the possible innocence of the woman in question one minute, and the next, had indirectly given his approval for his Chief Inspector to continue. This was all new to him and he accepted he might be in need of some enlightenment on how to conduct himself when dealing with the enigmatic highest-ranking gentleman in the future. He thought it might be a wise move to counsel Frederick Morgan, before exposing himself again in the office on the top floor. He wasted little time in gathering his hat and coat and hastily departed for Richmond, where both himself and Morgan resided.

After arriving for the second time that week at the same residence, the senior detective was allowed entrance by James the butler, who immediately escorted him through the house to Sally-Anne Morgan, who he found standing behind some potted plants inside a glasshouse attached to the veranda.

"How is he?" a bemused Richard Rayner enquired.

"Look for yourself, Richard," she suggested, pointing towards the far end of the garden, where the puffing figure of her husband could be seen running up and down in a vest and pair of old trousers, with Miss Longfeet standing closely in attendance grasping a large time piece in one hand.

"I have to watch from here because if he sees me, he gets embarrassed and things are bad enough as it is," the lady of the house explained.

"He doesn't seem much different to when I last called, Sal."

"Oh, I think he improves each day and he hasn't complained about his haemorrhoids for some time now or his desire to take one of those dreadful powders."

"At least that's reassuring news."

"The problem Frederick appears to have at present Richard, is his detestation of the woman who is trying to help him. He's already sacked Nurse Longfeet on five occasions so far, to my knowledge."

"Good grief."

"She doesn't seem perturbed in the slightest though and just carries on giving him instructions, to which he obeys, although reluctantly."

"Then he must know she means well, Sal."

"I'm not so sure. Here he comes, I think the nurse is bringing his exercise to a close."

Morgan staggered past where they were both covertly stood and disappeared into the back of the house, blowing and grunting and without catching sight of his wife in the glasshouse or his visitor.

By the time the Chief Superintendent reappeared, bathed and fully dressed, Richard Rayner was seated with Sally-Anne in the lounge, drinking coffee.

Morgan was evidently delighted by his friend's presence and confirmed as much by a warm greeting. He then turned to his wife and swore on a stack of bibles that if that cursed woman didn't leave her employment soon, he would commit suicide.

"Now Frederick, you don't mean that, myself and Richard were just saying how well you look and how you have improved under Miss Longfeet's tuition."

He turned to Rayner and suggested he began an Investigation into the nurse's background, insisting that in his view she was the kind of woman who had been married on several previous occasions, killing each and every one of her husbands to get her hands on their money.

Rayner smiled, obviously not taking his friend seriously.

"I joke not Richard, the woman is a masochist, brought to this planet by demons and has no given right to breathe the same air as we do."

The visitor chuckled and commented, "Surely, she cannot be as bad as that, Frederick."

"She bloody well is and if you were in my shoes, you would be in full agreement."

Sally-Anne stood and explained that it was time to get ready to leave for the circus.

"I suspect there is something Richard wishes to discuss with you

Frederick, so I shall leave you two gentlemen to get on with it."

After she had left, James the butler entered the room carrying a silver tray containing a jug of lemon water and empty glass. He poured and left the drink at the side of his master's chair, before turning to make his exit.

"Jimmy," Morgan quietly called to the servant, sticking a thumb in the air, as the butler turned to look at him.

Jimmy nodded, but the look of fear on his face told Rayner the story.

After he'd left the room, Morgan quietly predicted his head of the domestic staff would return very soon with a bottle of malt whiskey.

"He's my saviour Richard, and he's very good at ensuring the Goddess of Darkness isn't about when he brings me my only pleasure."

Now Rayner couldn't help but laugh at the Chief Superintendent's antics, made funnier by the fact he was acting like a naughty schoolboy under his own roof.

After both men had settled, the visitor described the course of events leading up to what he described as the biggest dressing down he'd ever received from the Commissioner.

Morgan continued to listen, putting a handkerchief to good use as he was still perspiring from his most recent enforced exercise.

When Rayner had finished his tale of woe, he asked for his friend's views on how he should continue in his relationship with the main man at Scotland Yard.

"You have to understand Richard, the old chap spends most of his time up inside those four walls of his and whenever he is given an opportunity to add some spice to his life or justify his own existence, he grabs it with both hands."

"By running people over the coals, you mean."

"On occasions yes, but you mustn't take it to heart, he benefits more from bollocking people than those on the receiving end might well do. What were his final words to you on this Annie Crockett affair?"

"He told me to keep him updated."

"Then there you are my old mucker, you have it. So, he ticked you off and I have no doubt he felt justified in doing so, but it was a way of maintaining his image and deep down he would know that you had good intentions. Obviously, he wants you to continue."

"He has a funny way of showing it."

"Don't we all, when we reach such dizzy heights. How far has your Inquiry gone by the way."

James the butler then re-entered the room, carrying what appeared to be a brass coal bucket. Watched closely by the two senior detectives, he carefully placed the receptacle at the side of the fire before taking from it two cut glass tumblers, giving one to each of them. Morgan winked an eye at Rayner who continued to watch in total amazement as the butler produced an opened bottle of malt whiskey, as if by some mesmerising magical trick and charged the tumblers.

"Shall I leave the bucket where it is sir?" James quietly asked.

"Yes, but cover it with one of those pillows Jimmy, just in case and well done my old mucker."

The butler nodded, completed his task and left the room,

Rayner, who felt he was very much a part of the conspiracy he'd just witnessed, mentioned his visit to see the woman's local priest. After taking a swallow of the intoxicating liquid, he described how Father Michael at St Patrick's had confirmed that Annie Crockett had been cursed with some personal problem prior to her husband's murder.

"He is bound by his sworn oath not to disclose any details though, so that's as far as we have got."

Morgan then asked whether the man living next door to the Crockett's had been interviewed; the individual who had been drinking with the victim on the same night he was murdered.

"Not yet, but I intend to speak with him. I need to unravel the motive behind Leonard Crockett's death and without the assistance of the lady in question, I'm finding it extremely difficult."

Although Richard Rayner knew exactly which path he intended going down, he welcomed the opportunity to bounce some of his ideas and concerns off Frederick Morgan, who was responding in a constructive and helpful way. For the Chief Inspector, it was like an exercise in revision and when he finally stood to leave, the Chief Superintendent offered one further piece of advice.

"Looking at this from my point of view, Richard, might I suggest the next-door neighbours and Annie Crockett's daughter hold the key to confirming whether or not the woman killed her husband. Usually, there is money involved, but in the absence of that, then you will find the motive is entangled somewhere in a relationship."

Morgan sounded like some wise old sooth sayer and Rayner was surprised by the way in which the senior man appeared to be so clear headed. He had never before heard the Chief Superintendent share such logical common sense and appreciated the advice offered. As he turned to make his exit, the door to the lounge was flung open and a determined Nurse Longfeet appeared. The visitor from Scotland Yard, calmly placed his empty tumbler on to a table. After all, he wasn't the subject of rehabilitation from drugs addiction and was beyond reproach or chastisement. There was no sign of where Morgan's drink had disappeared to and God only knew, how the Chief Superintendent had managed to conceal that so quickly.

In recent years, London had grown fairly rapidly into the most densely populated city in the country, with factories and other industrial facilities springing up just about everywhere. As a result, the capital was invaded by hordes of people; some seeking to create their own businesses and line their pockets with gold by dipping into this new found centre of wealth; others desperate to find work if only to survive. New communities appeared from nowhere, consisting not only of the local people born and bred in London, but imports of various denominations from Ireland and the continent, including Jews, Poles and representatives of just about every other European nation. The scourge of over-population soon became commonplace and lodging houses were eventually filled to the brim with numerous lost and starving strangers, looking for a means to live on a daily basis. In most instances, paltry wages were insufficient and there were many who were forced to turn to the streets to beg and get what scraps of food they could find, just to continue living.

Conditions for the majority became intolerable and unhealthy. Where workers lived, basic facilities such as the necessity for clean water, sewerage and adequate ventilation was absent. There remained a constant stench in the air from unclean sewage that eventually polluted the River Thames with human waste and naturally, a number of deadly diseases became rampant.

Both men and women turned to drink whenever possible, escaping from the trauma of deprivation in many of the backstreet public houses, or from a bottle of gin or other cheap spirit. Drunkenness on the streets was rife and the police were kept busy.

It was amongst those nests of poverty and destitution that Henry Bustle's informant, Spotty Finkel, sort shelter in a void house accessed from a narrow balcony overlooking a courtyard. Like so many other similar communal hovels, the same enclosure had an open sewerage system running through its centre. But at the very least, the itinerant had a roof over his head, albeit one amongst other aging and decaying buildings.

The insipid looking little man was just locking his front door, intending to spend an evening begging drinks at the Canal Bargee public house, when the Sergeant entrapped him on the balcony.

"A word in your cabbage patch, Spotty," Bustle demanded, referring to his informant's listening organ.

"Can't it wait Mr. Bustle, I'm on my way out. Time is money you know."

"You mean time is begging my little flea-bitten friend. Open up again, I need you to enlighten me."

The Sergeant followed the vagrant back inside the hovel where the stink of decay was prominent, an odour that Henry Bustle's nostrils had become accustomed to, having experienced the same presence and consequences of poverty numerous times previously. He found himself a wooden crate to sit on, which apart from a couple of other similar items and an old square shaped table that looked as though it had once belonged in a church, was the only object in the darkened room.

"For Christ's sake Spotty, it's like the bleedin' black hole of Calcutta inside here, haven't you got a candle or something to light so I can see your miserable face. Don't worry, I'll buy you a couple of unused ones in the morning."

"You'd better Mr. Bustle, this is the only one I've got left," the resident announced pleadingly and taking a small, much used stub of candle wax from his jacket pocket, before placing it on a cracked saucer and producing a match to light it.

Although, Henry Bustle never refrained from speaking harshly to the man, he did have a great deal of sympathy for any individual forced to live in such appalling squalor and without the money the Sergeant often handed over to his man, Spotty Finkel would in all probability, starve to death. Having said that, the Sergeant was also aware that most of that cash he parted with, went on drink but at least a glass of nourishing black ale inside his stomach was better than nothing.

Both men sat opposite one another, their faces illuminated by the flickering light coming from Spotty's only source. It was cold inside that small room and Bustle would have been tempted to have delivered a load of wood to use as fuel for a fire, except he knew only too well the same would be quickly sold off for the price of a glass of beer.

Surprisingly, the visitor noticed a large crucifix on one of the walls that hadn't been there when he had last set foot inside the room and declared that he hadn't known that Spotty Finkel was religious. The only time the little man would have attended a church was when there was every likelihood, he could steal some of the silver plate.

"Don't take the Lord's name in vain, Mr. Bustle," the squatter said, words that were ignored by the detective.

"I need to know something about the Poles and Ruskies working and hiding out in the city my old mate, so what can you tell me?" the Sergeant finally enquired optimistically.

The little man's eyes lit up, when he saw a ten-shilling note being placed on top of the badly scarred table. If only he could get his hands on that, he would be spending the next two nights on a park bench, paralytic drunk.

"What do you want with them, Mr. Bustle," he asked, snatching at the money, but unable to grab it owing to the detective's quick reaction.

"I'm looking for a woman who drives around in a posh carriage, black with a gold trim," the Sergeant divulged, "And if you can get her for me, Spotty, you'll earn much more than that ten-bob note."

His informant displayed that toothless grin of his and immediately asked quite bravely, what price the detective was willing to pay. He knew only too well that Bustle would never cotter any attempt to bargain when it came to buying information and was more likely to nail him to a wall and use him as a clock face. However, the Sergeant was obviously in a more understanding mood.

"Do you know anybody answering that description then," Bustle enquired, still grasping hold of the ten-shilling note.

"What's the carriage look like?"

"I've told you, all black with a gold trim and a coachman on top."

"I might know something Mr. Bustle," Finkel said, teasingly and holding out a palm, stretching his man's patience to the limit.

"Don't piss me about, you little runt. Do you know her, or don't you?"

"Am I right in saying, she's a frequent visitor to the docks then."

Henry Bustle got to his feet after hearing those last few words and demanded to know more, at the same time, releasing the ten-shillings back on to the table top that quickly disappeared into Finkel's woollen and well patched trouser pocket.

"It's gotta be worth more than that, Mr. Bustle. What do you want her for?"

Finkel's upper frame was lifted up off his wooden crate and grasped tightly with both legs dangling clear of the floor. The Sergeant's understanding mood had just evaporated.

"Three seconds is all you've got, Spotty."

"She's staying at the Dorchester with the nobs, Mr. Bustle."

"How do you know that?"

"Cos I've seen her and that carriage down at the docks and again outside the Dorchester. Smart young lady with a nice smile and always wearing grey clobber."

"Do you know who she is?" Bustle asked, lowering the man back on to the crate.

"Naw, why should I, but I could find out soon enough Mr. Bustle."

"Do that Spotty, and let me know at Scotland Yard." The Sergeant then placed a one-pound note on the table to join the ten-shillings already paid, much to his informant's utter delight.

Chapter Fifteen

When visiting 71 Denmar Street for the second time, Rose Pendry answered Richard Rayner's knock and wasted little time in inviting her gentleman caller inside. The lady had an enticing grin across her heavily painted face, only this time she was fully clothed, wearing a white blouse and ankle length badly creased olive skirt.

The Chief Inspector explained that he wished to speak with her husband and asked if the gentleman was available. He was disappointed when told that Charlie Pendry was at work and wasn't due back for his supper until eight o'clock. A seductive look was now dominant in the woman's eyes and the message being portrayed was quite clear; there was plenty of time for them to become better acquainted. But Rayner ignored the silent invitation and looked straight through the lady.

"What does your husband do for a living, Mrs. Pendry?" he asked, maintaining a level of authority in his voice and not giving her the slightest indication of encouragement.

"I would have thought a gallant man such as yourself would have already known that sir," she answered, smiling and bowing her head slightly in a sort of submissive manner, "He's a coster and works from his stall in Queen Street, near to Southwark Bridge." In other words, her husband worked as a costermonger, more popularly known as a street seller.

"What products does he sell?"

"Fruit and veg mostly and stuff like that, but he won't be able to help you much."

"Was your husband doing the same kind of work at the time Leonard Crockett was murdered." Richard Rayner's words were spoken abruptly and quite deliberately. He felt uneasy being there alone with this particular woman, especially when she undid the two top buttons of her blouse for no specific reason.

"He's worked on the streets since he was a kid, but had his stall on Westminster Bridge when that happened."

"Thank you Mrs. Pendry, I only have…"

"You can call me Rose if you prefer, Mr. Rayner." The look of enticement had returned, probably as a last throw of the dice by this self-opinionated female.

"Thank you but that won't be necessary. I only have one more question for you. When I last called, you told me that on that same night, your husband came home from The Bushell public house at half past ten, just after closing time."

"Yes, and he did."

"You are absolutely sure about that."

"Yes, I distinctly remember Big Ben striking the half hour as he walked through the door."

"Could that have been half past nine by any chance?"

"No, it was half past ten. He had his usual shot of whiskey and went to bed."

Rayner believed her but it meant that according to the landlady at The Bushell, Mrs. Dorothy Peterson, there was more than an hour unaccounted for between the time Charlie Pendry left the public house, to when he arrived home.

He thanked Mrs. Pendry for her help, but as she was showing him to the door, suddenly turned and faced her, reminding the lady of her previous remarks indicating that Annie Crockett had been a loose woman when suggesting she had a number of male callers.

"Can you recall any of those visitors in particular, Mrs. Pendry?" he asked.

She shook her head, obviously taken a little by surprise.

"Not really. Perhaps I exaggerated a little Mr. Rayner," she confessed, "Now I think about it, perhaps there was just one or two, but I cannot for the life of me remember much about them."

"Might I suggest that your claim is a complete fabrication and the truth is, Annie Crockett had no male visitors to her house during the time her husband was at work. The truth of the matter is extremely important to my Investigation."

The mischievous woman opened her mouth, as if to deny the allegation put to her, but then closed it before finally admitting she had been mistaken.

There was no doubt, Rose Pendry, was either a natural and lying trouble maker or had an intense dislike of the woman who once lived next door to her. After leaving, he wondered why on earth she had quite deliberately lied about the lady now serving a life sentence in Holloway and why would she wish to blacken the same lady's character in such a way. Unless of course, she was talking about herself, which from what he had just experienced was highly likely.

When he arrived back at Scotland Yard, he found Jack Robinson waiting for him with a notepad in one hand and pencil in the other. His young Sergeant's face was alight with enthusiasm and impatience to let his Chief Inspector know, he believed he'd had some success.

"Give me time to hang my hat and coat up Jack," Rayner pleaded, making good use of the coat stand near to the door of his office, before stepping across the room to his desk.

"Now then, what have you."

Rayner sat and listened intently, as his reliable detective explained that he'd confirmed the name, Natalia, was indeed of Polish origin and that a search of the appropriate records had revealed very little.

"However, about twelve months ago sir, there was an incident at the new Carrick Theatre involving a young lady who complained about being refused entry, having purchased a ticket to watch the opening production."

"I was there with Mrs. Rayner, Jack. It was 'The Profligate' by Pinero, and was an outstanding success I recall."

"Yes sir, Johnstone Forbes Robertson was the star apparently, both me and the wife are big fans of his." Robinson was referring to a well-known thespian and performer at that time.

"Sorry Jack, I've interrupted you. What about this young lady then?"

"Well, according to our reports she was with another small group of people who were all a bit tipsy and when refused entry, she showed her disgust by hitting one of the floor managers across the face and over the head with an umbrella," Robinson continued, "The police were called and she, with some of the others were arrested and later released.

"Was she charged?"

"No sir, according to the report they were all made to promise to be of good behaviour in the future and released, but her name was Natalia, and one of the other women with her was her sister, Lena Baranski."

"Was there any mention of their father being the Polish representative to the United Kingdom?"

"No sir, but if that was the case it might explain why they were never taken before the magistrates."

"What address did they give at the time, Jack?"

"The Dorchester Hotel sir."

"Well done, it seems that we need to speak with this particular Polish lady rather urgently."

There was a knock on the door, followed by the appearance of Henry Bustle. The older Sergeant also had a look of optimism on his grizzled face and explained how, according to his informant, Spotty Finkel, the woman they were seeking might be residing at the Dorchester Hotel.

Both Richard Rayner and Jack Robinson laughed, leaving Bustle looking just a little confused.

"I apologise Henry," the Chief Inspector offered and then explained what the younger Sergeant had just divulged.

As if fate came in threes, the Commissioner, Sir Edward Bradford, then entered the office and informed Rayner that, Miss Natalia Baranski, would be attending Scotland Yard to see the Chief Inspector at ten o'clock the following morning.

"I have no doubt Mr. Rayner, the lady's father, Bolak Baranski, will accompany his daughter so tread with caution."

"Yes sir."

It was raining quite heavily outside and the Morgan residence was in complete darkness. The pathetic looking figure stood in the darkness on the patio at the back of the house, waiting patiently until his friend appeared at the French windows. Silently, they were opened and the young man slipped inside, resembling a drowned rat.

Estelle stealthily led the way up the main staircase with her homeless associate following closely behind, shivering and soaking the carpet beneath his feet. Once inside her room he was stripped off and given towels with which to dry himself while she returned to the basement kitchen, where she found some soup left in a saucepan on the hob. She began to heat the food and was waiting for it to simmer when the figure of another man appeared unexpectedly in the doorway. It was James, the butler.

"I was feeling hungry, James," she quietly explained, "And thought..."

"It's quite alright Miss Estelle, I saw your visitor follow you up the stairs," he said, interrupting her, "But of course, I will have to inform your father."

The girl begged him not to, explaining that her father had enough problems of his own to be getting on with at present and which the butler was already aware of.

James listened carefully to the girl's pleas and eventually agreed to keep her secret on the condition that her young man, Raphael Dickens, slept in the stables at the back of the house and was gone by the time daylight arrived.

Estelle had no other option, but insisted her friend should have his hot soup first together with some bread to sustain him, before leaving the house.

The incessant rain had continued falling throughout the night and it was still an hour or so before the dawn was expected. Maisy Fletcher locked the front door of her backyard house in Finch Street, before pulling the hood of her cape over her head and leaving. She then scurried across the backyard, avoiding the miniature lakes that had formed, intending to reach the soup kitchen at St. Mary's Church early enough to help provide the Whitechapel homeless with their first meal of the day. It was a ritual, Maisy undertook each morning, walking the same route no matter what the weather, only on this particular morning her journey was to be interrupted by an unusual obstacle.

When she reached the enclosed entry that led down to Finch Street itself, the middle-aged early morning worker noticed a man lying, seemingly asleep on the loose bricks. At first, Maisy thought it was a drunk from the night before, sleeping off his intoxication and gave him a sharp kick, calling out for him to move so she could pass by. When she got no response, she cursed and stretched her legs out to step over the human obstruction. It was then she saw the pale bearded face staring up at her with an open gash across his throat. It was the body of a dead man, obviously the victim of a brutal murder and causing the charity volunteer to scream out in terror.

When Richard Rayner and Henry Bustle arrived in Finch Street, one of two constables guarding the entry told the Chief Inspector that the pathologist, Doctor Critchley, had been sent for. It was still dark and the rain hadn't eased, although where the dead man had been discovered it was fairly dry inside the enclosed entry. Both detectives followed the beams from their Bullseye lamps to where the corpse lay and were taken aback when catching their first sight of the victim. Lying there on the floor and peering up at them with lifeless eyes, was none other than the face of the docker, Blackie Jennings.

"My God, this is down to me, this must be the price he's paid for having been seen with me," Bustle suggested, "I wish now, I'd taken more care. He never harmed anybody in his life."

"You didn't kill him Henry, but what's he doing here, so far away from his workplace?" Rayner asked.

"He lives just around the corner in George Street, with his widowed mother," the Sergeant explained, "Never did no harm to anyone," he repeated, "And God only knows how the old dear is going to manage now."

Realising how much his friend was affected by self-incrimination, Rayner suggested he go and give the bad news to Mrs. Jennings, at the same time offering to go with him.

"No, I'll be okay," an absolutely distraught Henry Bustle answered, before turning and leaving the enclosed entry.

Richard Rayner couldn't remember the last time he'd seen his right-hand man looking so upset and genuinely felt for him. But there was work to be done and he began by treating the murder scene as he would any other, his first course of action being to search through the victim's clothing. There were a few small items recovered from the pockets of Blackie's jacket and trousers, but the most surprising was a well-worn cheap wallet containing a few shillings in coppers, ruling out any motive of robbery. His first thought turned to Tommy Herrick and his crowd of bully boys, who had seen the dead man talking to Henry Bustle at the docks; the same men who had taken it upon themselves to physically attack the Sergeant, but then doubted they would go to all this trouble just for the sake of revenge. In any case, Herrick would know he would be the first suspect Rayner would call upon. No, the senior detective instantly dismissed that group of malefactors from his reasoning.

Without further consideration, the detective checked Blackie Jennings's kneecaps and found them to be intact, unlike those of Joseph Kelly's, but the fact both men had been dockers disturbed him.

"It looks as though the cause of death is obvious," Doctor Critchley remarked, having stealthily approached Rayner without his knowledge.

"Good morning doctor," the senior detective answered, "Yes, so it does but I shall be interested if some kind of violent confrontation took place before he had his throat slit."

The doctor nodded and made his usual cursory examination of the immediate area around the body, whilst Rayner examined the entry from top to bottom. There were lights showing in the windows of the majority of the nearby houses, the residents obviously having been awoken early by Maisy Fletcher's screams and the activity that had followed. The Chief Inspector made the usual initial enquiries to find out if anyone had heard anything, but as was quite normal in Whitechapel, everyone claimed they hadn't.

Before arranging for the corpse to be taken to the mortuary at St. Mary's Hospital, the pathologist commented that he thought the unfortunate victim had been dead for about five or six hours.

"Which takes us to around midnight," Rayner suggested.

"Yes, certainly no earlier than eleven o'clock last night."

Rayner nodded, before making arrangements with the constables to have Blackie Jennings removed from the scene.

There was very little Maisy Fletcher could tell the Chief Inspector, other than the circumstances in which she had found the deceased man and Richard Rayner explained that he would arrange for someone to call later to take her statement.

The dawn had finally arrived when Henry Bustle returned, just as his senior officer was about to leave for Scotland Yard, and Rayner asked how the Sergeant had coped with Mrs. Jennings.

"She's distraught obviously and I managed to get a neighbour to stay with her, but the old lady's main concern now is where the next meal is coming from. I've told her I will help as best I can."

Rayner nodded, before climbing up into his carriage followed by Bustle.

"Scotland Yard sir?" his driver, Samuel Brown, enquired, grasping the reins in one hand and whip in the other.

The Chief Inspector was hesitant and then surprisingly directed his man to take them to St. Katharine Dock.

"All you'll see down there is the early morning labourers arriving," Bustle suggested.

"Yes," was all Rayner said in answer, unable to explain why he was feeling such a burning desire to visit London's dockland at that particular time, except he felt as if he was being pulled in that direction by some invisible magnet.

When they arrived, it was as his Sergeant had predicted, men were manoeuvring about on the quaysides having just arrived to begin their shifts. There was an early morning, low-lying mist across the vast expanse of water, giving the whole scene a ghostly appearance and Richard Rayner stood to one side in the shadows, with Henry Bustle at his side. The Sergeant had seen his senior detective immerse himself in such intensive concentration on many previous occasions and was well aware he needed to be left to his own mind-set, without interruption.

A cold breeze could be felt lifting off the water and both men pulled up the collars of their overcoats with Rayner watching and listening to the various activities of figures shuffling from one part of the dock to the other. He stood in silence, purposefully allowing the atmosphere to penetrate his inner-self. The sound of sliding doors opening and raised voices kept his attention. This was where two bodies of dead men had been found and a third victim had worked, until recently. The Chief Inspector's eyes continued to stare at the ever-growing numbers of dockworkers: the stevedores, warehousemen, watermen, lightermen, porters, coopers, riggers, pilers and other skilled and unskilled men responsible for the loading and unloading of the short-stay vessels now being moored. This was the lifeblood of the capital, where the produce and merchandise required to sustain the population arrived. But beneath the veil of industry lay its mysterious secrets, which included a link somehow between the three murders he was now charged with investigating. It was a conundrum he was determined to get to the bottom of.

In a strange and bizarre way, Rayner felt as if he was being challenged by every aspect of the scene confronting him. An invisible inducement to unlock the door to those same secrets London's docklands were so hideously protecting. It was then he saw the supervisor, Bartholomew Wright, wearing a brown cow gown and striding about with a board beneath one arm and called to him from where he was standing.

"It's a bit early for you Mr. Rayner, isn't it," the man quipped, looking surprised to see the flamboyantly dressed senior detective, so early in the morning.

"I thought I would let you know Mr. Wright, one of your men, Blackie Jennings, won't be coming in this morning. In fact, he won't be coming in ever again."

"Might I ask the reason why? I presume he's been up to some kind of mischief."

"No, he's been murdered." Rayner looked directly into the man's eyes, looking for the kind of response he would get from a man prepared for such tragic news, but all he saw was genuine surprise. He also watched a number of the workers who were close by, but there was nothing to indicate that any of them were anticipating what they had just overheard being disclosed.

"I take it sir, you will see to it that his elderly mother receives what monies are due to him."

"Of course, I'll see to it later this morning. Why, I mean how was he killed, Blackie was a good worker."

"Yes," Rayner said, imagining those same words being engraved on the latest victim's tombstone, 'Here lies a good worker'. Not exactly a satisfactory way of describing a man's whole past life, he thought.

"He was also a good man," Henry Bustle remarked, as they both turned to walk the short distance back to their carriage, with his senior detective sensing he could gain nothing more from remaining there.

Chapter Sixteen

The sound of Big Ben chiming out the ninth hour reverberated around London's busy streets, ensuring that everyone was aware the day was well underway. Richard Rayner stood facing his blackboard, scrutinising his own scribbled chalk relating to the Joseph Kelly murder. The hour was quickly approaching when the Polish woman, Natalia Baranski, would be arriving at Scotland Yard and he needed to compile a mental list of questions to put to her. Suddenly and without warning, a loud proclamation came from the doorway of his office, interrupting the Chief Inspector's concentration.

"God Bless all who work here, Rayner," the voice boisterously rang out in a Welsh accent, competing with Big Ben's chimes. It was Frederick Morgan, looking as though he'd just spent twelve-months working on a farm in the rural countryside. He'd lost weight and his appearance gave testimony to vastly improved good health and wellbeing. It was certainly the fittest the Chief Superintendent had looked since leaving the Army.

He was the last person Richard Rayner expected to see and his instantaneous reaction was to enquire what the Head of the Department was doing there.

"I'm completely cured now, Richard," the man suggested in a confident and enthusiastic voice, as if wanting everybody present in the building to overhear his announcement, "The Goddess of Darkness did the trick and

I've never felt fitter."

"Wasn't the treatment supposed to be ongoing for a minimum period of three months though, sir."

Morgan's freckled face lit up with the widest grin and he quickly retorted, "I only needed a fortnight, but don't worry my old mucker, all that nonsense is behind me now. I've learned my lesson and shan't be going down that crazy path again. Just you follow me mister and I'll show you how earnest I am."

The returning prodigal led the way back to his own office with Rayner following. He then opened the drawer to his desk and took out the package containing the Gold Remedy powders. Without hesitation he handed them to Richard Rayner and told him to throw them on the fire.

"See my old mucker, I shan't be needing them now and what's more, Sal got me some balm that works wonders with the old trouble up me backside. I'm as fit as a fiddler's elbow now and trust me, I can't wait to get back on the horse."

Rayner was dubious to say the least, but knowing Morgan the way he did, he was compelled to accept the senior man's word. His immediate problem though was the timing of the Head of Department's return to the fold. He hadn't got long before his anticipated confrontational meeting with Miss Baranski, and still had to deliver his daily briefing to the Commissioner. He shared that encumbrance with Frederick Morgan, hoping he would receive the response he actually did.

"Don't worry none about that, I'll have a word with the old man," Morgan offered, "Just put me in the picture about what's been going on, I can't wait to get stuck in."

The Chief Inspector parted with as much detail as he could in the limited time available, mentioning of course the most recent murder of the docker, Blackie Jennings, and explaining that Henry Bustle had gone to talk with some people at an Old Mariners Institution, to see if he could raise some charity for the dead man's mother.

"No bother, Rayner, you just arrange a whip round amongst the lads to support the poor old duck with my blessing. That should help her out for a bit."

Morgan was back and his old self-esteem had returned with all guns blazing. Whether such goodwill would last beyond the day was yet to be seen.

Both the Scotland Yard dandy and Jack Robinson found Miss Natalia Baranski seated in the front reception area. There was a man accompanying the lady but from his age and appearance, Richard Rayner could see it wasn't the woman's father, as the Commissioner had previously assumed.

After introducing himself and his colleague and thanking her for attending, Rayner suggested they could use a ground floor interview room to continue their conversation.

She was an impressive, medium sized young lady, who the senior detective guessed was in her late twenties with auburn hair tied up at the back and smartly dressed in a grey costume with white piping along the edges of her petite jacket. Miss Baranski wasn't what could be regarded as being beautiful, but she had an alluring kind of attractiveness showing little make-up on her face and Rayner detected a look of confident innocence in her hazel eyes. Either that or she was an accomplished actress.

The man who accompanied her was a little older, with dark brown shoulder length hair and mutton chop whiskers. He portrayed a look of arrogance and Rayner suspected he might just be the kind of individual who would be obstructive, when being questioned by someone in authority. When he asked who Miss Baranski's chaperone was, the man answered, "Jakub Baranski, Natalia's brother and I am here to represent my sister's interests. State your business with her Chief Inspector."

It was a declaration made in a guarded manner and Rayner viewed it as being a little strange in the circumstances, but continued to escort the couple into the room where there were four chairs and a small table.

"What is this about?" Jakub Baranski demanded to know, as soon as they had all sat down.

"I'm coming to that, Mr. Baranski," he explained, before turning to the woman and enquiring, "Could you tell me if you have ever been associated with a man by the name of Joseph Kelly, miss, a man who used to work at the docks."

"Heaven forbid, what makes you think my sister would associate with a docker, for Christ's sake," her brother asked, rather superciliously.

Rayner ignored him and continued to look in the woman's direction.

She shook her head and quietly answered, "No, Inspector."

"Pardon me, but it's Chief Inspector Miss Baranski. Could you describe for me the kind of carriage in which you travel about London please."

"God Almighty man, you'll be accusing her of driving the damned thing next," the obnoxious man suggested.

"I've never really taken much notice of the transport I use, that's when I use a carriage, which is rare, Chief Inspector."

"She hardly leaves the hotel," Jakub Baranski remarked, his interrupting tendencies now beginning to get under Rayner's skin.

The senior detective turned to the man and advised him that there was a need for his sister to answer the questions without further interference.

"I find your attitude dictatorial sir and typical of an imperialist authoritarian," the brother replied, accusingly, his words also being a little confusing and surprising.

"Then I apologise," Rayner calmly offered, before turning back to the lady and continuing with his questions.

"I understand you have frequently been seen travelling in a black carriage with a gold trim, is that not so, Miss Baranski?"

Her brother turned to his sister and advised her not to answer that question, not until they had been told of the purpose of the interview.

That obstructive advice was the last straw for Richard Rayner, and he turned to glance at his Sergeant.

"If you would be so good, Jack," he directed.

Robinson stood and without further warning, grabbed the brother by his collar and yanked him from his seat. The door of the room was thrown open and both the Sergeant and the interfering nuisance disappeared back into the reception area, with Jakub Baranski making all kinds of vociferous objections.

Rayner himself closed the door behind them before returning to his seat and apologising to the young lady, but emphasising that he needed her to answer his questions without any prompting one way or the other.

"You see Miss Baranski," he quietly continued, "We are making enquiries into the murder of Joseph Kelly, and from what a number of witnesses have told us, you have been seen in his company at St. Katharine Dock on a number of occasions."

"I've already told you, I have never heard of this man, Joseph Kelly. If I had, I would say so. These witnesses of yours are obviously mistaken...Chief Inspector."

Richard Rayner had always believed in scrutinising whatever circumstances were presented to him, with a sense of objectivity and in the belief that there were always two sides to a story. Whenever a suspect came to light in any of his Investigations his approach was always somewhat unorthodox, aiming to prove that person was innocent as a priority. If however, he failed to do so, then in most cases he usually unravelled sufficient evidence to prove their guilt. In this particular case, Rayner's approach was different, in that no matter how much Natalia Baranski denied having known, Joseph Kelly, he was convinced the woman was lying. What disturbed him was that her facial features and behaviour didn't support that supposition.

The Chief Inspector had hoped that by confessing to having had an association with the murdered victim, the Polish lady would have opened up further lines of enquiry for him to follow. Such optimism never materialised, leaving Rayner with no other option but to end the interview prematurely. He was also aware that there was no likelihood of the woman's resolve weakening by continuing to press harder, in fact quite the opposite, deciding more work had to be carried out into Natalia Baranski's background before confronting her again. One deciding factor was that the woman's denials appeared quite natural, not having been rehearsed.

After thanking Miss Baranski for her time and returning her to the custody of her brother, the Chief Inspector pondered for some time on his first meeting with the Polish couple. The defiant behaviour of her brother, Jakub, which the senior detective thought went beyond someone just looking out for the interests of his sister, was a poignant feature of interest to him. He felt that the man was in genuine fear of certain information being disclosed that Rayner had no knowledge of yet, and instructed Jack Robinson to try and find out more about Jakub Baranski's background.

"In particular, Jack, anything regarding his political affiliations or perhaps his involvement in any activist groups and what is our Mr. Baranski doing in London at present."

Henry Bustle had naturally faced a multitude of disappointments throughout his life and on occasions, bereavements, yet still found himself being deeply affected by the death of his friend, Blackie Jennings. In the self-incriminating belief that he had been indirectly responsible for the brutal murder of his associate, his sympathy soon turned to anger. His resolve and determination to find the gentle giant's killer meant leaving no stone unturned and he was prepared for an indefatigable search to find Blackie's killer.

The Sergeant was aware that the Bishop's Crook public house was where the latest victim of murder drank on a regular basis, not far from where Blackie Jennings had lived and not far from where his body had been found. That was to be the first location where Richard Rayner's right-hand man would begin his enquiries.

Apart from a small group of heavy looking malingerers sitting in one corner, who Bustle assumed were out of work labourers biding their time over a few pints of ale, the bar room was empty. Raymond Bull was the landlord, a tall man with a mop of dark brown unruly hair and an insincere grin on his pointed face, pushing what looked like the remnants of a moustache closer to his nostrils, stood behind the bar. His skeletal build reminded Henry Bustle of a hatpin.

When asked, the Sergeant ordered a glass of stout and remained standing and waiting to be served. Then leaning forward and keeping his voice very low, he mentioned his old friend's name to the landlord, enquiring when was the last time Blackie Jennings had been seen supping inside the establishment.

The grin disappeared and without showing the same amount of caution Bustle had demonstrated when asking the question, the man in charge of The Bishop's Crook demanded to know in a fairly loud voice, "And who says this Blackie Jennings comes in here?" He was obviously determined that his only other customers should overhear the conversation, which didn't go unnoticed by the detective.

"I do, Sergeant Bustle from Scotland Yard."

"In that case Sergeant, yes, Blackie's a regular in here," the landlord confessed, still speaking loudly enough for the group of heavies to hear every word.

"Was he in here last night?"

"He gets in here every night."

"Who was he drinking with last night?"

The landlord hesitated and then told Bustle that his friend was drinking with a couple of men he hadn't seen before, and in a manner that signalled to the Sergeant the 'hatpin' wasn't being completely truthful.

When asked what they looked like, the landlord gave a vague description of two rough looking customers, adding that Blackie had shelved out for the drinks.

"Why, has Blackie been up to something then, Sergeant?" he asked, still keeping the volume turned up.

"Did he leave with those same two geezers?" Bustle asked, ignoring the question.

"As a matter of fact, I think he did."

The man then unexpectedly leant over the bar and whispered in the detective's ear for him to meet him outside. As he did so, he nodded his head towards the group sitting in the corner.

Bustle finished his drink in one gulp, before turning away from the bar and making for the exit door. Once outside, he saw the landlord step out of the private door to the premises and walk up to him.

"I couldn't say too much in there Sergeant, you know walls have ears and all that."

'Especially with a mouth as loud as yours,' Bustle thought.

"So, tell me, who were these couple of blokes he was drinking with?" the detective asked, but before he could receive an answer, something hard struck him across the back of his head causing his knees to buckle for the second time in a short space of time.

As he fell to the cobbles, he managed to see there were two of them, a couple who had been drinking with the group of heavies in the bar room and both armed with cudgels.

Hobnailed boots rained in on his ribs, adding to the discomfort he was still feeling from his recent confrontation at the docks and just as before, Henry Bustle was incapable of regaining his feet. He covered his head with both arms, as their cudgels were brought down with a vengeance to inflict more harm to the Scotland Yard man.

Richard Rayner's driver, Samuel Brown, who had driven Bustle to that part of London, was minding the horse just a few yards away and upon seeing the Sergeant's predicament grabbed for a blunderbuss he kept stored away under the bench on top of the carriage. The constable blasted one shot in the air, as he hastily stepped across the pavement towards the violent confrontation. That warning shot was enough and the two assailants made off, running across some wasteland and disappearing inside some derelict buildings.

Rayner's driver helped his colleague to his feet, asking if he was all right and receiving only a grunt in reply. Henry Bustle's face was contorted more than usual and his eyes were ablaze with the most fearsome looking anger and thirst for revenge.

"Where is that bastard, Sammy?" the Sergeant demanded to know, looking like a raging bull and referring to the 'hatpin' who had obviously set him up.

"He fled back inside, as soon as that pair came on to you."

Bustle turned to go back inside the public house and Brown suggested he should go with him.

"No, keep an eye on that horse," Bustle shouted back, before returning to the bar room.

Two of the group with which his attackers had been drinking were still sitting in the corner and the Sergeant made a beeline for them, demanding to know who their mates were. Both men just looked at him with blank expressions. There was no sign of the treacherous landlord.

The injured detective then upturned the table in uncontrollable anger, causing glasses to smash on the floorboards, the contents also spilling out. Neither of the two remaining layabouts felt any desire to get involved with this mad man and hurriedly disappeared through the exit door, leaving Henry Bustle snorting fire.

The detective then leapt over the bar in search of the missing Raymond Bull, who he intended putting in hospital. He stood at the bottom of the stairs leading up to the private quarters with clenched fists, resembling a volcano about to erupt with imaginary smoke pouring out through the top of his head. The landlord's name was shouted out several times, but attracted no response.

"If you don't show yourself in ten seconds you back-stabbing bastard, I shall demolish every stick of wood in this place," he continued to yell.

Still the landlord failed to materialise, adding fuel to the fire already blazing inside Henry Bustle's head.

The detective then leapt back into the empty bar room and grabbed hold of a broom. Grasping one end of the handle with both hands, he swept it across the top shelf containing bottles of spirits. Everything came crashing down as a meek voice called out from the upper landing, threatening to call the peelers.

"I am the police, as you well know you piece of shit, show yourself and be a man for once in your life," Bustle answered, his fury still on the ascent.

The landlord appeared, looking like a petrified rabbit and with good cause. A large rounded woman, obviously his wife, was pushing him forward from behind where he was standing, his high cheek bones looking as though they were about to disintegrate.

"I knew nothing about that Sergeant, I swear," he blurted out, like a man pleading for his life. Never before had he seen such evilness in a human face and became tearful as he felt himself being lifted off the floor before being thrown over the bar, to land on the filthy floorboards on the other side.

As Raymond Bull struggled to regain his feet a boot dug into his side and he felt a rib crack.

"Leave him alone," the woman cried out, "He's already told you, he don't know nuffink about it."

The aggrieved detective ignored the plea and grabbed the landlord by his collar, wrenching him back into a standing posture. The publican was incapable of defending himself and stared into that face again, the one that carried a threat of more instant and intense pain. Blood oozing from a wound in the detective's forehead added to Bustle's already grotesque appearance. The landlord's whole side felt as though it was on fire, but was nothing compared to the look of utter rage in Henry Bustle's volcanic eyes.

"Names, or I swear you'll never walk again," the Sergeant threatened through gritted teeth and meaning every word.

"I've told you; I didn't know..."

The side of his face exploded as a fist crashed into it, sending the man back to the floor and the woman screaming as she retaliated by throwing two fat and exposed arms around Bustle's mid-drift. She was instantly dispatched away by an elbow and the detective's eyes never left the spreadeagled, groaning landlord.

"Names, you slimy bastard," the call came again, "Or, as God is my judge..."

"One of them was the Greek; I don't know his proper name but the other was Nobby Clarke." The victim of Henry Bustle's onslaught was actually sobbing in between speaking his words, but that made no difference to the Sergeant.

"I need to know the hovels they've come out of and I need to know them now."

The petrified, injured man shook his head and winced when seeing another closed fist being raised in readiness to deliver another devastating blow.

"Thirty-two Thomas Street, I think that's where the Greek lives, but honestly, I don't know where Clarkie hangs his coat and that's the Gospel

Chapter Seventeen

At least Bustle's pulsating urge for instant revenge had partially subsided. Unlike Richard Rayner's more exploratory and at times, long-winded approach, the Sergeant preferred taking a more direct route, finding out the truth by using his pugilistic skills to good effect.

He roughly manhandled Raymond Bull back to his feet and still maintaining a grip on his collar, spoke with his nose just an inch away from the 'hatpin's' swollen face.

"The way in which you answer my next question will depend on whether you stay here or come with me, matey," he aggressively explained, "Were those the same two men who were with Blackie Jennings last night."

The man nodded, knowing that any further falsehood would only result in another caning.

"If you've given me any shit mister, I shall come back and finish the job."

"I know that," the landlord confessed, in total capitulation.

When Henry Bustle returned to the carriage, Constable Brown suggested he should take him to a hospital to get himself checked over, but the Sergeant was having none of that.

"Go back to Scotland Yard Sammy, and tell Richard Rayner that I reckon both Jennings's killers are staying at thirty-two, Thomas Street. It's down near the docks."

"What about you, sarge?"

"I'm going for a walk to clear my head and tell the Chief Inspector I'll meet him there. And Sammy, thanks for giving me a hand."

The driver nodded and watched as the obstinate detective made his way along the cobbled street, walking just a little unsteady, before turning the horse's head back towards Scotland Yard.

Richard Rayner was staring out of his office window at the dappled sky above, before becoming engrossed by the erratic behaviour of fallen leaves being chased around the streets below by the Autumnal winds. This was his and Clarice's favourite time of the year and he reminded himself that he must take some time away from work and spend a couple of days at home, once he had dealt with the present investigative challenges. The sound of Morgan singing 'Men of Harlech' from the office next door was becoming irritable and frequent. The melodious arrangements were slightly out of tune, which didn't help much although quite rare for a Welshman.

The Chief Inspector turned to face Jack Robinson and genuinely asked what the younger man thought of the woman, Natalia Baranski.

"I'm not sure sir," the young Sergeant answered, "I know her father is an important person and find it difficult to make an assessment of his daughter. She seemed genuine enough but there's so much pointing towards her."

"I find her brother, Jakub, interesting Jack. Have we learned anything more about that young man?"

Robinson explained that Natalia Baranski's brother was known by the Foreign Office to frequently accompany his two sisters and father to London and that he was suspected of being an activist, opposing the way in which Poland was being internally governed.

"But according to them, he's fairly harmless and doesn't give them any cause for concern, sir."

"All wind and nothing else then Jack."

"Apparently so, sir."

Rayner then noticed the renditioning coming from next door had stopped and looked up to see the Welsh tenor standing in the doorway, describing what a grand day it was outside. The Chief Inspector didn't quite know if he preferred the old Morgan to this new version and was impatient to see for how much longer the reformed character would continue.

"Robbo, do us a favour son," Frederick Morgan begged, handing over a monetary note, "Fetch us a bottle of malt would you, I feel like celebrating." As far as the Chief Superintendent was concerned, the unsavoury threat of having Nurse Longfeet return to administer further treatment was sufficient to ensure he didn't revert back to his drug habit, and a drop of scotch could only be beneficial.

Before Jack Robinson could respond, Samuel Brown appeared in the doorway, standing behind the Chief Superintendent, looking a little flushed and concerned.

"From that agitated look on your face Samuel, I suspect you have something dire to tell us," Rayner acknowledged.

The constable related Henry Bustle's message to all three of them after describing the altercation between their colleague and two other men at The Bishop's Crook. He also emphasised the Sergeant's claim that the men who had attacked him, were in fact, Blackie Jennings's killers.

"Right Rayner," an impatient Morgan called out, determined to take charge, "Let's get moving. Robbo, get some of the lads together and follow us across there. Me and the Chief Inspector will go with Sammy here."

"Did Sergeant Bustle make any mention of firearms," Rayner asked his driver.

"No sir, only that he knew the identities of Blackie Jennings's killers."

All four policemen abandoned the office in some haste and Rayner's carriage was soon heading across London, in the direction of Thomas Street, Whitechapel.

The address relayed to them by Henry Bustle, was situated amongst a conglomeration of narrow streets, alleyways, yards and enclosed entries, similar to the one in which Blackie Jennings's lifeless body had been found. Number thirty-two was a dilapidated corner house, projecting a dismal appearance but typical of the impoverished and extremely run-down district. It was a two-storey building with newspapers hanging down from inside the windows and Rayner's driver was instructed to stop a few doors up from where the detectives intended visiting.

"I can't see Bustle," Morgan remarked, tapping the end of his walking stick in the palm of a gloved hand, "Where the bleedin' hell is he." The Chief Superintendent feeling the edge and impatient for some action.

"If I know Henry, there's every chance he's already inside," the Chief Inspector answered in a concerned tone of voice. He then suggested that his senior officer wait for Jack Robinson to turn up with the cavalry, whilst he made some surreptitious enquiries with the neighbours as to who was living at number thirty-two and Morgan agreed that was the right thing to do, having to restrain himself and biting his lip.

Number thirty wasn't in much better condition that the house next door and an elderly lady wearing a hessian sack around her waist, answered Rayner's call. Not wanting to alarm the woman, the Chief Inspector portrayed himself as being a doctor, having been called out to attend to someone living at number thirty-two, falsely declaring he couldn't get any answer.

"If he's not inside there, doctor, he's probably in one of the locals filling his belly," the old lady offered, referring to any one of the many corner public houses prominent throughout the district.

"Would that be Mr. Bacon?" Rayner asked.

"Naw, he ain't got no fancy bleedin' name like that: 'Is name's Paddy 'Egarty."

"Does he live alone madam, only if he is really sick he might be in need of help?"

"As far as I know he does. There certainly ain't no woman who'd put up with that idle layabout. 'E's nothing more than a bleedin' squatter and a roughneck at that."

Rayner did notice how spotlessly clean the old woman's doorstep was and caught a whiff of disinfectant coming from it. These people might be poor, but the majority took pride in their cleanliness and he guessed a day wouldn't go by without that same doorstep being subjected to a scrubbing brush. He tipped his hat and thanked the woman for her help. He then noticed the second carriage coming along Thomas Street, which would contain Jack Robinson and a few others and cautiously made his way to the front door of number thirty-two.

When Morgan noticed what his Chief Inspector was about to do, he stepped down from the carriage to join him still grasping his heavy walking stick in the hope he could put it to good use across somebody's head. After his period of rehabilitation, he was bursting at the seams to exercise the violent side of his character.

Much to Richard Rayner's surprise he found the front door slightly ajar and held a finger to his mouth, indicating to Frederick Morgan, they should enter as quietly as possible. He then pushed the door open and both detectives stepped inside to find themselves standing in a sparsely furnished front room.

It was dark inside and the bare floorboards were covered in dust and grime. Owing to the absence of any fire, the interior was bitterly cold and the sheet of newspaper up at the window did little to stop the cold draughts from penetrating into the dwelling, if it could be described as being that.

Both men stood for a moment in silence, listening to a wind blowing through the rooms upstairs. The building gave the impression of being vacant, until voices could be heard mumbling from somewhere towards the back of the house. Both Rayner and Morgan stealthily made their way into the back room on tip toe, ready to face whatever challenge they were about to confront. Amazingly, they found Henry Bustle sitting in an old well-worn armchair with springs exposed and protruding out from the arms. At his feet and lying face down on the bare floor and totally immobile, were two men, both with their hands handcuffed behind their backs, groaning and showing all the signs of having just been hit by a hammer from the amount of blood on their faces.

"Hello, Henry," Rayner placidly said, "I see you've been busy."

The Sergeant grinned in his usual customary way when just having claimed a physical victory and boasting a couple of missing teeth in the front of his mouth.

"God Almighty, Bustle, you get uglier every time I see you," Morgan remarked, disappointed he'd missed the action.

One of the prisoners moved his head to one side and complained to the newcomers, "The bastards broke my arm."

"One more word out of you my old mucker and I'll break the other one," Morgan threatened.

"Meet Albert Clarke, he's the mouthy one," the Sergeant remarked, "And this other is Patrick Hegarty, otherwise known as 'The Greek' and who pays the rent for this particular palace, or so he tells me."

"He's broke my fuckin' arm and I needs to get to hospital," the man named Clarke, continued to persist.

"I've told you to shut it," Morgan demanded.

"Bollocks to you, I've got rights."

"Okay sunshine, here's one of your bleedin' rights." Morgan then dug his toe into the man's side, causing him to yell out in agony.

"Are these the men responsible for the murder of Blackie Jennings?" Rayner asked, already convinced they were.

"That's them," Bustle answered, "And for trying to decapitate me back at The Bishop's Crook, earlier."

"It looks as though you've made up for that, Bustle," Morgan pointed out, enjoying his return back to real-life policing.

The sound of clambering feet coming through the front door could be heard and Jack Robinson, with three other detectives made their appearance, each carrying wooden staffs.

Richard Rayner directed the younger Sergeant to arrange for the man Hegarty to be taken back to Scotland Yard and Albert Clarke to be transported to hospital to have his injured arm seen to. Henry Bustle had undoubtedly done his job well, which came as no surprise to the Chief Inspector, knowing his right-hand man's natural habitat was in the back-streets of London's most notorious districts.

Rayner then explained to Jack Robinson that he preferred the younger Sergeant remained at the house, to thoroughly search it from top to bottom.

"You know what we are looking for, Jack."

"Yes sir."

As the group were leaving, Morgan directed that the front door wouldn't need securing as there was nothing inside to steal. In any case, there was no doubt both prisoners had been squatting there and whoever the landlord was, needed to be put in the picture.

On the return journey to Scotland Yard, Henry Bustle gave both senior detectives a description of what had taken place, prior to their arrival at the Thomas Street address. He explained that he'd found Clarke and Hegarty sitting in the back room of the house, when he entered from the rear garden.

"The boot was on the other foot this time," he remarked, "And just as they caught me by surprise outside that boozer, I sprang a little stunner on them, with a little help from an iron bar I picked up on the way."

"I'm surprised they're still breathing, Henry, from what Samuel told us had taken place," Rayner quipped.

"Well, I doubt they'll take on another copper in the future, Bustle," Morgan remarked, showing his bizarre sense of humour by chuckling. He would have much preferred to have found the Sergeant struggling with the two vagabonds, giving him the opportunity to bring his walking stick into play.

"That won't make much difference to them two, sir, they're as thick as dumplings and don't know any other way to live. They'd batter their own mothers for a couple of farthings."

"I fear they won't be given the opportunity to demonstrate their violent behaviour ever again," Rayner commented, "They are both for the hangman, but first we need their confessions."

"That shouldn't be too difficult sir," Bustle added, striking the palm of a hand with his fist.

"I think Henry, you've seen enough violence for one day."

All three detectives were amazed when Jack Robinson appeared, just a few minutes after they had arrived back in Rayner's office.

"I think this is what you were after," he said, handing a large hunting-type knife to the Chief Inspector, the blade of which, was still bloodstained.

"Well done, Jack, where did you find it?"

"Upstairs, under the bed, if you could call it a bed sir."

That particular discovery was exactly what Rayner had been hoping for and would virtually guarantee the two men in custody would be lawfully executed for the murder of Henry Bustle's friend.

The man Patrick Hegarty had said very little since being overpowered by Henry Bustle, and sat in the basement interview room at Scotland Yard in silence, looking extremely forlorn. He was no longer the same man who had struck the Sergeant across the back of his head outside The Bishop's Crook and was now looking quite pitiful, with both hands shackled together. Rayner and Bustle sat opposite him; the Chief Inspector confident the interview wouldn't be a prolonged affair.

"Tell me Patrick, why is it they call you 'The Greek'?" he finally asked.

The prisoner looked across at his interrogators and just shook his head. A trickle of dried blood was noticeable, coming from one corner of his mouth and both the man's eyes were slowly disappearing beneath some heavy swelling, obviously the result of Henry Bustle's presence being felt earlier.

"I was just wondering, being as you don't appear to have any foreign blood in you," Rayner added, knowing exactly what was occupying the man's thoughts. He decided to make his point at the very start of the interview.

"You do realise you are facing the death sentence for having murdered Blackie Jennings, Mr. Hegarty, but what baffles me is how you managed to overcome such a strong man as that."

"You've not got anything on me or that other blabbering piss head," he said, speaking in a broad Irish accent.

"You're wrong, Mr. Hegarty, it seems that just about everybody knows what you got up to last night, when you both met up with your intended victim in The Bishop's Crook. You were seen drinking with him and then left with the man, which means you two were the last people to see him alive."

"Just you keep spouting on mister, I've got all the time in the world to listen to this garbage," the man arrogantly answered, sitting back with both arms folded across his chest in total defiance, although his facial features resembled that of a defeated clown.

"Well, it's you that has just referred to your mate as being a blabbering piss head, so how long do you think it will be, before Mr. Clarke decides to escape the hangman by putting you up as the fall guy; a few minutes, or perhaps even seconds. You know how much he runs off at the mouth and I can't see him not trying to save his own skin when given the chance."

It was obvious from the solemn look on Hegarty's face that his associate, Albert Clarke, was his Achilles heel but he continued to obstinately shake his head.

Henry Bustle was tempted to add more misery to the prisoner's situation with his fists, but also knew that such a course of action would have been condemned by the Chief Inspector, who hadn't yet played all of his cards.

Rayner produced the bloodstained knife recovered by Jack Robinson and placed it on the table.

"I believe this is yours, Mr. Hegarty, and contains Blackie Jennings blood still on the blade."

From the expression on the prisoner's face, there could be no doubt the grotesque weapon belonged to him.

Following a short period of silence, the Irishman looked up and stared across at his accuser, still remaining silent but the fear in his eyes told Richard Rayner the suspect's resolve was weakening.

"You want to ask me something, Mr. Hegarty," Rayner calmly suggested.

"You mentioned something about escaping the hangman," he muttered, barely audible.

"So I did, and that's possible, provided we have your full co-operation."

"What kind of co-operation, you seem to have something worked out."

Rayner glanced across at Henry Bustle, who explained that there were a number of issues needed to be clarified, beginning with the reason why Blackie Jennings had been so brutally murdered.

"Money, that's all it was, we were paid fifty quid each to do the job but she didn't tell us why she wanted him done in."

"Who do you mean by she?" Rayner asked.

"A foreign woman, who just pulled us up in the street one-day last week. She offered us the cash up front and took us to finger the man she wanted taken care of down at the docks. She's the one you want."

"And she pointed Jennings out to you when he was working there?"

Hegarty nodded, adding, "As fancy as you like, she even told us where he drank at night and gave us the money there and then."

The Chief Inspector asked what kind of accent the woman spoke with and the prisoner confessed to not having a clue.

"I can't tell the difference between them foreigners."

"You said she took you to the docks to point out the man she wanted done in. How did she manage to do that?"

"In the carriage she was in."

"What kind of carriage was it?"

The self-confessed killer looked genuinely mystified and explained that he hadn't noticed that much.

"It was posh inside, I can tell you that much, with black leather seats and carpet on the floor."

"Was it black on the outside?"

"I think so."

"With gold trim?"

"I've no idea. As I said, I didn't pay that much attention."

"How was she dressed?"

Hegarty had to stop to think and shrugged his shoulders, before confirming the woman was dressed in grey and was wearing a hat with white feathers around the one side.

The description was identical to the hat worn by Natalia Baranski when she called at Scotland Yard to see Richard Rayner.

"She was smartly dressed for that neck of the woods, that's all I can tell you about her."

"Have you spoken with her since the murder?"

"No, there was no need, she'd already paid us but we did think about pissing off and taking the money with us without doing the job, but there again, it was me who thought there was something about the woman that got me to thinking she was the kind you wouldn't like to cross. So, that's why we went and done him in."

"One more thing Mr. Hegarty, how did you and Albert Clarke manage to overcome Blackie Jennings. I should have thought he could have chewed you both up and spat out the bones."

"It wasn't difficult, we got him that pissed inside that public house, he didn't know what day it was. Although he did have a go at us, once we got him outside but it wasn't hard to use the blade on him."

Rayner could see by the look on Henry Bustle's face that if the prisoner was allowed to continue with his description of the way in which the Sergeant's friend had been disposed of, there was every chance that Hegarty was about to get the same outcome. Standing from his chair, he told Bustle to take the man back to the cells.

"Will I be topped for this?" Hegarty enquired, not unexpectedly.

"Very likely," Henry Bustle said, with some satisfaction in his voice.

"But we shall inform the judge of your co-operation, Mr. Hegarty," Rayner promised, being a man of his word.

Chapter Eighteen

Patrick Hegarty's condemning version of the events leading up to the murder of Blackie Jennings, was the lever required to extract a full confession from his associate, Albert Clarke, who also hoped that by admitting the part he played, he might just manage to escape the noose. Both men denied having been involved in the murder of the unfortunate docker, Joseph Kelly, and Richard Rayner had no reason to doubt their word. However, he remained convinced that the woman, Natalia Baranski, was possibly the same female that Raphael Dickens had made mention of when witnessing the demise of Kelly. There were far too many coincidences for the senior detective to think otherwise.

Although neither Hegarty or Clarke were in a position to name the individual who had allegedly paid them to commit her atrocious and fatalistic deeds, Rayner believed he was seeking a callous and brutal female predator; his only doubt concerning Miss Baranski, was that his first impression told him she didn't fit that kind of character,

During the time the Chief Inspector's mind was focused on the Kelly Investigation, the teasing situation surrounding Annie Crockett's predicament continued to torment the acclaimed detective. Of course, it was necessary he should remain concentrated on tracking down the killers of Leonard Crockett, and Richard Rayner was well aware of the need for more leg work to be accomplished. Nevertheless, his conviction and belief that the woman currently incarcerated in Holloway Prison was innocent never left him and his determination to expedite what was still a mystery, never dwindled.

Charlie Pendry, the husband of Rose Pendry, who lived next door to the Crockett's at the time of the murder, had still to be seen and it wasn't difficult to find his place of business located on Southwark Bridge. There were just three stalls present and only one offering for sale fruit and vegetables. The victim's neighbour of ten years past, might well have been the last man to see Leonard Crockett alive and the need to speak with him had now become one of the utmost importance. Richard Rayner was anxious to find out exactly what kind of relationship the two men shared and both he and Jack Robinson found the man standing at the side of his stall, busy serving a customer.

From their position, the detectives could see the river traffic was as busy as ever, with steamers and sail vessels coming and going from the direction of Tower Bridge. In the distance the docks were visible, also portraying a scene of industrious shipping activity and the Scotland Yard men continued to amuse themselves by the sights, whilst patiently waiting for the costermonger to conclude his transaction.

Finally, Charlie Pendry stood alone, vociferously offering his products for sale to other passing pedestrians, until being interrupted by Richard Rayner, who made the initial introductions, suggesting, "I assume your wife has told you to expect me."

The street seller, who was wearing an ankle length brown duster, didn't look surprised and answered with the kind of cockiness that was typical of an individual in his trade.

"That she did, the old bag mentioned something about the murder of Lenny Crockett being looked into, again." Pendry spoke loudly, in a local accent.

Rayner didn't hide his look of surprise at the manner in which the man referred to his wife, but it was obviously a busy time for the stall holders and the Chief Inspector couldn't help but notice the number of shoppers now circling around their man's enticing display of produce. He decided to offer the self-employed costermonger some understanding and empathy by explaining he had a number of questions to put to him, suggesting the retail supplier might prefer attending at Scotland Yard later, after closing down his stall for the day.

With some relief on his face, the street seller appreciatively agreed and was left to continue serving his regulars. At least it had given Richard Rayner the opportunity to assess the man, even if that brief meeting didn't tell him much.

"Our Mr. Pendry appears to be quite a loud mouth, if you don't mind me saying so sir," Jack Robinson opined, as the detectives were walking back across the bridge.

"Yes, there doesn't appear to be much love lost between him and his wife, Jack, but at the moment we have bigger fish to fry."

As a result of the unexpected delay in speaking in depth to Charlie Pendry, Rayner decided it was a good time to confront Natalia Baranski for a second time, only now he was in possession of the fresh information and claims made by Patrick Hegarty and Albert Clarke. Although she hadn't been named, he was confident enough he had sufficient additional and telling intelligence with which to challenge the woman further, in the belief that Baranski, was the same person referred to by the condemned men.

Jack Robinson suggested that both Hegarty and Clarke should be made to confront Natalia Baranski, with a view to identifying her as the woman who paid for their services, but Rayner had other ideas.

"I truly believe such a manoeuvre would be futile Jack," he quietly answered, "Even if they did point the finger at Miss Baranski, I doubt they would give sworn evidence against her and if they did, I'm afraid it would be deemed as being highly unreliable."

The Sergeant hadn't regarded his notion in that light and was compelled to agree with the senior detective.

"However, I do believe a visit to the Dorchester Hotel is in order,"

Rayner announced, before climbing back in the carriage and giving his driver the appropriate instructions.

On the journey, the difference between the two men's characters was quite distinct. Robinson felt and acted like a coiled spring about to be released, whereby his Chief Inspector just smiled confidently and remained his usual cool and calm self. The Sergeant was expecting some resistance when the arrest of Natalia Baranski was made, especially being the daughter of Poland's diplomatic representative to Britain, but Richard Rayner was far less concerned. He had the law behind him and was totally satisfied the woman was responsible for the murders of Joseph Kelly and Blackie Jennings. The only problem he was faced with, was that he didn't yet know the reason why she was the main perpetrator of those two atrocities, if of course, that was the case.

Whether it was fate or sheer luck, when they entered the main reception area of the hotel, they found the woman they had come to apprehend standing at the desk, handing over the key to her room to the desk clerk. She was alone with no other person present and showed not the slightest sign of being perturbed when Rayner quietly approached her. In fact, the lady smiled when the senior detective stood before her, as if about to greet an old friend and had been anticipating his visit.

"Miss Baranski, I am arresting you for being involved in the murders of two men who I suspect were both known to you." He took note of her attire, a grey ankle length dress beneath a coat of the same colour, with white piping along the collar. However, the hat with the white plume attached was missing and her head was bare.

He took hold of her arm and as he did so, she told him she was about to go for a walk. Rayner just smiled back at her, before leading this calm and on the surface, gracious lady out of the foyer and into the waiting official carriage. His first reaction was that Natalia Baranski was an extremely cold-hearted young woman and suspected it was going to be difficult to get her to admit to the crimes she had committed. Time wasn't his ally either, the clock was now ticking and he assumed her father would be sending a whole team of lawyers to Scotland Yard, as soon as he learned of what had just taken place in London's most salubrious hotel. There was also that vociferous brother of hers, who he had no doubt would soon be making his presence felt with banners protesting his sister's innocence.

It was left to Henry Bustle to speak with Charlie Pendry later that day, when the costermonger finally appeared as requested by Richard Rayner, at the same time as the Chief Inspector and Jack Robinson were engaged with Miss Baranski. Rayner was anxious to begin interviewing the female prisoner, before her predicted entourage turned up.

"What surprises me, Natalia, is why you arranged for the killing of the docker, Blackie Jennings. He was a hard-working man who did no harm to anyone and yet, he must have been a threat of some kind to yourself. Could it be that your latest victim had gleaned some important information concerning the evilness of the business you have been engaged in?"

She remained exactly as she had done so during their last confrontation.

"I have never heard of the man," she answered, still looking extremely confident and displaying a perfect set of pearly white teeth. Her body language displayed no signs of anxiety and she sat upright with both gloved hands clasped together on her lap.

"And yet, we have arrested and charged the same two men you paid a total of one hundred pounds to, for committing his murder."

Rayner looked closely at the woman's expression, hoping to see some kind of reaction upon hearing that news, but there was none and she remained sitting there opposite himself and Jack Robinson, appearing to be completely indifferent to the allegation.

"You do not deny having hired those men then," he pointed out, trying to maintain the high ground in the exchanges.

"Mr. Rayner, I have no idea what you are talking about."

"On the last occasion we met, you denied everything I put to you and yet, the two men responsible for slitting Blackie Jennings's throat have both made statements implicating you as the person who paid them to commit the murder," he lied, "How would they know who you were and what's more, why should they make that claim if it was not true."

She shook her head, looking a little bewildered and re-emphasised, "I have no idea, Mr. Rayner, but I can assure you, I have murdered no one. I am not that kind of person. You sir, obviously think I am."

"Why should other witnesses tell us that they had seen you in the company of the first murdered victim, Joseph Kelly, if that was not the truth."

The woman just stared across the table at him, offering no explanation.

There was a knock on the door and Jack Robinson found the Desk Sergeant standing in the corridor outside, asking to speak urgently with the Chief Inspector.

"I'm sorry sir, but the woman's brother, a Mr. Jakub Baranski is upstairs in reception creating merry hell. He's got some kind of fancy lawyer with him."

"Alright Bert, I'll be up in a minute," the senior detective confirmed.

When Rayner returned to the interview room, he continued putting questions to the woman he suspected of being a person without any scruples, asking what exactly she did with her time when staying in London, and who were her closest friends and associates.

Natalia Baranski answered each question calmly and reassuringly.

Something was wrong. Never before had he been confronted by a guilty killer who was so convincing of their innocence. Rayner sensed that the young lady was far too confident; too blasé and far too genuine in appearance for an individual who should really have been displaying all the signs of being cunning and dishonest. And yet, all the evidence pointed towards her. In fact, it was overwhelmingly against her, but his sixth sense was telling him he had the wrong person. Perhaps some time spent alone in a police cell might just strip her of whatever shield she was hiding behind, if at all. He directed Jack Robinson to place the prisoner in a cell, before making his way up the stairs into the reception area.

Jakub Baranski stood looking like a man who had just paid a hundred pounds to purchase a boat with holes in the bottom. The look of immense anger in his eyes was obvious and as soon as he saw Richard Rayner appear, instantly began to demand in a screaming voice for his sister's immediate release.

"I'm afraid, I cannot do that Mr. Baranski," the Chief Inspector told him, "Your sister has been arrested for a double murder and we are still putting questions to her."

The man accompanying Natalia's brother was a silver haired gentleman, tall, slim and wearing a morning suit beneath a smartly tailored frock coat. He certainly matched Richard Rayner for smartness and placed a gloved hand on the Polish man's shoulder, suggesting he should now continue to converse with the senior detective on the young man's behalf. That seemed to quieten Jakub Baranski somewhat and he just grunted.

Rayner asked who the gentleman was, assuming his occupation was that of a lawyer and he was there to represent the Baranski family.

"I am Adam Stanek sir, Barrister at Law and representing the interests of Bolak Baranski and members of his family, including Mr. Jakub Baranski and his sister, Natalia." The man spoke articulately but in broken English and the senior detective assumed he was also of Polish origin.

"Is there somewhere perhaps more private, where we can continue with this discussion, Mr...?"

"Chief Inspector Rayner, and yes, if you would follow me gentlemen," Rayner replied, before leading the two visitors to the ground floor interview room in which he had conducted the meeting with Natalia Baranski on the previous occasion, when she had attended at Scotland Yard with her brother.

"May we see the evidence for which you are holding my client's daughter, Chief Inspector?" Mr. Stanek asked, looking quite clinical and obviously intent on securing the woman's early release. His politeness was typical of a legal eagle who was attempting to claw his way towards a position of strength.

Rayner briefly described the facts as he portrayed them, implicating Natalia Baranski in the murders of Joseph Kelly and Blackie Jennings.

"I'm sure you will appreciate, what we have been told is quite damming for the lady in question," he added, addressing the barrister.

"You've got the wrong woman," her brother blurted out, "Natalia has done nothing wrong." The man's claim was only what Richard Rayner had been anticipating and that showed by the Chief Inspector's look of disregard.

Stanek held up a gloved palm for Jakub to keep quiet and turned to the senior detective, explaining that in his view and from what he'd just been told, there was nothing sufficiently evidential to justify charging Natalia Baranski with any kind of crime.

"I strongly suggest Mr. Rayner, you either charge the lady now, this very minute, or release her. Failure to do so will result in my applying for a Writ of Habeas Corpus, sir."

Rayner knew it was a veiled threat being made by the lawyer. There was no way such a writ would be issued against him, when the subject had only been in police custody for a matter of minutes, especially as the crime she was being held for was one of the most serious nature, murder. He called the barrister's bluff.

"I'm afraid, Mr. Stanek, she will be remaining with us, so go and get your writ," he confidently invited.

"But you've got the wrong woman," Jakub Baranski bawled out, repeating himself, "Natalia has done nothing wrong."

"So, you keep telling me," Rayner snapped back, "But I will be the judge of that, sir, if you would allow me to do my job."

It was then a most surprising turn of events took place. The prisoner's brother unexpectedly sat on a chair and began to cry, an act that completely baffled Richard Rayner and Adam Stanek.

"Can I get you some water?" the detective offered, but the man just shook his head and continued to sob.

Rayner looked at the lawyer, who could offer no explanation and both men just stood there, waiting for Jakub Baranski to recompose himself.

Finally, the young man with the shoulder length hair looked up and pleaded one last time for the detective to release his sister.

"I cannot do that, for the reasons I have already explained," the Chief Inspector reiterated, beginning to recognise there was more to this young man than what appeared on the surface. Either he was convinced of his sister's innocence because he knew who the real killer was, or was far more unstable than Rayner had assumed.

"Then might I speak with Mr. Stanek in private, sir?"

Rayner nodded and left the room. It was a request he couldn't actually refuse.

Jack Robinson met his Chief Inspector in the reception area and the senior man enquired if Natalia Baranski had said anything else, when being placed in a cell.

"Not a word sir," the Sergeant replied, "You would think, with all the evidence stacked up against her, she would want to tell the truth and plead for clemency to escape the noose."

"Perhaps she is telling us the truth, Jack, perhaps."

After waiting for only a few minutes, the door to the interview room opened and the gentleman, Mr. Stanek, revealed himself, explaining that Jakub Baranski wished to make a verbal statement.

When both Rayner and Robinson entered, the young man was still sitting there with both arms stretched out across the table, looking a lot more subdued.

His lawyer explained that Jakub wished to share some information that might be beneficial to the Chief Inspector's search for the truth, but there was one condition.

"And what pray might that be, Mr. Stanek?" Rayner enquired.

"A guarantee that, what my client's son is about to tell you Chief Inspector, will remain within these four walls and will not result in any criminal proceedings being taken against him."

The senior detective smiled, explaining that confidentiality would not be a problem, however, he could not make any such promise regarding any reluctance to take official action against Jakub Baranski, should he implicate himself in anything that might be incriminating.

"Very well, I appreciate your candour sir." The lawyer then looked directly at the young man and nodded.

The young Polish activist sat back in his chair and began to breathe rather heavily.

"Before I disclose what I think you should know Mr. Rayner, I need to describe to you the difficulties we are experiencing in my own country at present," he said.

Both Rayner and Robinson sat down and the Chief Inspector waited patiently to hear the man's story, not really having any interest in the internal affairs of Poland, but if it had any bearing on the case, then he had all the time in the world.

Chapter Nineteen

Recalling his days as a student at Oxford, Richard Rayner was aware that Poland had been a country resembling a cake sliced into various sectors; being in the unenviable position of not having enjoyed an independent existence for the past one hundred years or so. The unfortunate and disunited land mass had been bastardised by Germany, Austria and Russia, but the senior detective had little knowledge of the internal politics governing the various partitions that were in place.

Jakub Baranski explained that his country's location on the Northern European Lowlands was of extreme importance to Prussia, but of extreme significance to Imperial Russia, because of its position to the rest of the continent.

"Following its defeat in the Crimean War thirty years ago, the Russian Tsar introduced a number of liberal reforms," the young man quietly explained, "Including the liberation of all impoverished people throughout the Russian Empire." He continued to describe how land reform followed and was opposed by many of the landed nobles, who as a result of the new reforms, lost a great deal of their power and wealth. Their objections were condemned by opposing activists like himself and other young partisans, including the known philosopher, Karl Marx, who strongly influenced a number of various rebellions.

"Imagine Mr. Rayner, if your country was controlled by outsiders who lived and reigned off the back breaking labours of your own people. My ancestors fought against such oppression, until alas, in 1864 the insurgency was crushed by the might of Russia, having failed to get the backing of other European governments. We were left to stand alone by the rest of our so-called allies."

Actually, Richard Rayner was aware of that fact, but until now, such history had been of little relevance to him although he could fully understand where this young man was coming from and sympathised.

"And you are about to tell me that such a revolution is about to be re-ignited," he suggested.

The young Baranski nodded and continued to explain that there were sufficient numbers of Polish men and women ready to fight and restore total independence for their country. In his view, they had leaders with the knowledge and attributes required to usurp the Russian oppressors and were waiting for the right time to come, when they would return to their country as a potent force of liberators.

"You sir, can have no idea of the amount of anger and frustration we feel at being a suppressed people. But we shall continue our fight for freedom and once we have restored that part of our country away from the Russian invaders, we are confident the rest of occupied Poland will fall easily enough."

Rayner glanced across at Adam Stanek, who sat there listening to Jakub's portrayal, as if he had heard it all before. Could Jakub Baranski be regarded as eccentric. Possibly, but the senior detective genuinely believed if the boot was on the other foot, he would most probably be feeling just as defiant and found himself strangely supporting the young Pole's sentiments. However, there were other matters that were a priority for Richard Rayner.

"As much as I sympathise with your beliefs and intentions Mr. Baranski, what has this to do with the murders of the two London dockers, Joseph Kelly and Blackie Jennings," the Chief Inspector asked, "And pray tell me how it assists your sister's predicament."

"There are cells of activists all over Europe Mr. Rayner, including in this country, all in hiding and waiting for the call to arms."

"The call to arms, you say, from whom?"

"I cannot tell you that sir, only to say that the central cell from where the Polish Revolutionary Army is currently based is in Paris, and it is there that arms are being gathered and plans are being made as we speak."

"Again, I ask you, what has this to do with the murders I am investigating and the reason your sister, Natalia, is currently sitting in one of our cells downstairs."

It was obvious the young man had reached a point in his narration, whereby he was reluctant to share more information and Richard Rayner was quite intent on pushing him, knowing that whatever puss-filled boil was driving this young man forward, it had yet to be lanced.

"There is a private club here in London where Polish sympathisers meet frequently. Its membership consists of one of those cells I have mentioned to you and I tell you in the strictest of confidence, that is where you should be directing your Investigation into those two murders."

Rayner moved forward in his seat and placed both elbows on the table, clasping his hands together and looking more determined.

"Are you a member of that organisation, Mr. Baranski," he asked, with a look of serious concern on his face.

But before the man could answer, Adam Stanek advised him not to.

"Forgive me Chief Inspector," the lawyer said, "It would not be in my client's son's interests to disclose that information and I must insist you do not press the matter further. He has made his statement and that should suffice, sir."

"Mr. Stanek, I am the invited recipient of young Mr. Baranski's tale of woe and to fully understand what it is he is trying to tell me I need to know everything. However, I understand and sympathise with your position and shall not press that particular point."

"Thank you, sir."

"It does appear however, that Mr. Baranski seems to have a great deal of knowledge concerning what has been going on and it is difficult to accept what he says, without recognising he plays an active role in what he is discussing."

"Might I remind you sir you gave your word there would be no criminal prosecution brought against my client."

"I gave no such thing, Mr. Stanek, as you well know. However, I shall promise this much, that I shall consider fully the co-operation Mr Baranski has given to us, when finally deciding what course of action to take next, following this meeting."

Rayner had already shown a great deal of respect to the lawyer, but he certainly wasn't going to place himself in a position that would be detrimental to the search for the killers of the two dockers. Of course, those responsible for cutting the throat of Blackie Jennings, were in custody and would hang for their misdeeds, but Rayner remained determined to identify and apprehend the woman behind the two atrocities.

The Chief Inspector then turned back to the young informer and asked for the location of the private club he had made mention of.

The man sat up straight and looked across at his lawyer. Rayner actually saw a veil of fear cover Jakub's eyes and waited for Mr. Stanek's response. He didn't give one.

"It's in Weymouth Street, Newington, near to the Elephant and Castle," Mr. Baranski whispered, both hands trembling, "Halfway down the hill on the left-hand side. Two houses converted into one with blue curtains at the windows. The premises are completely cloaked Mr. Rayner, and there is no sign outside."

"And you are suggesting the killers of Joseph Kelly, can be found inside those premises?"

The man nodded and confirmed, "Yes, certainly those responsible for Joseph Kelly's demise sir."

"And what of the woman we wish to speak to for arranging his death and that of the docker, Blackie Jennings. If that person is not your sister, Natalia, then will she be there also?"

"I've no idea. All I can tell you is that the woman you seek is not Natalia."

Rayner knew that Baranski was aware of the identity of the female killer, but realised anything short of threatening him with his own execution, wouldn't extract that information.

Having reached that point of the conversation and satisfied he had manoeuvred Jakub Baranski into virtually admitting to have known the killers Rayner sought, the boil had been lanced and it was now time to drain it.

"I need their names, Mr. Baranski," the detective demanded, trying to make his authority more emphatic.

"Mr. Rayner, I protest sir," the barrister cried out, standing from his seat, "You are inadvertently endangering the life of my client's son."

Rayner also stood and glared at the lawyer, but remained calm and deliberate, when he explained, "Mr. Stanek, I am conducting an Investigation into foul murder committed here in London, a city in which I might remind you sir, you and the Baranski family are invited guests. I have a responsibility to find those who committed those grotesque atrocities and will not have anyone, including yourself, stand in my way. Please do not give me cause to suspect you yourself possess credible information that could assist my Investigation and are intent on obstructing me."

The lawyer was obviously taken aback by the insinuation and shook his head before returning to his seat.

The Chief Inspector then looked down at the younger man and further explained that two men had already confessed to the murder of Blackie Jennings, indicating they had received payment for their part from a woman answering the description of Natalia Baranski. He also suggested that they were facing the hangman and asked the same question he had earlier put to the young man's sister; why should they lie about such an event?

"That in itself, is sufficient to send your sister to the gallows Mr. Baranski, now do you wish to enlighten me further on what you know about both those incidents."

The young Polish man bowed his head and began to speak to the tabletop.

"As I have already told you sir, Natalia had nothing to do with any of it. She is completely innocent." Again, he looked directly at his lawyer for guidance but Mr. Stanek shrugged his shoulders, inferring he had lost the position from which he could protest further.

Jakub continued to speak, lowering his voice even more so.

"However," he whispered, "My younger sister, Lena, is a member of the cell in Weymouth Street." He paused to take a deep breath, before continuing, "In fact, she is a leading member."

His legal representative instantly advised Baranski to stop talking, but his client's son quickly explained that he wished to tell all, rather than see an injustice being committed.

"I cannot see Natalia hang for something she hasn't done," he blurted out at the barrister, his voice betraying immense anger and frustration.

Richard Rayner remained silent, knowing just how much heartache this young man was experiencing and at least admired him for his honesty and intentions.

Much to the investigating detective's surprise, the disturbed young man then continued to explain that arms were being brought into London docks, having been purchased by the Polish Movement in Ireland. Once they had arrived, they were then later transferred to a vessel destined for Calais, where they were shipped prior to being transported to Paris by road. According to Jakub, Joseph Kelly had been assisting in the concealment of the weapons, before they were transferred to the French bound vessel.

Rayner returned to his seat and asked, "For what reason was he murdered?"

"As far as I know and it is only what I have heard, he was being paid an exorbitant amount of money, but was demanding more. According to my younger sister, Kelly threatened to disclose the activities of the organisation to the British Foreign Office and a decision was taken to silence him. There you have it, Mr. Rayner, and I shall never forgive myself for having told you but I had no other choice, if only to save my other sister Natalia, from being unjustly executed under your laws."

Richard Rayner sat in silence for a moment, digesting everything that had just been unexpectedly disclosed. He then asked the man, "When you say a decision was taken to silence Kelly, who made that decision?"

"Lena."

"I take it then, that your sister, Lena, was using Natalia's name."

"If you say so, but I have no knowledge of that."

"And what of the murder of the docker, Blackie Jennings, do you know the reason for his callous execution?"

"As far as I know, my people discovered he was working for you Mr. Rayner, and that cost him his life. As I told you before, my people have been ridiculed and suppressed for more than a century and will not allow for anything to stand in their way, when attempting to regain their freedom."

"Where can I find your sister, Lena, now Mr. Baranski?"

He shrugged his shoulders, before suggesting if she wasn't in her room at the Dorchester Hotel, she would most probably be at the club in Weymouth Street.

"I have said enough Mr. Rayner and do not intend helping you further," he insisted.

The Chief Inspector then instructed Jack Robinson to take Jakub to the cells, soliciting another immediate protest from Adam Stanek.

"As a result of his assistance, Mr Stanek, he will be released later together with Natalia Baranski, but I need him to remain with us for the time being, at least until we have verified all that he has told us."

"Do I have your word on that, sir?"

"Yes, this time, you do Mr. Stanek."

Jakub Baranski was taken to share the cell already occupied by his sister and the couple were provided with refreshments on the instructions of Richard Rayner.

Adam Stanek disappeared, having left Scotland Yard to report back to his client, Poland's representative to the United Kingdom and was satisfied that the Chief Inspector was a man of his word, that both the young man and woman would be released fairly soon.

As for Richard Rayner, he felt like a fly caught in a spider's web. Intelligence and knowledge were wonderful guidelines upon which a professional investigator could direct an Inquiry, but such information would not be regarded as circumstantial evidence, necessary to convict. He stood staring at the vast amount of data he'd recorded on his blackboard, examining a number of different options available to him. After just briefing Frederick Morgan on what had transpired from the interview with Jakub Baranski, the Chief Superintendent had suggested his preference was to raid the club in Weymouth Street without further delay. There lay Rayner's dilemma; should he follow that advice or would it be more prudent to seek further corroboration of what the young Polish man had told him. He stood for quite some time, juggling with both options.

The Chief Inspector considered the use of an undercover individual being planted inside the same club where, according to the informant, a cell of Polish activists was operating, but Rayner was aware such a manoeuvre would be difficult, if not impossible. Those he was intending to apprehend were dangerous people and what if his agent was discovered and paid with his life. As much as his preference was to take that course of action, the risk was far too great.

Observations on the building from a distance might prove to be successful, but for what purpose, he asked himself. It was highly unlikely that anything that went beyond seeing people enter and leave would result. He decided that option would provide very little and was therefore a non-starter.

Perhaps a search into the background of the institution and those responsible for its management might provide something of value. But there again, other than being an establishment where various members of a community visited for social purposes, what else would be achieved by going down that particular path.

Finally, Rayner decided there was no other feasible option but to do as Morgan had suggested and raid the club, in the hope of finding Lena Baranski there and subsequently obtaining a confession from the woman. He wasn't totally convinced that was the most effective way of progressing further, only because if he failed, no other way to advance the Investigation would be open for him. However, the senior detective was left with no other choice and if they failed to find the woman at the club, then there was a good chance she would be at the hotel.

It was yet another wet and miserable evening, when three official carriages left Scotland Yard, each filled with uniformed constables and sergeants. The leading transport included Frederick Morgan, Richard Rayner, Henry Bustle and Jack Robinson, each of them armed. Sergeant Robinson had earlier identified the exact location of the Polish Club in Weymouth Street, having been dispatched there by his Chief Inspector during the daylight hours and directed the coach driver to within a hundred yards of where the private club was situated.

Frederick Morgan was like a popping weasel, feeling a rush of adrenaline and impatience to be part of the climax to the Investigation.

"What if the woman we are going for, is armed as well, Rayner?" the Chief Superintendent asked, checking the loads in his own revolver.

"Then what action we take will depend upon how she responds to our visit sir, that's of course, if she is there."

"Naturally, but it might be to our advantage to take her alive. We shall need her to name the others involved in this little caper of theirs otherwise it might mean locking the bleedin' lot of them up."

Rayner looked confused and explained as best he could that he suspected it wouldn't make much difference whether they took out the complete membership of the group of Polish activists or not.

"All we would be doing is to delay whatever plans they have in Paris. I'm sure there will always be plenty of others to fill their shoes sir. I am more concerned with catching the killers of our two dockers."

"So am I, Rayner, but one thing puzzles me, why do you think these reprobates decided to spike Kelly's kneecaps, before killing him?"

"I can only imagine it was meant to deter others from threatening their Cause. After all, if what Jakub Baranski has told us is correct, we are dealing with extremists who strongly believe in what they are doing and not your ordinary run of the mill villains."

The convoy of carriages stopped in the darkness of Weymouth Street and without further delay, officers could be seen stealthily making their way up the incline, heading towards the targeted premises, with Jack Robinson leading the way. Those men who had been so instructed made their way towards the back of the two houses in question, some carrying axes and others grasping their truncheons.

The detectives could see that lights were showing from behind the heavy curtains on the ground floor and Rayner was the first to approach the front door, with no intention of knocking or delaying matters by making introductions. Both Morgan and Bustle stood behind him, ready for what would take place once they gained access.

"I've a feeling this is going to be like Armageddon," the others heard Morgan whisper, communicating his most optimistic hopes.

Chapter Twenty

The door at the front of the premises was secured on the inside by a bolt halfway up from the ground and which yielded to one kick from Richard Rayner's highly polished boot. Albeit, the outside gave the appearance of two separate houses, the interior was very different as the detectives discovered when finding themselves standing inside a large spacious room. A carpeted floor lay beneath small clusters of ornate tables and chairs, the majority of which were occupied by men and women. A drinks bar could be seen in the far corner, attended by a smartly dressed young gentleman. The first impression was that the private club was most certainly more resplendent than the average meeting place, where ordinary people sought the social company of others.

As soon as the presence of the Scotland Yard detectives was realised, the atmosphere inside the room abruptly changed from being convivial, with individual conversations ongoing, to one of immense apprehension. When a line of stern-faced uniformed officers entered through a back door and positioned themselves regimentally around the perimeter of the room, people became agitated with a number of the patrons standing from their seats. Vociferous requests were made as to what was going on and a sea of bewildered and confused faces stared at the uninvited intruders.

Richard Rayner's first impression, having made a quick visual examination of the scene, indicated the absence of any kind of unlawful practices taking place and from the ages of the women present, there certainly wasn't any individual lady resembling the description of Miss Lena Baranski. It did appear that they might well have been misled by the information provided by Jakub Baranski.

During the general kerfuffle, a small bald-headed man with grey mutton chop whiskers seemed to come from nowhere in particular to approach the senior detectives, looking extremely annoyed. The gentleman instantly demanded to know, speaking in pigeon English, who they were and what was the meaning of such a daunting and 'unwarranted' trespass. His manner was like cannon fodder to Frederick Morgan.

"I'm Maggie Hughes and this is Ann Marshall," the Chief Superintendent sarcastically jested, pointing his walking stick at Henry Bustle, and referring to a couple of well-known female thespians who were popular on the London stage at the time, "And that geezer there is, Richard Rayner from Scotland Yard, who's here to nick you for keeping an unlicensed drinking parlour my old mucker." Morgan's recent personal problems hadn't diminished his humour and the grin on his face became transfixed.

"But I am licensed," the man insisted, confirming he was the club owner.

"No, you're not, you lying little toad, I've checked."

During those initial brief exchanges, Rayner made a more detailed visual examination of the gathered assembly, most of whom remained staring in disbelief at the constables who were looking menacingly back at them and was more convinced that the lady they sought wasn't present.

"Alright, all of you take a deep breath and stay right where you are," Morgan shouted out, "This is an official police raid and we are looking for Lena Baranski. Step forward miss and let's not have any bother."

No one responded to the demand and Rayner watched closely the reactions of those gathered.

"It doesn't look as though our girl is here," the Chief Superintendent whispered, frustratingly, a fact the Chief Inspector was already aware of.

Rayner noticed a flight of stairs leading up to an upper level and pointed them out to Henry Bustle, suggesting upstairs needed to be searched. He then led the way across the room, followed by his Sergeant but just as the two detectives made the bottom step, the sound of a gunshot reverberated around the building, taking everyone by surprise. There was no doubt the report had come from above their heads.

A number of screams followed and both detectives took the stairs two at a time before reaching an upper landing, partially illuminated by a burning oil lamp attached to a wall. Quickly but cautiously and with their handguns grasped in their hands, they moved down a dark narrow corridor, until they could hear a woman sobbing in one of a number of rooms. Again, using extreme caution they stepped inside and found a young lady standing crying with both hands raised to her face. She was looking down at the body of another young woman lying on the floor at her feet. In the dead female's hand, a gun was still being held and human brains could be seen splattered across the bare floorboards. Richard Rayner knew at that precise moment they had found the woman they had been seeking.

When the distressed lady saw the detectives she went hysterical, screaming out a few inaudible words and causing the Chief Inspector to nod towards Henry Bustle, who quickly grabbed hold, doing his best to calm her. Rayner then made it his business to take the weapon from the hand of the corpse, which was a small single shot percussion pistol; the likes of which the senior detective hadn't seen before. He turned to the hysterical woman and asked who the dead lady was, requiring confirmation of what he already knew. By then, they had been joined by Frederick Morgan and Jack Robinson.

The insuppressible woman was in shock and found it difficult to express herself.

"Control yourself miss," Rayner demanded, "We need to know who this lady is."

The woman took a deep breath and with some effort, declared, "My best friend, Lena."

"Miss Lena Baranski?"

"She didn't want to face you people and you are the vermin responsible for this." She spoke with venom and hatred in her voice and spat on the floor, before being man-handled and led back downstairs by Sergeant Bustle.

Rayner remained crouched over the young woman's corpse and looked into a death mask that reflected a great deal of anguish. He felt a wave of sympathy towards her, thinking only of a wasted life, until being reminded that Lena Baranski had been responsible for committing such horrendous acts of barbarism.

"Right then, the whole bloody lot of them can be taken back to Scotland Yard," the Chief Superintendent decreed.

Rayner rose to his feet and looked hard at Morgan, explaining, "There must be thirty of them at least, where in God's name are we going to put them all."

"We'll double them up in the cells Rayner, four or five to each cell."

"Might I suggest we just take their names and addresses. I shall be sending a full report to the Foreign Office and they can take whatever action is necessary. After all sir, it seems that our Investigation into the murders of Kelly and Jennings have been concluded by the unfortunate death of Miss Baranski."

"And what about the thugs who helped her to bump off Joseph Kelly, my old mucker. Don't tell me you're suggesting they should go scott free."

"I believe in all probability they were local heavies, hired to do a job in the same way as Clarke and Hegarty were and the only way we will identify them is if they are put in. I doubt they are likely to be connected with this gathering, otherwise why would the woman pay two locals to dispose of Jennings, instead of using the same men who helped murder Kelly, if they were activists."

Morgan nodded his acquiescence, acknowledging the Chief Inspector was making a valid point. Further action should now fall within the remit of the Foreign Office and security forces, to consider the implications of what they had been told by Jakub Baranski. Richard Rayner's only regret was that, by committing suicide, Lena Baranski had taken with her the answers to a number of poignant questions, but it was too late to do anything about that now.

"A successful conclusion then Richard, to a nasty Inquiry," Morgan stated, as they were making their way back to their carriage.

"I'm not so sure sir," Rayner answered, "I would still have liked to have known why Lena Baranski used her sister's name when dealing with Joseph Kelly."

"Obviously to cause some confusion my old mucker."

"Perhaps."

As expected, it was with great sadness both Natalia and Jakub Baranski received the news of their sister's demise, their only comfort coming from Richard Rayner keeping his word and releasing the couple from the cells. But before leaving Scotland Yard, the older of the two sisters remorsefully disclosed to the Chief Inspector that she and Lena Baranski, had never really been lovingly close confidantes.

"I speak to you with a heavy heart, Mr. Rayner," she confessed, "But the truth is, my sister was jealous of the way in which my mother and father regarded me as being their favourite daughter."

"I understand," Rayner said, listening to the young lady intently, but having some difficulty in accepting such a situation had existed.

Natalia went on to explain that her sister had a harsh, uncaring streak that often resulted in acts of cruelty, the likes of which brought shame to her family. She described how on one occasion, Lena had taken a knife to a new coat bought Natalia by their parents, albeit, the younger sister had received a similar gift.

"As much as I tried so hard to placate her, she never accepted we were on equal terms, thus I suspect was the reason she used my identity when planning and committing those terrible deeds."

Of course, such behaviour helped to explain a lot to the senior detective and Richard Rayner had to accept the pain inflicted on Joseph Kelly, was indeed the masochistic tendencies of the woman who had ordered his death. As far as he was concerned, that particular Investigation was now finally closed and the way was open for him to concentrate on the bizarre circumstances surrounding the woman who had been languishing in prison for the past ten years or so.

"What a jumbled affair that was sir," Henry Bustle remarked, as both detectives made their way up the stairs and back to the Chief Inspector's office.

"I believe Henry, Lena Baranski wasn't just driven by hatred towards her sister. I suspect her mind had also been corrupted by the detestation she and her family felt towards those who invaded their country and that same hatred deposed her of any thought beyond doing what she thought was right, no matter how depraved or violent."

Bustle then made mention of Charlie Pendry, the Southwark Bridge costermonger he had interviewed earlier and who Richard Rayner had momentarily forgotten all about.

"And what did he volunteer to you Henry, about the night Leonard Crockett died?"

Bustle explained that initially, the man denied leaving the public house earlier than closing time, adamant that he had remained there drinking until ten o'clock. But when the Sergeant explained that the landlady, Mrs. Peterson, had sworn that Pendry had left an hour earlier and that his wife had confirmed he hadn't arrived home until ten thirty that same night, he retracted his first remarks.

"What was his final story," Rayner asked.

"He told me that he now remembered going for a walk after leaving The Bushell in Denmar Street, as he wasn't feeling very well but couldn't think of anybody who might have seen him and who would support his story."

"In your opinion, what kind of a man is he and most importantly, do you believe him."

"No sir, he was lying, but we might find it difficult to disprove what he says."

"I think we should revisit Denmar Street in that case; I'd like to get to know the neighbourhood a little better."

Each time James the butler took food from the kitchen to the young fugitive hiding amongst the hay in the stables, he feared the wrath of his master, should he get caught out. Of course, the man who had served the Morgans' since they had first moved into their Richmond residence following their marriage, knew only too well that if the man who paid for his loyalty and service ever discovered what 'Jimmy' had been up to, it could very well result in his instant dismissal. He realised he was a fool to succumb to the outlandish wishes of Miss Estelle, but had a great deal of sympathy for the itinerant who always appeared to be a lost soul with nowhere else to lay his head. In addition to that, there had been something persuasively benevolent about the way in which the girl had pleaded for the butler's assistance. In any case, young Raphael Dickens only required shelter off the streets during the hours of darkness and had usually disappeared again, well before daylight. From then on, it was anybody's guess as to where he remained concealed to evade the police or anyone else looking for him, only returning to the Morgan's stables as dusk approached.

When James appeared, carrying a tray of the usual bowl of hot soup and bread, he found the two young people crouched down on the floor towards the back of the wooden structure. Estelle was sitting at the side of her friend, trying toilsomely to persuade him to surrender himself to Richard Rayner. She was overheard to explain to 'Ralphie' he could trust the Chief Inspector and would at least be safe from pursuit during the time he was in his care, but the young fugitive was still a fair distance from trusting any policeman, even the celebrated detective.

The butler quietly supported what his master's daughter was suggesting, before placing the tray on the ground.

"You should listen to what Miss Estelle is saying," he advised, "You can't stay here for ever my boy."

The young man ate like a wolf with a bone, while the girl continued putting various suggestions to him with the butler listening and waiting to take the tray back to the kitchen. In between concentrating on the food, Ralphie occasionally nodded, encouraging the master's daughter and servant to believe he was slowly becoming convinced by what they were now both persuasively suggesting.

Suddenly their small world appeared to disintegrate, when all three were taken by surprise and the air instantly filled with menace, as a loud voice boomed out from the open doorway.

"What in hell's name is going on here then." It was Frederick Morgan standing there, his figure partially bathed in moonlight penetrating through the stable entrance.

In disbelief, Estelle got to her feet and began to tremble.

James the butler's first thought was whether he would be allowed to stay another night before being dispatched in the morning and Raphael hurriedly scraped his last piece of bread around the soup bowl.

Three pale and bewildered faces then stared back at the last man they wanted to see at that very moment.

"So, it seems there's been some bloody conspiracy going on in my own house," Morgan continued in a hostile voice, moving forward into the light of a burning oil lamp resting on top of a board dividing two stalls, both occupied by horses.

"Father, we have only been trying to help this..."

"Jimmy, explain yourself," Morgan demanded, ignoring his daughter and sounding like a judge wearing a black cap and about to impose the ultimate punitive sentence.

"I can't sir, except to apologise, but..."

"James was acting under my instructions father," Estelle confessed, doing her best to mitigate on behalf of the friendly butler and realising his head would be the first to roll.

"And you, you little squirt, I suppose you've been hiding your carcass in here since doing a runner from the Rayners household," Morgan angrily assumed.

The petrified lad shook his head and stood to his feet, allowing the empty soup bowl to fall to the ground and break.

"Right then, I'll deal with you two in the morning," Morgan directed, before moving towards the itinerant fugitive, "As for you, you're coming with me to Scotland Yard forthwith my old mucker and let's not have any trouble or you'll be feeling the lash."

Raphael Dickens stepped back in fright as the Chief Superintendent reached forward to grab his arm, but in doing so, knocked the oil lamp over with his elbow. The lamp fell to the ground and immediately ignited a pile of straw gathered at the foot of one of the wooden supports.

"Bleedin' hell," Morgan cried out, as the flames quickly shot up the wooden structure as well as seeking more impetus from the straw covered floor.

Both master and butler tried to douse the fire with their feet, but to no avail, as within a few seconds the blaze began to take hold. By the time they had grabbed a couple of horse blankets to tackle the fire, it was hopeless and all seemed to be lost. In sensing the immediate danger, the horses began to whinny and kick at the wooden doors securing their individual stalls. It was only a matter of time before the whole building became an unpreventable inferno.

Morgan shouted to Estelle to go to the house and fetch help and for Jimmy and the squatter to help get the horses out. The way the fire was spreading, they had to act quickly.

"And Estelle," her father shouted above the noise of the crackling fire that would soon destroy the livestock if action wasn't taken quickly, "Fetch some buckets with you and hurry girl."

Raphael Dickens's way with horses was a gift and he'd always found he had a close affinity to them. Quickly but calmly, he began to lead them out of their stalls to safety, talking softly and reassuring them, as the smoke began to thicken. On the other hand, both Morgan and his butler had great difficulty in pulling the horses away from the blaze until the homeless vagrant took the reins from them and finished each job successfully, as if being capable of hypnotising the mounts.

Between them they managed to get six frightened horses away from the imminent danger without harm or injury, although that achievement was undoubtedly the result of Raphael Dickens ability to converse with the animals. By that time, the remainder of the household was in attendance, including Sally-Anne, and formed a bucket chain as James the butler aimed a hose pipe at the scorching flames. However, it was all to no avail and the heat and smoke became intolerable, with one of the stable boys being sent to fetch the Fire Engine as the daunting job of trying to save the building continued.

Morgan felt like Moses trying to turn back the waves of the Red Sea, but without having the same success. It was all too little, too late, a hopeless task and by the time the official Fire Brigade were in attendance, most of the stable had disappeared beneath a wall of flame. When the roof finally caved in amongst a shower of sparks the master of the house told everyone to stop, realising that the structure had been lost.

"Well, it's only wood and straw," Morgan was overheard to say to his wife, "But it could have been much worse, Sal."

Everyone spent the rest of that night fighting the fire and when the first light of the following dawn eventually came, the master of the house stood staring at the charred remains. Firemen walked about the devastation, dousing what hot tinder remained and Sally-Anne stood to one side of him with an exhausted Raphael Dickens on the other.

"There's nothing more can be done now, Frederick," his wife suggested, looking up into her husband's blackened face, "Why don't you go and get some rest while you can, I'll make some arrangements to have all of this cleared and we can keep the horses at the circus until a new stable is built."

Morgan reluctantly agreed and turned to wearily walk back to the house, just as the pathetic figure of Raphael Dickens also turned away to seek out the exit gates.

"Wait," Morgan called out to him and the lad turned to face his nemesis, obviously fearing the man was about to carry out his earlier threat to take him back into police custody. He was certainly devoid of sufficient strength to run away.

"You did well tonight boy," the Chief Superintendent continued, "Without you, we might very well have lost one or more of those horses, so thank you for that."

The boy just nodded and turned to leave, but was stopped by Morgan, who invited him to have some breakfast.

"Yes, come on back to the house and have something to eat before you go," Sally-Anne suggested, having guessed who the strange lad was.

"Or stay, if you want to," her husband added, "There's something you need to know about those blokes who have been chasing after you."

Chapter Twenty One

The coming of winter seemed imminent, as low-lying black clouds moved down from the north, bringing with them rain, later turning to sleet. Both Richard Rayner and Henry Bustle stood exposed to the inclement weather on the corner of Denmar Street outside The Bushell public house, where Frank Crockett had visited just prior to his untimely death. The Chief Inspector was determined to continue the Investigation in a manner that, in his view, should have been conducted ten years previously.

Rayner had remained sceptic as to whether, on the face of things, those detectives initially attending at number seventy-three Denmar Street, might well have been too ready to accept Annie Crockett's guilt. He suspected they could have been far too disparaging towards their suspect after recovering the kitchen knife in the back garden, leaving a number of questions unanswered. Was it possible they could have quite easily jumped to inaccurate conclusions when hearing what Priscilla Crockett had told them about her mother cleaning the kitchen floor. Such assumption was understandable and would have been more convincing to Rayner, if that same version given by the daughter had been tested more rigorously by the detectives.

There was also the fact that Annie Crockett had made a statement of admission, one that was later retracted at her trial. Was it not possible that the woman had confessed to the murder in fear of the predicament she had found herself facing, before reality eventually persuaded her to deny responsibility? In Richard Rayner's inquisitive mind, he truly believed she had been a sacrificial lamb, placed on the altar of justice for purposes of self-gratification by those in charge of the case. Such possibilities required further and more detailed scrutinisation, beginning with basic investigative methods.

Now it was time to wear down some of that boot leather Frederick Morgan had earlier mentioned and the senior detective suggested he and Henry Bustle should knock on alternative doors along the street.

"We are only interested in talking to people who lived here at the time of the murder, Henry," he directed, "And you know what questions to put to them."

Bustle nodded and pulling his cap down over his ears as protection against the biting wind and sleet, began the laborious task of visiting each household, with Rayner replicating the same actions.

After the first hour had passed, both detectives were feeling a little dejected. Only one householder had been present at his current address ten years earlier, an old man who could not tell them anything about the night they were interested in. Of course, the gentleman remembered the incident very well, but had nothing to offer about the murder itself.

Just as midday was approaching, the Sergeant knocked on the door of an elderly woman who appeared, grasping a walking stick in one hand in such a manner, there was a distinct possibility she would wrap it across Bustle's head. With some urgency he quickly told her who he was and produced his identity card, thankfully calming the lady down. Bustle then asked how long the lady had lived there, at number twenty-six.

"Twenty years thereabouts, duckie," she answered, withdrawing her hostile weapon and boasting a full set of missing upper teeth, "Me husband turned his toes up some five years ago now and I've been a poor widow woman living on my own ever since. What did you say your trick was again young man?"

"Bustle ma'am, Sergeant Bustle from Scotland Yard. We are making enquiries about the night the man who lived at seventy-three was murdered."

The woman shook her head, saying, "A terrible thing was that, Sergeant Bristol, and it was his missus that done him in, would yer know. You'll have to speak up a bit though young man, I'm as deaf as a post."

"Did you see or hear anything unusual that night ma'am?" Bustle asked, raising his voice.

"Nope, can't say as I can remember, but my Ernie got pissed off at all that ruckus going on in the entry, him with his bad chest an' all."

"What kind of ruckus would that have been then?"

"I couldn't tell yer, I never heard nothing, but there was nothing wrong with my Ernie's hearing, about the only thing that still worked for him mind you." She cackled at her own humour, before continuing, "According to him, there was a couple of layabouts playing up in our entry and he went outside with his stick and told them to piss off. That's what he told me any roads."

Richard Rayner joined his Sergeant, having just drawn a blank from the house on the other side of the entry the elderly woman was referring to and Bustle repeated what the lady had just told him.

"You're a bit of a toff for a copper ain't yer son," the widow remarked, when the Chief Inspector was introduced to her.

Rayner just smiled and asked how she remembered it was on the same night as Leonard Crockett was murdered, that her husband had disturbed two men causing a disturbance inside the entry. She was quite specific, telling him she was certain because her husband had later heard Rose and Charlie Pendry arguing out in the street and it was her Ernie who had called the police.

"Of course, we never knew then that the woman next to that pair had done her old man in, at the time. We heard about that off one of the peelers afterwards."

"Did your husband describe either of these two men he found fighting in the entry, Mrs...?"

"Wardle, Fanny Wardle, and he never had to because he told me one of them was Charlie Pendry. He didn't see the other one, I can tell you that straight. That Charlie Pendry must have been off his head that night."

"Did you mention any of this to the police at the time, Mrs. Wardle?"

"Naw, we didn't pay much mind, except Ernie was pissed off at all the racket going on with the Pendry's before he fetched the peeler."

"I shall need to have your statement taken from you, if that's okay. Would it be alright if I sent one of my best men to take it?"

"I ain't going anywhere ducks, I've been here on my own since my Ernie passed on, God rest his soul. 'Ere, send one of them good looking buggers with all his tea and sugar in working order." She cackled again, bringing yet another smile to Richard Rayner's face.

Frederick Morgan was in his office when the two detectives returned to Scotland Yard. He resembled a man who had been up all night fighting a fire and quickly confirmed, that had been exactly what he'd been doing. After describing the ordeal he and his household had been subjected to, the Chief Superintendent made mention of how the blaze had started, confessing to having found the fugitive, Raphael Dickens, being hidden by his daughter and butler in the dark recesses of the stable.

"The whole place was gutted," he continued, "But in fairness that kid was a great help, Rayner, and saved a couple of the horses for us. He certainly showed me a thing or two about how to talk to the nags and calm them down."

"Did you tell him about Lena Baranski and that there's no longer any further need for him to worry, sir."

"Yes, and I've done more than that, I've hired him on as a stable boy doing a few odd jobs until the new stable is built. He was secretly being fed and watered by that underhanded butler of mine, Jimmy, who's had the bollocking of his life. He won't be doing anything like that again, I've made sure of that my old mucker."

Rayner was surprised the butler had kept his job, but then remembered how 'Jimmy' used to covertly supply his master with whiskey during the reign of Nurse Longfeet. Turning the conversation to the subject of Annie Crockett, the Chief Inspector hinted they were getting nearer to confirming the woman's innocence.

"You do know Rayner, the only way she will be released is if there's somebody to take her place," Morgan suggested.

"I'm aware of that sir and have an idea of who that individual will be."

"Who?"

Rayner looked confident until that point, but then explained that he wasn't quite ready to reveal the real killer's identity.

"I need more time just to tie up a few loose ends before making an arrest."

"Well, whoever you've got in mind, the old man will have a bleedin' fit if you're proved to be right my old cock-sparrow. It's best you tell me."

"I need to make a few more enquiries first just to be certain, but from what a witness has just told myself and Henry, Charlie Pendry, the next-door neighbour had a fight on that same night with Leonard Crockett, after they had both been seen drinking together in the Bushell."

"Ah, and that hasn't been mentioned before, I take it."

"No sir, but I need to have another word with Annie Crockett's daughter before we have another talk with Mr. Pendry."

"Don't tell me you think she was involved?"

"No sir, but if she overheard her mother and father arguing from her upstairs bedroom, or thinks she did, then she might have mistaken that altercation for an argument that took place outside in the street between Charlie and Rose Pendry, according to our witness that is."

"What difference would that make, if the lass was mistaken."

"It would negate an important and telling inference given to the jury, that Annie and Leonard Crockett had been involved in a violent encounter just prior to the murder."

"Yes, of course my old mucker."

"And that's why I need to speak with the daughter again. I'm assuming the barney between the Pendry's would have taken place not far from the girl's upstairs bedroom and about the same time she thought it was her own mother and father."

Morgan glanced across at the wall clock and requested he be kept updated, before bringing the conversation to an end.

"I've got to lay my hands on a builder who can reconstruct the stables for us."

Richard Rayner smiled to himself, accepting that there were other important matters to be dealt with, apart from investigating a ten-year old murder.

Before leaving Scotland Yard to visit the circus in Bermondsey, Rayner instructed Henry Bustle to bring in Charlie Pendry and to take Jack Robinson with him.

"What condition would you like to find him when you return sir?" Bustle asked, teasing his Chief Inspector.

"In one piece Henry, and capable of answering a few more questions, if you please."

Bustle feigned looking hurt, but was only joshing.

The afternoon matinee was coming to an end by the time Richard Rayner arrived at the Pratchett and Longfellow Circus and it was noticeable that Sally-Anne Morgan was absent. The detective assumed she would be busy dealing with the aftermath of the fire and waited patiently for the audience to vacate the Big Top, before approaching, Emily Pratchett.

Miss Pratchett confirmed that the young lady he'd come to speak with was busy in the artists enclosure with the other Petroni's and offered to bring her to him.

It was a busy time of the day for the circus people and the arena and seating had to be prepared in readiness for the main event that was to take place on the evening. Fresh sawdust was being spread across the floor and a few casual labourers were busy picking up rubbish when Priscilla Crockett appeared, looking as glamorous as she had on the previous occasion.

Rayner quickly explained the reason for his visit, indicating that they were getting close to proving her mother was innocent of her father's murder.

The young woman remained as unmoved as when he'd last spoken to her and asked if he was aware of the identity of the real killer.

"It's too early to say miss," the detective answered, "But we have an idea who might have been responsible. But putting that aside for the moment, I intend visiting your mother again soon and was hoping that you might now wish to accompany me."

The girl shook her head in utter defiance, but without speaking.

"I believe your mother has a closely guarded secret concerning the real killer of your father and at the moment, she's unwilling to share it. I thought that by seeing you again, after all these years, it might just persuade her to be more co-operative with us."

Priscilla Crockett looked hesitant and the Chief Inspector became hopeful. Unfortunately, that optimism was quickly dashed when she told him she was incapable of seeing her mother again, after everything that had happened.

"It was a nightmare that took me many years to recover from Mr. Rayner, you must understand and I genuinely fear that to face my mother again would bring it all back to me. I just couldn't stand that. Perhaps later I might feel differently."

"I understand miss, it was just a thought. I want you to cast your mind back again to the time you overheard what you thought was your mother and father arguing downstairs."

"Yes."

"Did you hear anyone else arguing or causing some disturbance in the street outside your bedroom window, at any time during that night?"

She gave the question some thought, before shaking her head and declaring, "No, nobody."

"Is it possible that the people you thought were your mother and father were in fact Mr. and Mrs. Pendry from next door, arguing in the street."

"It was my mother and father."

Guessing just how far Charlie and Rose Pendry's voices would have carried at night, Rayner was surprised the girl had heard nothing, but was forced to accept Priscilla's adamant denial. From an evidential point of view that didn't help her mother's cause and the senior detective felt frustrated by the outcome.

He thanked the young lady and turned to leave, when the trapeze artist surprisingly enquired about her mother's welfare and how she looked on the last occasion he'd visited the prison.

He smiled reassuringly and told her that, Annie appeared to be okay but he believed she was still missing her daughter very much. Perhaps that was the first sign of the young lady's resolve softening and perhaps a little later she might feel more like attending the prison.

When he returned to Scotland Yard, Charlie Pendry was waiting in the basement interview room contained inside the cell block. He looked nervous and Rayner wondered if it was as a result of Henry Bustle's presence. The one thing his Sergeant detested more than anything else, was a liar. Put a thief in front of him, even a murderer and Bustle would show them some respect, but he had always claimed that a liar was the lowest form of life, who you could never trust and Pendry fitted into that category, as far as the Sergeant was concerned.

The senior detective sat opposite the man for a short time, assembling his thoughts until finally deciding upon the way he intended to question this particular enigmatic individual.

"I'm losing money while sitting here Mr. Rayner," Pendry complained, before the Chief Inspector had spoken a word, "So, what can I do for you?"

"I'm interested in your relationship with Annie Crockett, Mr. Pendry."

The man looked surprised and quickly asked the senior detective what exactly he was getting at.

"For how long did you continue your relationship with the woman who lived next door to you, or are you going to deny that."

"I don't know what you mean and object to your insinuation sir."

Henry Bustle had judged the costermonger correctly. The man was lying, which Richard Rayner recognised immediately.

"Are you the reason Mr. Pendry, why Annie Crockett has just spent the last ten years of her life in prison." Every question the Chief Inspector threw at him seemed to have the same effect as a snake sinking its stinging fangs into the street seller.

He leapt from his seat and raised his voice, aggressively continuing to repudiate all that was being suggested; his face contorted by what Richard Rayner believed was nothing more than an act and a poor one at that.

"Sit down, Mr. Pendry," he told the simulating protester, unmoved and with a voice of the utmost authority.

The interviewee did so, huffing and puffing and clasping both hands nervously in front of him. He then glanced back up at his antagonist and asked if he was going to be charged with any offence.

Rayner knew exactly what was coming next and told him that whether or not he was to be charged, was dependent upon how he answered the next few questions.

"Your future Mr. Pendry, will be based on whether you are honest or persist in continuing with this charade."

"Then I'm free to go," Charlie Pendry claimed, standing again from his seat.

"Henry," Rayner said, looking towards his Sergeant.

With no further ado, the Sergeant's shovel-like hands pushed down hard on Pendry's shoulders, forcing him back to his seat.

"Let me explain Mr. Pendry, what I believe took place on that night when Annie Crockett's husband was so brutally murdered with a kitchen knife."

Rayner sat back in his seat, remaining quite unperturbed and deliberate when continuing to allege that Leonard Crockett, discovered his wife was having an affair with their next-door neighbour and went purposefully to The Bushell public house to confront the man now sitting opposite him.

Charlie Pendry was now resembling a frightened sparrow, having lost much of his pomposity.

"You left The Bushell early that night and waited up a closed entry to waylay your man when he later followed you out. It was then you attacked Leonard Crockett and plunged that knife into him a number of times. You were disturbed by a Mr. Wardle, and somehow managed to carry your victim off." He paused to look for any reaction from the man, but saw only fear in his eyes.

"Now, Mr. Pendry, you tell me how you managed to get Crockett's dead body into that pickling barrel and have it transferred to the docks in the hope it would never be found."

The street seller placed his head in both hands and solemnly claimed. "No, no, no, you're wrong, I didn't kill Lenny Crockett." There were beads of perspiration on his forehead and Rayner remained convinced the real killer was sitting right there in the interview room.

Pendry sat back and raised both arms in the air, proclaiming, "Okay Mr. Rayner, I'm not going to get topped for something I didn't do. I'll tell you the Gospel truth, but I swear to God, I didn't kill Lennie Crockett."

The senior detective had guessed right in his version of events that took place on the night of the murder, up until the meeting outside the public house between the two men.

"What Lennie found out was that his missus was pregnant and he thought I was the father."

That surprised Rayner somewhat, although he had wondered if something had taken place as a result of Annie Crockett's association with another man, remembering what the priest, Father Michael Day, had told him about the woman having personal difficulties and being distressed.

"And were you responsible for making her pregnant, Mr. Pendry," Rayner calmly enquired.

"According to Annie, I was, but it was Crockett who threatened me when we were together in The Bushell." Pendry paused and took a minute or so, pondering over what his next disclosure should be.

He was prompted by Richard Rayner to continue talking and his next words shook both the Chief Inspector and Henry Bustle, in a similar fashion to the building collapsing around their heads.

"I know that on that same day, she went and had an abortion Mr. Rayner, and it was that which made Lennie Crockett insanely jealous. He told me if anything happened to his wife he would kill me and that's when I stormed out of the pub."

"But you didn't go straight home?"

The man shook his head, "No, I thought matters needed addressing." He paused yet again, provoking Henry Bustle to thump him on the back of his neck.

Pendry continued in a nervous voice, "Look, I didn't want Crockett coming around our house and performing in front of the missus, so I waited for him to leave the pub."

"And you confronted him?"

"Naturally, but I tried hard to deceive him into thinking it hadn't been me what had got his missus up the stick, but he was having none of that."

"And you fought?"

"It was mostly mouthing off at each other, although he put one on my chin and I stuck one in his bread basket, but that was all. When the geezer showed up complaining about the racket, we both left and I went straight home, as did Lennie as far as I know. But Mr. Rayner, there was no knife involved and I swear on all the Gospels, I never laid another finger on the gent. Why should I for Christ's sake, it was me who was in the wrong."

"You were overheard arguing with your wife in the street after that."

"Yes, I forgot about that. She wanted to know how I'd got the lump on my face and when I told her I'd bumped into a lamp post, she reckoned I'd been going with Annie Crockett and used a rolling pin on me. She kept tanning me outside the front of the house and eventually I spent the rest of that night under a park bench. I never saw Lenny Crockett again after we left that entry."

A short period of silence enveloped the room until Rayner stood up and instructed Henry Bustle to place Charlie Pendry in a cell.

"How in God's name can I convince you, Mr. Rayner," the despairing man enquired.

"You already have, Mr. Pendry."

"Then why am I being kept here?"

"Because I haven't told you yet, of what it is you have convinced me is the truth."

Chapter Twenty Two

She still looked vacant, pitiful and unemotional, typical of a woman who had been domiciled behind bars for the past decade or so. Annie Crockett sat at the table in the same visitor's room watched over by the same escorting guard, and portraying an individual who had surrendered all hope of freedom long ago. Richard Rayner couldn't avoid feeling some emotion towards her.

After introducing Henry Bustle, the Chief Inspector genuinely enquired if she remained in good health and whether she had given any further thought to the circumstances leading to the reason she was still living her life in filth and indignity.

Annie remained defiant and shrugged her shoulders, offering nothing more than a glance across the table.

Henry Bustle immediately formed the opinion that his Chief Inspector had a mountain to climb, if only to get the lady to converse with them and was wondering why Rayner was going to all this bother, seeing no sign of appreciation. Surely, she must know he was only trying to help her, if only for his own satisfaction and not for any reward or other gratuity.

"Priscilla sends her love," Rayner lied, in the same way as he had done so before.

In response, the woman convict continued to look blankly at him, as if she had only agreed to the meeting out of courtesy.

"Since we last spoke, Annie, both myself and Sergeant Bustle have been making a number of enquiries into your case and I am now in possession of a lot more information I had no knowledge of before."

Rayner knew that the lady could just stand up and leave at any moment during the interview and realised it was imperative she remained with him, so continued to speak cautiously and sensitively.

"Would you mind if I put a number of questions to you, just to clarify a few points for my satisfaction."

She nodded, very slightly and certainly not showing any interest whatsoever in what this official from Scotland Yard was saying to her.

"Firstly, I wish to discuss your next-door neighbour, Rose Pendry. Do you remember the lady?"

She nodded again, looking vaguely inquisitive.

"How did you get on with her, Annie?"

The woman looked surprised by the question and answered quietly, almost in a whisper, briefly explaining that she couldn't remember having any difficulties with Mrs. Pendry.

"And her husband, Charlie, how did you get along with him."

She visibly frowned, but shook her head, curtly replying, "Okay, I suppose."

Rayner detected a note of negativity in her voice, as if annoyed by the mention of that last person. The senior detective then went on to philosophically describe how, on occasions, individuals could make mistakes by the way in which they prioritised various matters they believed to be important, but that in reality, weren't as paramount to their lives as they might have believed.

"For example, falsely believing that a person is worthy of protection, when in fact they are not and making unnecessary sacrifices as a result of that same belief."

"Please come to the point, Mr. Rayner," she pleaded, marginally raising her voice.

"Very well, Annie, allow me to do just that. I believe you had an arrangement with Charlie Pendry, is that true?"

"If you mean, did I have an affair with Charlie, yes."

"And according to our Mr. Pendry, you became pregnant by him." Rayner nodded his head, inviting an affirmative reply, but she didn't answer and looked up at the ceiling. He was still wary about forcing the woman to leave before disclosing any further information on what he was desperate to know. But the Chief Inspector thought it best to speak from the heart and then see how the meeting panned out.

"Annie, you have spent virtually the last ten years in this place for a crime you didn't commit and now you are very close to being set free, to return to a normal life and to do as you wish. You do understand that, surely."

"I know that, Mr. Rayner. Don't you think I have carried that burden with me since first coming to this dreadful place of confinement and degeneration." She was speaking far more articulately than at their last meeting, which indicated to the senior investigator, Annie Crockett had received an education before meeting and marrying her departed husband. He was learning something about this woman every time she spoke to him.

"Then be honest with me, did you have an abortion, as Charlie Pendry has told us."

The lady's eyes reminded Rayner of a shark's, staring back at him completely devoid of feeling or emotion when she answered, "Yes."

"On the same day as your husband was killed."

She nodded and her eyes dropped, showing the first sign of remorse.

He knew it would be pointless asking who the abortionist was; there was no way in which she would disclose such information to him and in any case, he wasn't there for that purpose but did mention that she must have been feeling very ill, after undergoing such a backstreet ordeal.

Annie Crockett continued to look at him, her eyes silently asking what was the point of his questions.

"I also understand Annie, that your husband found out about both the abortion and who the father of your child was. Pendry has confessed to fighting with him prior to his murder."

She smiled, which was extremely uncharacteristic of her, as far as Rayner had seen so far and he dared to enquire what it was she found to be so humorous.

"I wasn't aware that Lenny had a fight with Charlie over me. I regret that and wish he hadn't."

Rayner paused, needing to word his next questions with the utmost care and knowing he'd reached a vital stage of their conversation.

"Are you absolutely certain Annie, it was your husband who walked back in the house that night and not Charlie Pendry?"

She looked confused by the question before realising finally, the direction in which Richard Rayner was going. The Chief Inspector was trying to put a rope around Charlie Pendry's neck. She sighed and allowed her shoulders to drop, sitting back on her seat. The chains on her wrists clattered, as she did so.

"It was my husband, Mr. Rayner," she then confirmed, honestly or so it appeared.

"You see, Annie, I believe it was Charlie Pendry who stabbed your husband to death during an altercation they had in an enclosed alley just up the street from where you were living. I also suspect that Pendry then solicited your assistance in helping him to remove and hide the body."

"You are wrong sir," she said, surprisingly convincingly.

"I also believe Annie, that Pendry possibly handed the knife he'd used to commit the murder to you, asking for you to get rid of it for him and as a result, you threw it into your own back garden. Am I correct?"

"No."

"The blood you were seen cleaning off the floor by your daughter, had come from that same knife and it was your husband's blood you were cleaning up."

"Is that what Charlie Pendry has told you?" she asked, shaking her head with a distinct look of distrust on her face.

"No, it's what I am assuming, which if true, means you have already paid more than the full price for the part you played in helping to dispose of your husband's body."

"It was my blood I was cleaning up off the floor, Mr. Rayner. I was haemorrhaging after the abortion." Again, her eyes revisited the ceiling and she exhaled with a slight groan.

"Annie, we know what happened and who killed your husband, so there is no longer any need to continue with this charade. Why in God's name are you protecting a man like Charlie Pendry. It's time to tell the truth and relieve yourself of the burden you have been carrying for so long."

What Rayner had feared might happen, did so and the female prisoner then unexpectedly stood from her chair and turned to the prison officer, requesting that she be returned to her cell. The interview had come to an abrupt end and Richard Rayner had failed in his mission to obtain the truth from the lady. Anxiously and in desperation he made one last verbal plea, as she stepped away from the table.

"Annie, you owe Charlie Pendry nothing. If you walk away from me now there's every chance you will never see your daughter again," he quickly suggested.

She turned and looked back at him. He could see her eyes welling up. A small tear fell down one side of her pale face and it was then, as if Richard Rayner had suddenly been struck by the glaring light of truth, he discovered Annie Crockett's coveted secret.

"I will say this only once Mr. Rayner," she announced, "Charlie Pendry had nothing to do with my husband's death or the abortion I had that day. If you charge him with murder, you will be as good as hanging an innocent man."

"My God, Annie, I hear what you are saying," he snapped back at her, standing from his seat, "Yes, I believe you are quite right. How could I have been so naïve. I can see it clearly now; Priscilla killed her father when he was beating you up in the kitchen."

Henry Bustle stared across at the Chief Inspector, astonished by the claim just made and Annie Crockett began to sway before collapsing on the floor.

She was carried by all three men back to her chair and the prison officer was sent to fetch a glass of water. In fact, the guard was still absent when the woman prisoner regained consciousness from her faint and the only face she saw, was that of Richard Rayner's.

When the officer returned, the Chief Inspector helped the distressed inmate to take a few sips of water, before waiting for her to recover sufficiently to continue their conversation.

"I apologise for causing you so much distress Annie," Rayner quietly said, grasping one of the woman's shackled hands on the table top, "But I do need to know the truth and by all the Saints, I now know it was your daughter who took hold of that knife and used it to protect yourself."

Annie Crockett just looked at him.

He continued by suggesting that when her husband came home that night, having just crossed swords with Charlie Pendry, Leonard Crockett set about her, causing a disturbance overheard by Rose Pendry next door and Priscilla who was upstairs. When their daughter reached the hallway, what she saw wasn't her mother cleaning up blood from the kitchen floor, but her father physically and mercilessly attacking his wife.

"I assume that Priscilla screamed for him to stop and when he carried on hitting you, she picked up the kitchen knife and struck him down in a frenzy. He must have died from his wounds there and then on that kitchen floor and you wasted little time in cleaning it up, before the police arrived."

The woman didn't deny the synopsis put to her, but insisted that she had in fact been haemorrhaging as a result of the abortion and was still suffering when her husband returned home. The tears began to cascade down the stricken Annie Crockett's face and she held up both hands to hide her shame.

"But then Annie, how did you manage to get the body put into a barrel of vinegar and transport it to the docks?" Rayner felt some strange sensation of guilt, knowing how much pain this woman had suffered in the past but he needed to extract every detail of what took place on that fateful night, if he was going to secure the convicted prisoner's freedom.

Slowly, she lowered her hands and looked directly at Rayner. The tears had stopped and now she looked hard and angry.

"She was a mere infant Mr. Rayner, no taller than my waist and I have sacrificed my life for her. Not once has she visited me; not once has she written or sent any well-wishing message to me, her own mother. The first I ever heard of my own child was when you told me about her on that first occasion you came here, so when you said she had sent her love, I knew you were lying."

"That was wrong of me, Annie, and I apologise, but how did you manage to dispose of your husband's body in the way you did?"

"You need to put that question to Rose Pendry."

"I'm asking you, Annie."

Again, she looked reluctant at her inquisitor before announcing that why shouldn't she implicate others; individuals who had shown her no gratitude or commiseration during the time spent behind bars.

"Rose overheard Lenny rowing with me and of course, learned about my affair with her husband. She came to the house intending to create havoc, but when she saw what had happened, changed her mind."

"Did Mrs. Pendry know that Priscilla had killed her father?"

"No, I told her that I had done him in. Surprisingly, she then offered to help me; why, I have no idea. Charlie kept two barrels of pickling vinegar at the back of their house, connected with his business and it was Rose's idea that we should use them. She provided the transport and we both took the barrels down to the docks. The coachman helped us with the lifting without knowing what was inside and we left them on the quayside down at the docks.

"And what of Charlie Pendry, Annie?"

"Charlie had been thrown out of the house that night and knew nothing about any of it."

The truth about the Investigation had been beyond Richard Rayner's reasoning, coming as a complete unforeseen surprise. And yet, as Henry Bustle pointed out when they were leaving the prison, if it hadn't been for the Chief Inspector's sixth sense and persistence, Annie Crockett would have been destined to have spent the remainder of her days incarcerated in what could only be described, as an officially recognised hellhole.

Priscilla Crockett had her own caravan separate to that used by the Petroni family and was resting in between shows when the knock on the door came. From the look on Richard Rayner's face, she knew instantly the reason he was there.

"Yvonne Petroni, alias Priscilla Crockett, I am arresting you for the murder of your father, Leonard Crockett," the Chief Inspector solemnly announced, "You are coming with me to Scotland Yard where you will have the opportunity to answer to that charge."

"You've spoken with my mother," the girl abruptly answered.

Rayner nodded, before instructing Henry Bustle to put the handcuffs on the young woman. Her career was at an end and whether she would escape the noose for the most serious of crimes, after such a lengthy period of time, would be a matter for the courts. But in a strange way, Richard Rayner felt he had achieved nothing beyond of course, revealing the truth and correcting a gross miscarriage of justice.

Once back at Scotland Yard, the lady who would only have been eight years of age when she killed her own father, showed no pretence at not remembering the incident. She quite readily admitted what she had done, recalling clearly and with clarity exactly what had taken place and confirming what had earlier been put to her mother by Richard Rayner. She did say that she expected justice to be done and that she would hang for her crime, but the senior detective doubted that would happen. Ironically, mother and daughter would be changing places as a result of the senior detective's refusal to accept the verdict of guilt following the original trial.

There was a bright blue cloudless sky above and the ground was covered by an early morning frost when the main gates of Holloway Prison opened to allow Annie Crockett to walk through them, a free woman for the first time in ten years. She was greeted by Richard Rayner and Jack Robinson, both detectives congratulating her on her new-found life without bars and locked doors. She looked far different from the woman the Chief Inspector had visited inside the prison walls, radiant with eyes that portrayed happiness and joy, emotions that Rayner knew were long overdue.

The lady accepted the offer of Rayner's carriage, explaining that she intended finding some lodgings before looking for employment. But first, she was going to spend the day walking around London, visiting the sights and generally becoming accustomed to mixing with crowds of people again.

As the carriage made its way towards Piccadilly, Rayner asked if she had learned any trade during the time she had spent in prison and Annie laughed, confirming that convicts, male or female were never taught anything other than how to swab out their cells and keep their persons clean.

"But I used to spend hours knitting, Mr. Rayner, and have become quite proficient at that particular skill. There wasn't one prison officer's wife I didn't knit a cardigan for," she confessed, still chuckling.

"Could you teach the subject?" Rayner asked, suddenly having an idea.

"What I don't know about the use of knitting needles and wool now sir, isn't worth knowing about," she boasted, truthfully.

"Then, I might just have a suggestion to make that could help you return more quickly than you think, to a normal existence." Rayner was thinking of approaching Frederick Morgan's daughter, Estelle, to see if the Ragged

School where she taught, would be interested in employing a teacher with knitting skills. He thought they would and it was to be his last favour to the lady, Annie Crockett, to help her take her first step back to some normality.

About the Author

John Plimmer was a high-profile Detective Superintendent with West Midlands Police during which time he investigated over thirty murders, all of which were detected. He studied Law and Philosophy at Birmingham University and has been a feature writer for both the Sunday Mercury and Evening Mail newspapers. Plimmer has also written numerous articles published in various magazines, and has been involved in script writing for some of television's most popular dramas.

He is a prolific novelist and to date has over fifty books published. Some of his works include 'Brickbats and Tutus' - the biography of Julie Felix, Britain's first black ballerina, and Backstreet Urchins – a humorous account of life in the Birmingham slums of post war Britain.

The eight book 'Dan Mitchell' series involves international espionage and murder, and his popular Victorian Detective Casebook series describes the adventures of Richard Rayner and Henry Bustle of Scotland Yard.

The Secret of Annie Crockett is the eighteenth in the Victorian Detective's series. Others include:

The Victorian Case Review Detective

The Graveyard Murders

A Farthing for a Life

The Bullion Train Robbery

Rayner's Ripper

The Fourteenth Victim

The Pie Man

25 Augustus Street

Murder and Revolution

Life and Death – The Final Torment

The Seven Daughters of Diongenes

Fire & Brimstone

The Richter Claim

The Black Mamba

The Daisy Chain Murders

Morgan's Revenge – the sequel to The Daisy Chain Murders

The Warwickshire Assassin

The Secret of Annie Crockett

The Pharoah Hunter

Printed in Great Britain
by Amazon

87835484R40139